THE CAPTIVE BRIDE

★ ★ ★ ★ THE HOUSE OF WINSLOW / BOOK 2 ★ ★ ★ ★

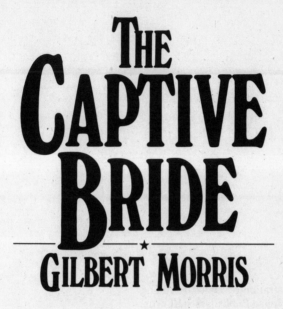

THE CAPTIVE BRIDE

★

GILBERT MORRIS

BETHANY HOUSE PUBLISHERS
MINNEAPOLIS, MINNESOTA 55438

Mor

Cover illustration by Dan Thornberg.
Bethany House Publishers staff artist.

Published by Bethany House Publishers
A Ministry of Bethany Fellowship, Inc.
11300 Hampshire Avenue South
Minneapolis, Minnesota 55438

Printed in the United States of America

Library of Congress Cataloging-in-Publication Data

Morris, Gilbert.
   The captive bride.

   (The House of Winslow : bk. 2)
   Sequel to; The honorable impostor.
   I. Title. II. Series: Morris, Gilbert. House of Winslow : bk. 2
PS3563.08742C3   1987   813'.54   87-15782
ISBN 0–87123–978–7 (pbk.)

To Stacy Lee Smith

Who makes being a father
the easiest task in the world!

THE LIBERTY BELL

🔔 🔔 🔔

THE HOUSE OF WINSLOW SERIES

★ ★ ★ ★

GILBERT MORRIS spent ten years as a pastor before becoming Professor of English at Ouachita Baptist University in Arkansas and earning a Ph.D. at the University of Arkansas. During the summers of 1984 and 1985 he did postgraduate work at the University of London and is presently the Chairman of General Education at a Christian college in Louisiana. A prolific writer, he has had over 25 scholarly articles and 200 poems published in various periodicals, and over the past years has had more than 20 novels published. His family includes three grown children, and he and his wife live in Baton Rouge, Louisiana.

CONTENTS

PART ONE

BEDFORD

★ ★ ★

1659

CHAPTER ONE

POWER IN THE BLOOD

★ ★ ★ ★

"Catherine, there he is—Matthew Winslow!"

The speaker, a short young woman with sharp features, grabbed at the arm of her companion. The pair had just turned off the narrow path that followed the curving coastline onto the main road leading up to the settlement.

Her companion, a tall, willowy girl of twenty, turned a pair of curious dark eyes on the horseman approaching from the other road. She wore a simple blue dress set off by a white collar, but its plain cut did not conceal her fine figure, and there was a boldness in her direct gaze that most young women of Plymouth did not possess.

"So that's the young dandy that's been interrupting your dreams, is it, Martha?"

"Catherine! If you ever breathe a word—!"

"Oh, don't worry," the tall girl laughed. "Your secret's safe with me." She gave the rider a closer look and tapped her chin slowly. With a light of speculation she murmured, "So this is the famous Matthew Winslow who's broken the hearts of half the young women in Plymouth!"

Martha suddenly giggled. "*Half*? Catherine, I don't think there's a maid in all Plymouth who hasn't set her cap for him!"

The taller girl gave an impatient shake of her head, and her lips tightened. "And his head is probably as big as that horse he's riding, I'd venture. Martha, he may be the answer to a maiden's prayer in this little place, but in Boston—"

"Shhh! Here he comes!" Martha gave a tug at Catherine's arm, then shook her head in wonder, saying in a whisper, "I knew he'd come! It's almost witchcraft the way he finds a pretty woman, Catherine—you could blindfold him, and he'd still know."

The two women had reached the dusty road that led up to the fort just as the object of their conversation arrived from the opposite direction. He looked up, saw the pair, then touched his horse with his spurs, driving the animal toward them. Wheeling the jet black stallion around, he dismounted with a motion so easy and fluid that he seemed to flow to the ground. The horse tried to throw his head up, but was held by an iron grip; the handsome rider swept his hat from his head, then bowed in a courtly gesture.

"A good day to you, Miss Martha."

His words were directed to the shorter of the two, but Catherine Brent knew instantly that she was the object of his attention. It irritated her, for she felt like a quarry of some sort—he the hunter and she the trophy he sought. As she heard Martha say, "This is my cousin, Catherine Brent, from Boston," she gave Matthew Winslow a direct stare.

Her eyes scrutinized the young man before her—tall, over six feet, with a shock of rich auburn hair. His face was bronzed, wedge-shaped, the wide mouth lifting at the corners as he smiled at her with a frank inspection. His ears were rather small, his nose straight, and there was a suggestion of tremendous strength in the corded neck and wide hands. He was wearing a red velvet coat and breeches, yellow waistcoat with ruby buttons, and shoes with gold buckles. The brown hat held under his arm, had a large yellow plume, and despite the summer heat he wore a cloak of dark maroon.

What a dandy—a fop! Catherine thought at first, but when she met his eyes, she was thrown off guard. He had the bluest eyes she had ever seen—blue as the sky overhead, blue as the cornflowers growing beside the road. But the power in those eyes made her feel as if his gaze had *touched* her physically!

"I trust your stay will be a long one, Miss Brent," he said in a deep, slightly husky voice.

In spite of herself, she felt her hand going out to him as he stepped forward and touched it with his lips. She suddenly hated herself for the thrill that swept through her. Snatching her hand back almost rudely, she said haughtily, "I fear there is little in this place to hold my attention, Mr. Winslow." *That ought to put him in his place*, she thought with some satisfaction.

He was not crushed, however. On the contrary, he smiled. "Plymouth is a small place, as you say." She felt the power of eyes laughing into hers. "But if you will permit me to call on you—and on Miss Martha, of course," he continued, "I would like to show you a side of Plymouth you've missed."

Catherine opened her mouth to say, "There's nothing in this town that attracts me in the least."

Instead, she said, "That would be very nice, Mr. Winslow."

She hated herself for that response, and had the impulse to reverse her words, but Martha broke in, saying, "You can come tonight if you like, Mr. Winslow."

He pulled his horse around, then swung into the saddle easily. "Nothing would please me better, but my uncle is arriving from England. I see his ship in the harbor there"—he motioned to a three-masted schooner at anchor in the bay—"and my parents will expect me to stay at home tonight and help welcome him." He wheeled the horse around and gave a sudden smile, calling out as he left, "I'll be there tomorrow!"

"Insolent puppy!" Catherine said waspishly. Somehow she felt he had bested her, and she found herself wishing for to- morrow. She'd put him in his place!

Martha looked at her friend and smiled. "I know what it is, Catherine. You think he's too proud, and you'll give him a taste of humility. That's it, isn't it?"

"Why—!"

"You think that hasn't been tried?" Martha glanced up the hill as the black stallion grew smaller, then shook her head with a smile of despair. "Isn't he the most handsome thing you ever saw—proud or not?"

"Well . . ." Catherine said grudgingly, "I will admit he's the most attractive minister I've ever seen."

"Oh, he'll never be a minister! That's his parents' idea, not his," Martha shrugged. "He's their only son—the last of the Winslow name, you see. His father, Reverend Gilbert Winslow, came over on the *Mayflower* and so did his mother. You know how it can be though, Catherine. Being a minister's son doesn't give a man a calling from the Lord."

Catherine tapped her chin thoughtfully, then said with a gleam in her eyes, "Well, I'm looking forward to Mr. Winslow's call tomorrow." She laughed suddenly and added, "Those blue eyes of his—they've got more of the devil in them than a minister ought to have."

Edward Winslow caught sight of Gilbert and Humility standing in the front ranks of the crowd and raised his hand in response to their greetings. The long journey from England had stiffened his joints, and the monotonous diet had stripped some flesh from his bones, but he was still portly as he stepped out of the *Fortune's* small boat to the shores of Plymouth. He took a few steps, then began to sway, the earth seeming to reel beneath his feet. Gilbert rushed forward and grabbed him in a firm embrace, steadying him.

"Careful, Brother Edward!" the younger man said with a grin. "If you stagger like that, our sharp-eyed elder will think you've been lifting the bottle a bit too much!" There was a light of affection in Gilbert Winslow's cornflower blue eyes, and since hugging among relatives was not common in the family, he took the opportunity to give his brother a rough hug under the pretense of holding him steady.

Edward Winslow felt a warm glow, as he always did on seeing this younger brother of his. In the past the two of them had been estranged, but since that epic journey on the *Mayflower* and the first terrible winter endured together in Plymouth Plantation, the two of them were extremely close. The long periods Edward had to spend in England in the service of the government were the harder to bear for his separation from Gilbert and his family.

Clapping Gilbert on the shoulder he said, "By heaven, it's good to set foot on solid ground!" Then he turned to Humility and put out his arms to embrace her. She, too, was his favorite, and he concealed his shock on seeing how poorly she looked. "Well, here's my favorite sister-in-law!" he said fondly, and as she came into his arms he noted that she had shrunk to almost nothing since he had sailed for England two years earlier. Her eyes were sunk back into her head, and there was only a faint trace of the rare beauty that had been the cause of several fights on board the *Mayflower*. Her complexion, which had always been radiant, was faded to a sallow color, and the once rich blonde hair was thin and dry, shot through with streaks of white. *Very sick—Gilbert kept it from me*, Edward thought as he looked down on Humility.

"Well, well, come along," Gilbert said quickly, noting the shocked look in Edward's eyes. "You must be starved after two months of biscuits packed with weevils, Edward. Humility began cooking as soon as the mast came in sight."

"Lead me to it!" Edward cried, and the two men linked arms and started up from the beach to the settlement that crowned the low hill. As they reached the first street that ran parallel to the shoreline, Edward paused, looking at the neat cottages, each on a good-sized lot. The cold fingers of winter had not yet touched the land, and the thick grass that would be dry and gray in another month glowed with an emerald sheen that almost hurt his eyes. Taking in the white-sided houses with neatly thatched roofs, some of them half-timbered just as in an English village, Edward murmured, "Doesn't look much like it did when Captain Jones put us off the old *Mayflower* the first time, does it, Gilbert?"

"No. That was—let me see—thirty-nine years ago, was it?" Gilbert shook his head and said ruefully, "You know what I said to Miles Standish that day, Edward? I said, 'Miles, this is as close to hell as I expect to find on this earth!' "

"What did Captain Standish say?"

"Oh, he swore a great oath—you know how Miles was in those days! Said it was a paradise on earth compared to some of the places he'd soldiered." Gilbert shook his head. "Poor old Miles. Been in his grave for twenty years now. I still miss him."

Humility joined the conversation, saying quietly, "I rejoice that he came to know the Lord before he was taken."

"That's true, sweetheart," Gilbert said, turning from Edward to gaze fondly down at her. There was, however, a sadness in his fine blue eyes as he shook his head and murmured, "Not too many of us left—the Firstcomers!"

"Well, *I'm* left, Brother!" Edward said heartily. "But if we don't get some of Humility's cooking inside this hollow stomach of mine, I can't speak for tomorrow!"

They made their way up the main street leading to the town, past the single street intersecting it. Houses lined both sides of the main street, each with a small, fenced-in garden, now mostly gone to seed. At the point where the two main streets intersected, four small cannons were mounted on swivels. Pigs roamed freely about the streets, serving both as the main meat diet of the colony and also as four-footed garbage collectors.

They passed the cross street and turned into a small house with a high-pitched thatched roof. It was sheathed with unpainted clapboard—short boards handmade by splitting a log lengthwise, then shaving it down to the proper shape with a drawknife. "Come in and let's hear what's happening in England, Edward," Gilbert urged.

The room they entered was dark, illuminated only by two small windows ten inches square, sealed with glass instead of the oiled paper used by many. Humility moved to a cavernous fireplace that took up half of one wall. It was three and a half feet deep, and so high that a tall man could walk around in it. The back was lined with rounded stones, and the inside studded with iron hooks, bars, and chains suspended from a wooden beam.

As Gilbert and Edward sat at the table talking, Humility took some of the goat's meat she had roasted on a spit and put it on hollowed-out wooden trenchers. She filled three large drinking cups with fresh milk and set out a sharp knife for each of them. Adding a wedge of cheese, she then pulled the loaf of bread baked in an outdoor iron-box communal oven close to the fire.

"All ready," she called, and the three of them took their places and bowed their heads. Gilbert prayed, "Thank you, gracious Lord, for this good food, and for the safe journey of our brother, in the name of Jesus Christ."

Edward reached out, cut a huge slice from the loaf with his knife, then laughed, "Gilbert, you have the shortest prayers of any minister in America! I trust your sermons are not so brief, or the congregation will feel led to seek another preacher who will give them their money's worth!"

Humility had gotten up to get salt and paused to lay her hand on Edward's shoulder. He could not help noticing how thin and frail it was as she said with a smile, "He is guilty, Brother Edward, I fear. A shame that the best preacher in Plymouth speaks no longer than an hour when others with nothing to say last for three or four!"

Gilbert sliced off a liberal portion of meat, held it impaled on the point of his knife, then said with a smile, "True. It all stems from an incident that occurred when I first began preaching. I heard someone say in a loud whisper, 'Is he done?' And then someone else said in a disgusted voice, 'Yes—but he's still preaching!' I think that made me choose to stop when I had nothing else to say." He shoved the portion of meat into his mouth and began to chew it slowly.

"A dangerous precedent!" Edward chuckled. "Now, tell me how it goes—I'm hungry for news."

As the two men sat there chewing the tough meat and washing it down first with milk, then with ale, the more common beverage, Humility leaned back against the wall and observed them. Though the Winslow blood was evident in both men, time and circumstance had sculptured them differently, and she was a little amused to see the variations.

Edward was sixty-five, six years older than Gilbert, and slightly taller. He was far heavier, his full face still red; the chestnut hair that had glowed in youth was still thick and only faintly tinged with gray. He had a smooth, good-natured face, a neatly trimmed moustache, and eyes of a penetrating blue. He was wearing a fine lawn collar turned out from his throat, tied beneath with a silk, red-tassled cord. A corduroy coat with a double row of silver buttons and silk breeches in the Dutch style completed his outfit. He had an air of authority, and his years of dealing with kings and later the Lord Protector, Oliver Cromwell, had given him a rather ponderous dignity.

Turning to look at her husband, Humility saw a man not greatly different in some ways than the young blade she had met forty years earlier. The face, to be sure, was somewhat lined, but the athletic movement was little slowed by time. He still had the broad, bronzed brow, and the face that tapered down to a jutting chin adorned with a small white scar was only slightly heavier than on the day they had met. Tall and muscular, he wore the plain, dark clothing of the Puritan minister, with pewter buttons and a broad, starched neckcloth folded over his shoulders.

He turned his head to smile at her, and her heart leaped, as it always did, and then a longing to be well again swept her. She had always been his equal physically, despite the burden of child-bearing. But now a stranger seeing them together for the first time might take her for his older sister. The memory of that time when she walked by his side, brimming with health (and beauty, so they said!), was more than Humility could bear. She rose and said, "You two will want to go visit the governor. I'll not go with you this time."

Edward got to his feet at once and said, "We should call, I suppose, but we'll be back soon. I'm anxious to see my nephew. He'll be here for supper?" His astute eyes did not miss the glance exchanged by the pair, and he said quickly. "Well, I've a month to see that young rascal—no matter."

Gilbert said, "Go lie down, dear. I'll take care of this when we come back. Don't argue—'Wives, be in obedience to your husbands' as the Book teacheth." He kissed her and then led the way out of the house and down the street toward the governor's house.

"How bad is it?" Edward asked at once. "What does Fuller say?"

Gilbert bit his lip and cast a glance over the iron-gray billows rolling ponderously over the docks below. "Bad enough, Edward. Sam said when she first fell ill, it was the result of too much bathing. He's always said that noxious vapors from winds and waters make bathing very dangerous." He smiled at the thought of Sam Fuller, their only physician since the *Mayflower* touched the New World. Then a gloomy light clouded his bright blue eyes and he said heavily, "But it's serious, Edward. She goes down every day! Whatever it is, it's draining her life before my eyes!"

Edward reached out and gripped his brother's arm, saying only, "God is able, Gilbert!"

"Yes, He is."

For the next three hours the two men went from house to house as Edward performed his duty to pass along the news from England. He had been governor of Plymouth, in addition to his offices for the Crown and later for Cromwell, so there was a certain amount of awe in the attitude of some. Others like John Billington, who had long resented Edward (or any other man of authority), and latecomers to the settlement, were less impressed.

Governor Bradford, of course, was pleased to see him, and they spent the bulk of the day with him. His house was larger than usual, more than twice as large as Gilbert's. Bradford was a compact man, and since the beginning had been the driving energy that kept Plymouth intact. After hearing some minor news he said, "Come, Brother Winslow, get to it. What will happen now that Cromwell is dead?"

"His son, Richard, sits in his place." Edward shifted uneasily, then added, "I fear him, Mr. Bradford. He is not a strong man, and the English have not lost their taste for monarchs."

Bradford's intelligent eyes searched the face of the other, and he nodded slowly. "My thinking exactly."

"You think Charles will be brought back?" Gilbert asked.

"His royal trunk has been packed for some time, Pastor Winslow," Bradford smiled grimly. "And if Charles sits on the throne of England, we all know what his thought will be concerning such men as ourselves."

"He will remember that it was the Puritan forces under Cromwell that beheaded his father and drove him to exile," Edward nodded. He looked sharply at Bradford and added, "It is well that we are here, with an ocean between us, is it not, Mr. Bradford?"

"Yes—but our brothers in England are not so protected," Bradford answered. He shook his head, and there was a sadness in his voice as he said, "I fear there will be a shaking soon in England."

They left the governor's house and made their way up the hill, speaking of the dangers that beset their brothers in England, and as they turned down the street and caught sight of Winslow's horse, he said, "Matthew is home." He added drily, "Most of us hitch up a steer or a dry cow to do our traveling—my son has some disdain for such primitive customs."

"I see what you mean, Gilbert," Edward responded, noting the horse tied to the fence in front of the house. "Where did he get the money for such a fine stallion?"

Gilbert shrugged and said as they passed through the gate, "Not from me. The price of that horse would pay my salary for six years. Matthew doesn't work, so he either stole it or he gambled for it." He put his hand on Edward's arm, saying in a low voice, "I felt it necessary to ascertain which, and I am pleased to report that it is the latter. It would have been disgraceful if a minister's son had stolen, would it not?"

Edward noted the edge of sarcasm in Gilbert's voice, and it saddened him. He had stood by grave after grave where the stillborn children of Gilbert and Humility were buried, and he knew the deep grief that had almost destroyed them both. When the last child had survived, they had poured themselves into the boy with such an intensity that Edward had always feared the result should the child have followed the others to an early grave. He had not been unaware, being a shrewd observer of human nature, that Matthew had been blessed with a strong body and cursed with a rebellious spirit.

Gilbert opened the door, and as Edward stepped inside and was greeted with a rush from his nephew, he thought for the ten thousandth time, *It's Gilbert at seventeen!* It was an eerie resemblance, for young Matthew had the same sharp features, the cornflower blue eyes that all Winslow men seem to have, he moved the same, had the same smooth gait of the natural athlete—balanced, almost sensual, with not a fraction of wasted motion as he crossed the floor.

"Uncle Edward!" *Even the same voice!* he thought, and the hard hand that crushed his was corded with muscle as were the arms and shoulders. "My word, it's good to have you back!"

"You're looking well, my boy." Edward smiled at the young man, "I haven't seen such fine clothing since I visited Bond Street in London."

There was some embarrassment in the young man's eyes as he said, "Well, Uncle, I suppose I am a bit of a peacock—but I've been to Boston, and they expect such things there."

"Some do," Gilbert said quietly. His brother saw the young man's face flush and the quick flare of resentment in his blue eyes.

Edward had not been a diplomat for nothing. He said with a laugh, "I remember your father wore an outfit much like this when he was a student at Cambridge. I believe Father took a rather dim view of it, eh, Gilbert?"

A startled look crossed Gilbert's face, and then he threw his head back and roared with laughter. "I haven't thought of that in forty years, Edward!" He threw a smile at Humility and said ruefully, "Father threatened to have me put in the stocks if I ever wore such a garb in his presence!"

"Father was a stern man," Edward said gently, and he saw the remark had its intended effect on his brother.

Gilbert nodded, and there was a softening of the lines around his mouth as he looked at his son. "He was that." He said no more, but the angry air that had filled the room faded, and young Matthew shot a grateful look at his uncle.

"Now, let's hear what you've been up to since I've been away. How's the Latin and the Greek? Still giving Mr. Littleton fits?"

"I'm bound to say," Gilbert said as he sat down beside Humility, "that it's rather the other way around." He gave a fond glance at the young man across the table and smiled. "I mean to say that Matthew has surpassed his teacher."

"And *that's* what I want to talk to you about, Uncle."

"Oh, not *now*, Matthew," Humility protested. "Your uncle is weary from his long voyage."

"Let the boy talk, Sister," Edward said easily. He leaned back in his chair and considered the eager face of the young man who at once began to pour out a plan he had obviously spent much time conceiving. In brief, he would either go to school in England or he would die!

Edward asked, when he could find a gap in the young man's flow of words, "You want to enter the church, Matthew?"

"No, the law!"

His uncle gave a quick look at Gilbert and Humility, and the disappointment on their faces was plain. He saw at once that this family, so precious to him, was on the razor edge of disaster. If the young man had his way, he would be embarking on a path odious to his parents; in addition, they would lose him forever—at least, Humility would! The study of law was a long, arduous process, and he knew in his heart that Humility would never live to see her son again if he left on such a mission.

"Mr. Shakespeare has given us many fine lines, my boy," Edward remarked slowly. "My favorite is not well known, but reflects my own views."

"What line is that, Uncle?"

"First we kill all the lawyers!" Edward remarked. "A sentiment I hold firm concord with after dealing with the breed for a lifetime and finding not enough honor for a squad in the whole profession!"

"The army then!" Matthew cried, his eyes piercing those of his uncle. "I'm not fit for the church, and the law, you say, isn't fit for me. Let me go for a soldier, Father!" He turned and held out one strong, square hand in a strange pleading gesture to Gilbert.

"Son, you can't mean that!" Gilbert protested, drawing nearer to Humility in an unconscious attempt to protect her, adding, "Your uncle will tell you it's impossible!"

"Why is it impossible?"

"Think, Matthew!" his uncle said intensely. "There *is* no army in England for you to serve in." His face grew stern and he slapped the wooden table with a sharp gesture. "The Model Army of Cromwell was the finest body of fighting men on earth—but Cromwell is dead, and there is no man alive who can rally those troops. Within a year—if God doesn't do something—Charles II will be the ruling monarch of England, and if you think the son of a Puritan minister could serve in *that* army, you're a simpleton!" He had half risen in anger, but it was not at the boy in front of him, but at the fate of the England he loved. Now he settled back and forced himself to be calm.

"Not the army, Matthew." It was a rare thing for a Winslow man to beg, but there was a pleading note in the older man's voice as he said, "Matthew, give the church a try. You're young and think you have to have excitement. Very natural in a young fellow such as yourself. Your father was much the same," he added with a smile.

"You've hit it, Uncle!" Matthew said at once. "I've heard stories all my life of you, Father! How you were the best swordsman in England, and how you fought duels and—"

"Son! Son!" Gilbert held up his hand and there was a horror on his face. "Don't call those days back! For heaven's sake, do you think I'm *proud* of them?" He shook his head, and let his head fall as he whispered, "I'd give my life to wipe out those wild days."

Humility put her arm around him and said, "Hush! I won't hear it, Gilbert. You were not evil. You used your sword, yes, but in every case it was to right a wrong."

"That's true, Brother," Edward added. He waved his hand at the young man in front of him, saying, "He has your blood, Gilbert, and perhaps some of the faults that Winslow men seem prone to."

"Are you saying he *should* go?" Gilbert asked in astonishment.

"No, certainly not! It's not my place to make such decisions for your family." Then Edward rose and said, "I find myself more weary than I thought. Would you mind if I took my rest a little early?"

"You're sleeping with me in the loft, Uncle," Matthew responded quickly. "I'll go make things ready."

As he skimmed the stairs with agility, Humility suddenly sobbed, and Gilbert put his arms around her. "He's going to leave us!" she said in a broken voice.

Edward looked at the couple, not knowing what to say. He averted his head, and his glance fell on a sword hanging from a peg driven into the wall. He stepped to the wall, removed the sword and held it in his hands. "I haven't seen this in some time," he remarked quietly. It was a rapier made by Clemens Hornn, once the greatest swordmaker in England. He stroked its shallow guard, gleaming like a closing flower carved in steel, then traced the blade down to the tapering, murderous point.

"The boy has your skill with this, Gilbert," he remarked quietly.

"Would God I'd never let him touch the thing! I would not teach him, as he begged me to do. But others did, and I allowed it—"

"You can't keep the boy locked up in a cage, Gilbert!"

"Yes, but—"

"Man, don't you remember *anything* about your youth?" Edward asked sharply. "You of all men ought to understand a little of the struggle the boy's going through!" He slapped the sword back on its peg, then turned and observed the pair with compassion, but with a severity in his face.

"You were forced into the church, remember? And what good did it do you, Gilbert? None! You gambled and ran after wenches day and night! And whom did you hate for it?"

Gilbert raised his head and said slowly, "You. I thought you talked Father into putting me into the church."

"And whom do you suppose Matthew will hate if *he* is forced to follow the same path?"

Gilbert's face was pale, but he said steadily, "Me, of course. Do you think I haven't thought of that?"

Humility drew out of Gilbert's embrace and stared at Edward. "You have a thought, don't you, Edward?"

"I fear," Edward shrugged, "there's no easy answer to this business—there never is! But you *must* see that it can't go on. Sooner or later the boy will go bad if he doesn't have some liberty."

"What—what sort of 'liberty' do you mean?" Humility asked.

"Not the law—and not the army!" He paused and began setting things in order in his mind, a custom they recognized. Finally he said, "Let him come to England with me—not to Lon-

don, but to a small town where he'll be out of *some* temptation.
I have a friend there, the pastor of the church. He was quite a
worldly man at one time. Served as a Major in the Royalist Army
for a time, and was pretty much of a gambler, a drunkard and a
blasphemer. But that's different now. He's 'Holy Mr. Gifford'
now."

"But—what would Matthew do there?"

"Study business, perhaps. At least that could be the excuse
for his going. I have a man there who does very well in that way,
and we could set Matthew under him. But I hope for better
things."

"Such as?" Gilbert asked.

"Such as Matthew growing older. And under the influence
of a man like John Gifford, he will, I pray, find his way. I dare
hope you will receive him back a candidate for the ministry in a
few years."

Gilbert glanced down at Humility with a strange look on his
face, and Edward added at once, "As a matter of fact, it might
be well for all of us to go. Why, it would be very good for you
to go back to England—see old friends—"

"Gilbert could never leave his church, Edward," Humility
said. She stood there, thin and worn, but there was a light in
her eyes that reminded both men of the fire she had had in her
youth. "We will pray," she added quietly. "God will give us His
mind on this."

As Edward turned to mount the stairs, Gilbert asked, "What
place is this—where Reverend Gifford lives?"

"Bedford."

"A small place?"

"Very small," Edward assured him. "Matthew will be bored,
but he will be safe. Nothing ever happens in Bedford."

CHAPTER TWO

LYDIA

★　★　★　★

The 200-ton *Fortune* rose and fell with the rolling waves under an iron-gray sky. The crew stood by to weigh anchor, waiting only for the couple who had come aboard to have a final word with young Matthew Winslow.

Gilbert held Humility in a firm grasp to steady her against the motion of the ship, and with the other he held to the rail. His bright blue eyes scanned the face of his son as if he sought to find in the handsome features some portent of the boy's future. He raised his voice against the rising wind, saying, "God guide you, my boy. God make His face to shine on you." The strong baritone softened to a lower pitch, and he held out his free hand to grasp that of his son, and he said, "Be faithful to God, Matthew! Never fail Him—never!"

Matthew nodded, marveling at the strength in his father's right hand, and he moved forward quickly to throw his free arm around his mother. As he bent to kiss her faded cheek, the thought that he might never see her again on earth swept through him, cutting his spirit more sharply than the stinging winds whipping across his face. He bit his lip and said impulsively, "Mother, if you ask me to stay . . ."

Humility raised her face to his, the dark blue of her eyes dominating her wasted face, and put one unsteady hand on his cheek. "You would never be happy here, son," she murmured so quietly that he had to lean forward to catch her words. Her hand lifted to push a lock of his reddish-blonde hair back from where it fell in his eyes. There was something so familiar in the gesture that the lump in his throat grew unbearable and his eyes stung with unshed tears.

"Only a year, Mother," he finally whispered, gathering her in his arms and fighting off the dismay her fragile form triggered in him. "Just a year!"

"Time to go," Gilbert said quietly. "The captain must catch the tide."

Humility pulled away from Matthew's grasp and looked up one last time. "Christians never say goodbye, son," she said, and touched his cheek once more. "Just until we meet again."

Then she turned and Gilbert handed her down the ladder into the boat, aided by a burly sailor. He started down, and when just his head and broad shoulders were visible he caught his son's eye, raised his hand in a curious gesture, as though he were flourishing a sword. A smile broke the austerity of his face, making him look very young in the clear sea air, and he called out loudly, "Be faithful, my boy! Be true to God—and to yourself!"

Then he was gone, and Matthew turned blindly and walked toward the forecastle. He heard the thumping sound as the sailors shoved the small boat off, but did not stop until he had found a place of solitude along the forward rail. The first mate cried out, "Weigh anchor!" and the rattle of the chains struck sharply on his ear. He bent over the rail, his lungs filling with the sharp briny air faintly mixed with the odors of land, the loamy smell of raw earth. "Hoist the mainsail!" came the cry of the mate, and slowly the ship heeled over, her prow turning away from the land.

As the sails slid up, the wind caught them, and filled them with puffs of air that cracked like whips. The riggings creaked, and suddenly the ship caught the breeze and lifted like a living thing to breast the waves, leaving the land behind.

"Give them a wave, boy!"

Matthew wheeled to face his uncle, who motioned toward the receding shore. "See? They're waving at us."

Matthew turned to see the small figures of his parents, still in the boat, both of them lifting their arms in a gesture that was sadder than anything he'd known all his days. But he lifted his arms and waved strongly, continuing until the small boat touched the shore. As it did the ship shifted and he could see the small craft no more.

"I'm a fool, Uncle Edward!" he said bitterly, his lips twisted into a grimace of pain. "What kind of man would leave his mother behind, sick as she is?"

"A *young* fool, I suppose," the older man said gently. He put his arm around Matthew's shoulders in a gesture of affection, which was unusual for him, and added, "Never grieve over past decisions, Matthew. There'll be no end of it if you do—and it never changes things."

His uncle's words stayed with Matthew in the three weeks that followed, as the *Fortune* nudged her way across the rutted surface of the gray Atlantic. For a few days he kept to his cabin, surfacing only to eat, then to stand beside the rail, his eyes fixed on the unseen land they were leaving far behind. He made a lonely figure, but his uncle was wise enough to let time heal the worst of the parting grief. Finally, since no emotion can be sustained forever at such a pitch, Matthew began to recover, and day by day as the ship drew closer to England, his spirit lightened.

He spent the days watching the sailors scamper like monkeys up the shrouds to trim the sails. He listened for hours to his uncle tell of the first voyage in the *Mayflower*, of the hardships of that terrible first year when half the colonists died. "We finally had to bury our dead at night—so the Indians wouldn't know how we had dwindled to nothing," he told his nephew one night as they stood at the stern watching the broken reflection of stars shatter like diamonds in the wake of the ship.

"I marvel any of you ever had the courage to go," Matthew said.

His uncle thought about it, then raised his fist and struck the rail with a sudden sharp blow. "We had to have God, Matthew!"

"I—I thought it was land and freedom."

"No! It was God that we hungered for!" The older man paused, then smiled gently in the silver moonlight. His eyes gleamed and he gave a small laugh. "We were all fools for God in those days!" Then he told more about how Matthew's father had found God, and had turned down a life of ease in the service of Lord North to become a poor preacher. "He could have married Cecily, Lord North's daughter," he added idly. "He was quite a ladies' man in those days." A thought struck him and he said slyly, "Like you, I suppose."

Matthew flushed and was glad for the covering darkness. He changed the subject quickly. "Tell me about Bedford."

For the rest of the trip the two talked a great deal, but after they landed at Southampton, made the trip by coach toward the north, Matthew's spirits were dashed by his first view of the small village his uncle indicated. "There it is, boy. That's Bedford."

"It's . . . small, isn't it?" Matthew said. Perhaps if he had not seen Southhampton first, he would have not been so disappointed. Bedford was composed of a scattering of half-timbered houses, all with thatched roofs. They followed only a very slight sort of plan, seeming to have been thrown like a group of dice to rest at random where they landed. The one road more or less connected many of the houses, but in the center of the village, Young Winslow saw, was a more structured look. "That's the Mote Hall," his uncle said, indicating a large two-story building with high-pitched gables crowning the over-hanging second stories. "Most of our large meetings take place there."

The coach stopped in front of a tavern with a large red lion on a sign, and they got out. "Let's have something to eat before we get you settled." Edward gave orders concerning their trunks, and they went inside the Red Lion where they were met by a snaggle-toothed man with a white apron tied around his prodigious stomach. "Mr. Winslow! Yer back again ter see us?"

"Just a brief visit for me, Williams, but my nephew here will be staying in your town for a time. Now, can you feed us?"

The question insulted the innkeeper and he sniffed, saying, "And did yer ever go hungry in the Red Lion, sir?"

"No, indeed not, Williams!" Master Winslow laughed, and the two sat down at a huge oak trestle table and talked until the meal was brought. After the ship's diet, the fresh meat and vegetables set before them were delicious. They were wolfing down portions of cold beef, chunks of fresh bread larded with fresh yellow butter, and boiled potatoes when a man entered the inn.

"Mr. Winslow, welcome back to Bedford!" He was only of average height, but held himself so straight that he seemed tall. His hair was brown, coming down low on his forehead, and his thick brows shaded intelligent brown eyes that held a quizzical look. He moved his head with quick, sharp movements that matched his words, a curious jerking as if his neck were caught in a tight collar and he was attempting to free it.

"Well, it's good to see you, Pastor." Winslow rose and the two gripped hands. "This is my nephew, Matthew—my brother Gilbert's son, from America." He watched as the two men shook hands, and added, "This is Pastor John Gifford, Matthew. You'll be a member of his congregation while you're here."

"I'm pleased to meet you, Pastor." Matthew liked the sharp-featured preacher at once and added, "I trust not to be an additional burden to your cares."

"Oh, I expect young men to be troublesome!" Gifford's eyes twinkled and he gave a slight wink at both men. "When I was your age I was studying for the gallows—but I trust you're a more settled young man than I was."

"Nay, that's past praying for, Pastor Gifford!" Edward laughed. "Fast horses, pretty women, and a duel now and then to put a little spice in the day—that's our boy!"

"Now, Uncle Edward!"

"All in jest, my boy!" Winslow laughed, holding up a hand. "Matthew will be living with Asa Goodman, an apprentice, to learn some of the world of business." He glanced out the door then added, "It's getting a little late, by the way. Will you walk with us as we go to Mr. Goodman's Pastor?"

"I can fill you in with the news on the way," Gifford agreed. The three men left the Red Lion and threaded their way through the maze of cottages in the dying light of the sun. Matthew listened as Gifford spoke somewhat gloomily of political conditions. When the pastor mentioned the possibility of the restoration of Charles to the throne, Edward broke in quickly, "It's coming, Pastor. We may as well get ready for tribulation."

They turned down a dirt lane and Gifford hailed a man sitting in front of a low-roofed cottage. "Ho, John, here's someone for you to meet!"

As the three men approached, the man arose, releasing the small children he had been holding in his lap. He was a tall, portly man, perhaps thirty years of age, Matthew judged, with broad shoulders and a full, round face. His eyes were not large, but had a penetrating quality, and Matthew felt that he was being carefully weighed in the balances as the large man gave him a direct stare.

"John, this is Matthew Winslow, Edward's nephew. Edward, this is Mr. John Bunyan—one of our more promising lights among the ministry."

"Why, I'll deny that, Mr. Winslow!" Bunyan said looking at Edward, a smile touching his full wide lips beneath a reddish moustache. "I'm just a tinker with a longing to speak of Christ." Bunyan had one of those clear tenor voices that carry over long distances without losing any clarity, and there was some sort of magnetism in the man, Matthew saw—a quality he had observed in Governor John Bradford of Plymouth. It had nothing to do with attractiveness, for neither man was particularly well favored. Neither was it a quality of voice, for though both men spoke clearly, they did not thunder as some men felt compelled to do to exert their authority. Whatever it was, Matthew knew that both men had that indefinable quality of leadership; men would listen to them and be led by them.

"John's become quite a traveler since you left, Edward," Gifford said. "He's been preaching all over the country—and with very good response."

The praise bothered Bunyan and he shifted uncomfortably. "Well, if Charles comes back as king, we'll none of us be doing much preaching, will we now?"

"Too true, John," Edward said heavily. "He'll clamp down on our churches—especially men like Pastor Gifford here."

"Perhaps you could come to America, Pastor Gifford," Matthew suggested. "And you, too, Mr. Bunyan."

"We can't *all* leave England!" Gifford snapped. His quick eyes flashed fire and he jerked his head in a series of quick motions as he added, "I was on the Royalist side in the war against the Crown—but this time it'll be different."

"There'll be no new war, Gifford," Edward said at once with a shake of his head. "The English *want* a king—demand one, in fact. And no matter what Charles promises—and I've heard that he's promised no revenge against those who executed his father—there's a host in France who fled the country one jump ahead of Cromwell. And it's *their* turn now, mark my words!"

There was a sense of gloom in the older men that galled Matthew, but he said nothing. He had come to England to find an escape from the boredom and monotony of Plymouth, and it appeared as if he was jumping into a very hot fire. Excitement and adventure were on the horizon, and these friends of his uncle spoke as if Doomsday had been announced!

"Well, you must come with me on some of my preaching engagements, Mr. Winslow." Bunyan interrupted Matthew's thoughts with a nod and a wide smile. "You won't hear much in the way of a preacher, but you'll see some very fine countryside and meet some choice saints."

"I will indeed, Mr. Bunyan," Matthew answered.

"Come, we must go," Edward urged. "Good night, Mr. Bunyan."

As the three men walked away, Gifford stated, "He's a rare one, John Bunyan. Born to preach!"

"Aye, I'm sure he is," Edward agreed. "But he'd better stick to mending pots and pans if Charles comes back."

"John? He'll not do that!" Pastor Gifford shook his head and indicated a house set off in a clump of towering yew trees. "There's Asa Goodman's house." He was silent until they reached the steps, then added quietly, "No, Bunyan is just the sort of man that the Royalists will hunt down. He's a man the people listen to. He's got a gift of moving people—just what the King will be dead set against!"

Winslow knocked on the door, and it was answered at once by a short man with weak eyes who peered at them suspiciously, then as he recognized them, cried out, "Why, it's *you*, Mr. Winslow. Come in! Come in!"

The three men entered, and Matthew made the acquaintance of Asa Goodman, his wife, Ruth, and their two daughters, Chastity and Faith, ages sixteen and eighteen respectively. He was shown to his room, a small one on the second floor, containing little other than a bed, a desk and a washstand. As they came down, he saw his uncle making for the door, but he stopped long enough to say, "I must make another call, Matthew. Mr. Goodman will lay out your duties." He left with Pastor Gifford, and Matthew spent the next hour explaining to Ruth Goodman that he had just eaten and could not hold another bite.

As he sat at the table, sandwiched between Chastity and Faith, he told them about America, but had great difficulty convincing them that elephants were really not a danger to the population. All the family had been reading travel books, and they hung on his every word as he told them of the Indians; the girls were especially avid for blood-curdling stories about their savagery. Matthew knew of none, but they were so pitifully anxious that he invented several to satisfy them.

He escaped to his room as early as possible; removing a small book from his pocket, he sat down at the desk and dipped a pen into an ink bottle, then began writing:

> The year of our Lord, 1659, 6 August, Bedford.
> My first night in Bedford, and I have purposed to keep this journal a record of my new life—and to be as brutally honest as a man can be!
> My poor mother! Shall I never see her face again? I fear not. And I shall carry the picture of her face that last time on the *Fortune* to my grave! How much capacity we have to hurt the ones we truly love!
> If there is such a price then, to my leaving home and parents, I resolve to make it worth the candle! The future is a book whose pages I may not read, save one at a time. The times are troubled. Fear is already in the air. Bunyan, Gifford, my uncle—all are like men standing on the brink of an awful chasm, blindfolded, not knowing what lies before them, but convinced it is a dark day for England—for the Puritans, at least!
> And what will *I* do? Little enough, I suppose. Perhaps I will be a dry and dusty man of business like Asa Goodman. At any rate, I am here, and it is an adventure—I will not be bored to death!

But Matthew was, in fact, terribly bored after the excitement of living in a new land wore off—which was about one month. Bedford was, he admitted ruefully, much the same as Plymouth. He soon learned his duties with Asa Goodman, and since his uncle had left for London two days after depositing him in the small village, there was no one to talk to. Oh, Goodman was not a hard driver, but he had no thought of anything except business. Pastor Gifford was a man of wit, but he was a busy man, ranging far in his pastoral duties. He enjoyed the meetings on Sunday, thinking Gifford the best preacher he'd heard, by far, but the days grew long and the nights grew lonely.

He wrote a bitter note in his journal:

> I might as well have stayed in Plymouth! When Uncle Edward returns, I will make him send me to London or somewhere else on some sort of business. I will be bored out of my head with this place if nothing turns up this week! Please, God, Give me *something* to do in this place!

The day after this plaintive prayer, Matthew sought out John Bunyan in desperation. "Take me with you next week when you go to preach!"

Bunyan gave him an understanding look, then nodded. "Bored with it, are you, Mr. Winslow? Well, it's a small village. Nothing exciting now. Let's see, I go to Elstow next Sabbath. It's my old home, and there's a goodly congregation with no real pastor. Would you like to go there?"

"Yes! Tell me the time and the place, and I'm your man, Bunyan!"

The tall tinker laughed and punched Winslow on the arm, "Well, you might be a help. Can you sing?"

"I'll do my best," Matthew grinned. "Anything for a little variety."

"Be here at dawn next Sabbath, lad," Bunyan nodded. "And be in much prayer for the service, you mind?"

That was on Thursday, and it was with a spirit of release that Matthew met Bunyan as first light began to bathe the little village. "Come now, we go long shanks!" Bunyan said with a smile, and the two set out at a fast pace for Elstow, which lay only eight miles from Bedford. As they walked, Bunyan spoke quickly, sharing with the younger man some of his early history. He had been a terrible sinner as a young man, had served in Cromwell's Model Army, and after the war had been converted to Christ by John Gifford's preaching, then had begun preaching himself a few years earlier.

The sun was bright as the two men entered the small village of Elstow, and Bunyan greeted everyone they met, leading Matthew to a large barn-like structure on the north side of town. To

Matthew's surprise, the place was full. He found himself a seat on one of the backless benches, and for the next three hours, listened spellbound to this mender of pots preach the most powerful sermon he'd ever heard in his life!

It was a strange sermon, and at first he could not tell why it seemed so different. Finally he realized that it was the strange quality of imagination that linked the Scriptures and the message together. Bunyan had the gift of the storyteller, and he employed it in a masterful manner, yet so simply that even the small children that sat there through it all must have understood it.

And it was when he spoke of Jesus—mostly as "the Man"— that Matthew was most moved, for Bunyan had such a love for Jesus Christ that it communicated itself to his hearers. Matthew had never heard such poetic figures, and such plain devotion in a preacher!

He was carried away with it, and when Bunyan called a halt at noon, he moved forward to stand with him. Twisting his head to look at the preacher he felt his foot step on a soft object, then heard a faint cry of pain.

"Oh—pardon me!"

Then he found himself looking into the eyes of the most beautiful woman he'd ever seen!

She was not tall, her black curls not reaching far above his shoulders, and the tear-filled eyes so black that the pupil could hardly be discerned. She bit her lower lip, and swayed helplessly, so that he took her arm without a thought, saying, "Oh, what a clumsy oaf I am! Here, let me help you to a chair."

"It's . . . all right." Her voice was low and husky and there was a trace of an accent which seemed to Matthew quite charming. She tentatively tried her foot, winced, then said, "Perhaps I'd better sit down."

"Let me help you!" As Matthew guided her through the crowd, he could not help noticing that in spite of the drab gray gown she wore, she had a splendid figure. He helped her ease herself down onto a bench, then stood there feeling like a fool. "I say, can I get you anything?"

"No, it will be quite all right." She looked up at him and he thought that he had never seen such coloring! Her lips were like crimson petals against her pale skin, and the enormous eyes and arched brows were bewitching. She suddenly laughed and said, "Don't be so silly! You only stepped on my foot."

He let out his breath in relief, then shook his head. "It's such a small foot, my lady, and mine are so large."

She smiled and shook her head. "I'm all right—oh, here comes my aunt." As she pronounced her words with a distinct French accent, Matthew turned to meet the woman who came to stand beside them.

"Are you all right, Lydia?"

"Yes. I just twisted my ankle, Aunt," she said, turning her large dark eyes on Matthew, who quickly explained, "My fault completely. I'm so clumsy!"

Then John Bunyan appeared, saying, "Ah, have you met?"

"No."

"This is Miss Smith and her niece, Lydia Carbonne. This is Matthew Winslow. I believe you are acquainted with his uncle, are you not?"

The mention of his uncle softened the rather severe look on Miss Smith's face, and she nodded. "Of course." She gave Matthew a direct look and said, "You resemble him greatly."

"Oh, all the Winslows look alike," Matthew remarked with a shrug.

"There are refreshments outside," Bunyan offered. "Will you join me?"

He led them all outside where tables were set up and soon filled with cold cuts and fresh bread. Bunyan and Miss Smith were soon in conversation, and Matthew found himself sitting by the niece, who was eating with a healthy appetite.

"You'd better fortify yourself, Mr. Winslow," she said with an arch smile. "Pastor Bunyan hasn't really begun yet. We'll have the second half of the sermon after lunch."

Matthew Winslow could have been eating sawdust instead of cold beef! He was gazing into the blackest eyes he'd ever seen, and it took all his powers to keep his mind on the conversation with Lydia.

Realizing he was staring at her like a fool, he took himself in hand and began asking her about her background. He learned that she was an orphan, her mother and father (French, of course!), having died in a plague. She had then been taken in by her spinster aunt, Martha Smith. The sermon interrupted the conversation, and he was forced to content himself with glimpses of her beautiful face and form as Bunyan preached.

All too soon it was over, but Bunyan might have preached on the gray beard of Daniel's Billy Goat for all Matthew knew!

One thing he *did* know, however—he was invited to tea the following week at Miss Smith's!

On his way back to Bedford, Matthew was like a drunk man. His jovial mood didn't entirely fool the tall preacher, who gave him a quiet smile as they arrived at the street where Matthew turned to go to the Goodmans'.

"It was a fine sermon, Mr. Bunyan," Matthew said warmly, shaking his hand.

"What did you think of the second part?" Bunyan asked with a straight face. "Was it as interesting doctrinally as the first?"

"Why . . ." Matthew saw the faint smile on Bunyan's lips, and returned it. "Why, as to that," he said, "it was true enough—and the congregation was very fine."

"Yes, she was, wasn't she?" Bunyan stated. Then he laughed. "You'd best sit on the front row next Sabbath, Brother Winslow. I can't compete with a beautiful woman like Miss Lydia Carbonne!"

Matthew flushed, but finally grinned. "You have sharp eyes, Mr. John Bunyan."

Bunyan clapped him on the shoulder and said, "I was young myself once, you know!"

That night Matthew's journal recorded one line:

Lydia—Lydia—Lydia—Lydia—oh, Lydia Carbonne!

CHAPTER THREE

A Young Man's Fancy

★ ★ ★ ★

"Lydia, you must stop seeing this man at once!"

From where she sat in front of a small table brushing her hair, Lydia Carbonne looked up defiantly at the tall figure of her guardian. Her full lips compressed and a rebellious light smoldered in her dark eyes. She had heard this statement in one form or another for the past two months from Martha Smith. At first she had submitted with a sigh, but now she shook her head, causing the mass of raven-dark ringlets to sweep her shoulders.

"There's nothing wrong with seeing Matthew Winslow."

"There's something wrong with a young girl making a spectacle of herself over a man in public!"

"That's not true! He walks me to the meetings, he comes here to tea, sometimes we walk together—is that what you call making a spectacle of myself?"

Miss Smith stared at her niece in despair. "You're every bit as stubborn as your mother!" She shook her head and wondered for the thousandth time how her sister Mary could have been so foolish as to marry a Frenchman. Her mind flew back to another time, another place, when she had faced the mother of this fiery young woman in precisely the same way.

In this same room, less than a year after the death of their father, Mary Smith had met a dashing young foreigner, Andre Carbonne, had fallen in love with him, and agreed to marry him.

Their mother had been a woman of no force, prostrated by the death of her husband, so the lot fell to Martha to do her best to stop the match.

"He's not even of your faith," she had said in horror to Mary. "Your children, God forbid, will be brought up as idol worshipers!"

"Not all Christians are outside the Catholic church!" her sister had shot back, and from that instant Martha Smith knew there would be no hope of changing the girl's mind. "We're going to be married and live in Dover, Martha. We love each other, and I must have him!"

Now, twenty years later, Martha Smith had the eerie feeling that her sister Mary, dead along with her husband and buried in the soil of France, somehow stood before her. *She's Mary come back again!* she thought helplessly. *The same beauty—and the same rebelliousness—like the sin of witchcraft!* The thought shocked her, and she said quickly, "You don't know this man. He's a stranger to us."

"I *do* know him, Aunt Martha," Lydia shot back at once. She gave one more pull through her luxurious hair with an ivory comb, rose and came to stand by the older woman. Placing a hand on her aunt's arm, she modified her voice and said quietly, "Don't be afraid. I know it broke your heart when mother married out of the faith. It—it was hard on her, too, you know—to be cut off from her family."

"It was her choice, Lydia."

"I know, I know, but she had to follow the man she loved. Can't you see that?"

"Oh, Lydia, it's just that I'm afraid for you!" Martha Smith had never married, and this girl had been the daughter she'd never had. Now she was losing her, and fear filled her at the thought that tragedy might strike her down. "Will Howard wants to marry you, and I'd hoped you'd make a match of it with him."

"I don't love him, Aunt. I never could."

The statement left no room for argument, and Martha Smith stood there looking at Lydia, and finally asked the question she had not dared to ask before: "Are you going to marry this man?"

"If he asks me, I'll marry him."

Yes, the same as Mary! Martha Smith thought instantly. *Mary stood in this very room, and she looked me right in the eye and said the same thing. "I'll marry Andre if he asks me."*

"Will you talk with Pastor Gifford about this? Will you at least do that for me?"

Lydia smiled and suddenly pulled her aunt's head down and kissed her cheek. "Of course I will. And you may have nothing to worry about, Aunt Martha. He may never ask me." A thought struck her, and she smiled, adding, "Matthew is spending so much time with John Bunyan these days, he may forget me entirely!"

The object of their conversation was, as a matter of fact, sitting in the Bunyan cottage at that very moment, engaged in conversation with the head of the house on the very subject of matrimony. It was not, however, Matthew's marriage that they spoke of, but Bunyan's.

A light rain was falling, so instead of sitting outside the front door on a stool as he worked, Bunyan was seated at the table putting a series of small rivets in a utensil made of pewter. He held it up to the light and then looked across the table at Matthew and asked, "Some tea, my boy?" He glanced across the room where his daughter Mary was seated on a stool sewing. "Mary, would you brew a little tea for Brother Winslow and me?"

"Yes, Father." Matthew turned to watch as the girl rose, moved unerringly across the room to where the teapot sat on a table and began making the tea. Her blindness was a source of constant sorrow to Bunyan, Matthew knew, though the big man seldom mentioned it. But now there was a veiled grief in his eyes as he watched her.

"She's like her mother, Matthew. I wish you could have known her." All four of Bunyan's children were by his first wife who had died in childbirth. "She was a godly woman, indeed," he went on, tapping the head of a rivet carefully, then holding it up again to the light.

"I suppose you had a hard time, as most newly married couples do," Matthew remarked.

"Hard? Why, I suppose it was," Bunyan remarked. "I had nothing, but she had a marvelous dowry which she brought to our marriage."

"Indeed?"

"Yes, Matthew. I became a wealthy man with that dowry."
His lively eyes twinkled and he rose to go to a bookcase nailed
to the wall. Taking down two books, he returned to the table
and placed them carefully before his guest. "There it is."

Matthew picked up the worn volumes and read the titles
aloud: *"The Plain Man's Pathway to Heaven* by Arthur Dent and
The Practice of Piety by Lewis Bayly. I don't know these books,
John."

"Well, they're solid gold, my boy, solid gold!" Bunyan
smiled. "You know I found the Lord in a most unusual way."
He touched Matthew's arm, adding with a smile, "Perhaps I've
told you the story before—but *I* want to hear it again."

"How was it, John?"

"Why, I was in the army, you know, and we were about as
holy as soldiers ever get. You can thank Cromwell for that! Sermons every day, and God help the poor devil who cursed and
used the name of the Good Lord in vain! He'd be tied over a
cannon and whipped until he was raw! But it paid off, my boy."
His eyes grew dreamy as he leaned on his hands across the table,
thinking of the past. "We went into battle singing hymns of
praise to God. I think that frightened the enemy as much as our
guns! Well, anyway, I was mustered out and went home to Elstow. There I found Sarah, married her and we set up housekeeping. But I was a wild fellow, Matthew, aye, a very wild
fellow!"

"What form did this devilment take, John?"

"Oh, playing stupid games like tip-cat on the Sabbath, ringing the church bell at odd times, midnight and such, and the
worst was my filthy tongue. Oh, I was one for cursing in those
days! But then one day I was walking along the street in Elstow
and there were three or four poor women sitting beside a door
into a room, talking about the things of God. I thought they
spoke as if joy did make them speak; they spoke with such a
pleasantness of Scripture language and with such appearance of
grace in all they said that they were to me as if they had found
a new world!"

"A new world, John?"

"Aye, nothing less than that!" Bunyan shook his head, marveling at it all, then went on in a low voice. "I knew nothing of Jesus Christ—except what little I'd heard in sermons. They spoke of Him as a dear friend whose company they shared. Well, I had to have that, Matthew, I had to! So I was drawn to their company, these poor women, into the fellowhship of which they were a part. It was like a voyage to a new world, indeed, and when I met Mr. Gifford a few months later, I was so hungry to find God that I moved my family here to Bedford, just to sit at his feet. And I've never regretted it."

"He's a fine preacher."

"A man of God indeed." They spoke of the preacher until Mary brought them two large cups, filled them with tea, and allowed herself to be drawn into Bunyan's lap as he drank the steaming beverage. "Good to your poor old father, you are, sweetheart!" he exclaimed, giving her a hug. "And what a helper to her mother—I tell you, she's a marvel, Master Winslow!"

"I know." Matthew watched as the two sat there, Bunyan holding the child close, her blind eyes turned up to his seeing ones.

The two of them sat there listening to Bunyan's talk until Elizabeth came in carrying an empty basket on her arm. "Still preaching at the poor boy, Husband?" she said with a smile. Elizabeth Bunyan was a tall full-bodied woman of twenty-three with the rosy cheeks and clear eyes of the Saxon blood. Her hands were roughened with work, but she had a natural winsomeness which Matthew admired. She had married Bunyan, taking on the care of his four small children, when she could have made a much better match.

Bunyan rose at once, embraced her and said, "Now you sit down here and let me spoil you!" She smiled and obeyed. He brought cakes and tea to her, leaving a trail as he went. Matthew was amused to see that the tinker, so exact and careful in his work with metal, was so careless in his service.

She told him of the poor people she'd seen that afternoon, and he shook his head sadly over each case. It was a pleasant scene, and Matthew, for all his desire to wade into action in the wide world, thoroughly enjoyed soaking in the atmosphere of the family group. The smaller children came in, clinging to either the father or the mother, and Matthew reached out and pulled

Mary to his lap, laughing at her protests that she was too big.

Finally, the children left to play, except for Mary, who helped her mother prepare the evening meal. "Looks like the rain has stopped," Bunyan observed. "Let's take a walk before supper."

They walked around the village streets, and Bunyan observed slyly as the neighbors all greeted young Winslow along with himself, "You've become quite a fixture here, Matthew. How long has it been since you came—two months?"

"About that."

Bunyan said suddenly, turning to face Matthew, "You're completely taken with the Carbonne girl."

"Well, she's a charming young woman—"

"Faw!" Bunyan snorted. "Don't you think I have eyes? Even Mary, who can't see a thing, asked me when you two were getting married."

Matthew stopped suddenly, then turned to lean against a rock wall that encircled a snug cottage. He pulled a piece of moss from between two smooth stones, stroked its silky texture, then tossed it to the ground. "I didn't come to England to get married, John. I came to find—" He paused and once again he plucked a shred of the emerald green moss and seemed to be lost in thought as he stroked it with the tip of his finger. "To tell the truth, Brother Bunyan, I don't know *what* it was I came to find. I thought maybe it was adventure—for I've always wanted that! But these last few days in this place have made me uncertain."

Bunyan nodded sagely and said, "I know, boy, I know. Didn't I run off when I was only a lad to fight in the war? And there's some of that in you. You'll not be a man content to rust unburnished, I tell you! But war—that's not the answer." He shook his head and looked up as a swallow sailed gracefully to land in the chimney of the house beyond the wall. "No, men tire of that. But there's another kind of action, the warfare of the spirit. Jesus calls us to arms, you know. He urges us to put on the whole armor of God, to train as athletes for the race. Being a Christian isn't a soft, easy life—especially in this poor country of ours, in the year of our Lord 1659."

Matthew tossed the shred of moss to the ground and looked at Bunyan with excitement in his bright blue eyes. "I think I'd like to be part of that struggle, John."

Bunyan took in the lean form, the eager wedge-shaped face turned toward him, and then he shook his head sadly. "It won't be easy, you know. I don't think we can win this war. Some of us won't die in our beds—and some will go to prison or be driven beyond the sea."

"I'm not afraid of that!"

"No, not now, perhaps. But I tell you flat out, Matthew Winslow, the only ones who will survive this coming darkness will be those to whom the Lord Jesus Christ is a living reality! Can you say that's true of you?"

Matthew dropped his head, and there was a silence on the air so profound that he could hear the far-off cry of a curlew. The silence ran on, broken only by the tinkle of bells on a few sheep in a distant meadow.

When he raised his head, there was a mixture of sadness and desire in his face. "No, John," he said slowly, "I can't say that. I've been watching the people here, and I confess to you— as I have to Pastor Gifford—Christ is not formed in my heart. Not *yet*! But I'm willing to throw myself into this battle you say is coming."

Bunyan straightened his back and looked carefully into the eyes of young Winslow. He liked what he saw but was not ready to say more than, "It's a beginning, Matthew. God will guide you—and as I said, you'll not be a dusty man of business! The spirit in you, why, it's far too strong for that!"

"I—I've been confused about just about everything, John, but one thing I'm sure of is that I want to marry Lydia Carbonne."

Bunyan stared at the young man, then shook his head. "Be sure of yourself, Matthew." He held up his hand to cut off the protest that leaped to Matthew's lips. "In the first place, you're young and have no profession. Now, I hear that you may do well in business, so Asa Goodman says. But that's not enough for a marriage."

"But I love Lydia!"

"There is one thing that few people know about Lydia, Matthew, not even her aunt suspects it."

"What is that, John?"

"She seems flighty, not at all serious about her religion, but I tell you she *is*! Even her aunt mistakes her; being so much opposed to her mother's marriage, she chooses to think that the French strain has corrupted the English piety. Tell the truth now, son, do you not think the young woman to be somewhat frivolous—though very beautiful?"

"Yes, I suppose so, but—"

"You are mistaken, and you will find out that there is a will of steel in her makeup. I have had more than one talk with her about her commitment to the Lord Jesus Christ, and I tell you she will not be happy with a husband who is less of a Christian than she is."

"And you think I am not enough of a Christian to be her husband?"

Bunyan smiled and put his large hand on the young man's arm. There was a mixture of love and judgment in his direct gaze. Then he said, his voice low but firm, "I think you have not found yourself yet, my boy—and you have not found your God. I travail much in prayer for you." Then he slapped the broad shoulder of the young man, saying with encouragement, "You will find your way! Now, let us go inside."

The two went into the cottage, but for once Matthew had little appetite for Elizabeth's good cooking. He played with his food, then after supper spent some time with the children. Finally he left, thanking the Bunyans for their hospitality. When he went up to his room, he picked up his journal and struggled to put down on paper what was happening to him.

October 3, 1659. Bedford.

This country is in a fever! There is no government, and the talk is all of the restoration of Charles to the throne. Pastor Gifford says it will come within a month, and each Sabbath he exhorts the congregation to prepare their souls for the terrible times he says will come then.

And what will *I* do? Run home like a cur with his tail between his legs? Deny the faith and join the Church of England? It would be so easy!

And what of Lydia? I have not let myself think of it, but here in this room on this night, I set it down so that it will give me strength and purpose to stand when the tribulation comes: By my soul, I love this woman. *You are young—you don't really know yet—you have no profession!* They will say this, and more.

And what is my answer? I love this woman. That is my

answer, and I know that even if she does not love me, I will go to my grave with her image in my heart. Yea, though I never see her again in this world, she has spoiled for me the image of all other women—no, not the *image*—the *reality*!

What will I do then? I will do this one thing. I will take my courage all rolled up like a ball, and I will go to her and I will say, *Lydia Carbonne, I love you with all my heart. I want you to share my life, my bed, my heart for all time on this earth.*

She will probably say no. That is *her* decision. Mine is made—to offer her my name and my strong right arm—and my heart—so help me God!

Slowly Matthew closed the journal, cleaned the tip of the quill, and placed it on the desktop. His face was slightly pale, and as he knelt beside his narrow bed, instead of the rather ritualistic prayer that usually closed his day, he lifted up his face and for a long time waited for some answer. Finally he got into bed and lay there staring at the low ceiling.

Lydia thereafter said of Matthew's proposal, "It was the most *unusual* proposal any man ever made or any girl ever received!"

The scene was the small chapel in Elstow. The audience was the congregation of Separatists gathered for the customary Sabbath morning sermon. Since the church had no pastor, John Bunyan had been asked to bring the sermon, and he had just started his seventh major point when Matthew Winslow came in, his face pale as paper. Ordinarily he took a seat at the rear of the church, but on this occasion he swept the congregation with a swift glance, and finding Lydia sitting in the second row with her aunt, walked steadily across the pegged wooden floor and plunked himself down firmly beside her.

Lydia was startled, for the Elstow congregation held to the old ways, men seated on one side, women on the other. Her large eyes flew open as Matthew sat down beside her, and she felt her aunt stirring angrily on her other side.

Matthew leaned forward and said something in a faint whisper which she did not understand, primarily due to the fact that Brother Bunyan was preaching about hell, and it was the usual custom to raise the volume considerably when the subject was under consideration.

He leaned forward until one of her black tresses touched his cheek as he whispered into her ear, but at the exact moment he repeated himself, Bunyan slapped the desk in front of him and gave a resounding roar.

Lydia was confused, having no concept as to what urgency could warrant such behavior on the young man's part. She turned from him, only to have her arm firmly grasped, pulling her back to face him again. This time he raised his voice so that she understood him *very* clearly!

Indeed, every living soul in the congregation heard him, for just as he raised his voice, Brother Bunyan suddenly stopped speaking. And into that sudden and absolute silence that fell over the church, Matthew Winslow said in a clear, urgent voice: "I said, *will you marry me, Lydia?*"

The loud question drew a sudden gasp from Lydia's aunt, and she jerked around, causing her large Bible to drop to the floor with a *thud*! A hum swept through the room, and John Bunyan, who had heard the guns of war with more aplomb, stood there behind the sacred desk staring at the couple.

Lydia was stunned. The silence that followed seemed to roar in her ears as she became conscious of the stares burning into her from all sides. Her lips parted and she wondered if she had heard him correctly. Surely no man would be so forward as to propose to a young woman under such circumstances!

But apparently Matthew Winslow was exactly such a man, for he seemed totally unaware of the gaping audience, and said again, "Lydia, I love you and want you to marry me!"

She stared at him, her face flushed, tears of vexation filling her eyes. "No!" she snapped indignantly, and with a suddenness that caught everyone off guard, she rose and rushed out of the church, leaving Matthew staring into the angry eyes of her enraged aunt.

Turning from the irate woman, and without a glance at either preacher or congregation, he dashed out, his heels drumming rapidly on the wood floor.

As the door slammed behind Matthew, Pastor Bunyan looked with startled eyes at his congregation, took a deep breath and then continued as though nothing had happened. "Hell," he stated firmly, "was created for the devil and his angels—not for men!" He cast one furtive look at the door where the pair had escaped and added enigmatically, "God made other things for men—such as marriage." But his attempt to recapture the attention of his flock was hopeless.

Outside, Lydia ran along the narrow street, crying with humiliation, stumbling over the cobblestones. As she turned the corner onto the lane where she lived with her aunt, strong hands grabbed her from behind.

"Let me go!" she cried, trying to free herself from the iron embrace. "I hate you, Matthew Winslow!"

But he just stood there holding her as she beat her fists against his chest, tears running down her cheeks. Finally she stopped and, in a gesture of surrender and helplessness, fell against his broad chest, moaning, "What will I do? What will I do?"

Placing his hand under her chin, he drew her face upward. She had never seemed so beautiful to him.

"Why did you do such a thing to me?" she cried.

Pulling her close, he said passionately, "Because I love you! And I'll have you, Lydia, or die in the attempt!"

She gasped at his boldness, but had no time to do anything else, for he suddenly bent his head and kissed her intensely. Then as his kisses grew gentle, she found her arms going around his neck. How long they stood there or who drew back first she never knew, but when they looked at each other in breathless wonder, she whispered, "I love you, Matthew Winslow! I'll never love anyone else!"

She took a deep breath and released it. One hand went up to touch his cheek tenderly; then she smiled with trembling lips and murmured, "I never knew love could be like this."

"Nor I," Matthew responded quietly. "But it's only the beginning, sweetheart!" he said triumphantly. "Only the beginning! Why, we've got a whole lifetime to love each other!"

Then she said something that startled him, so unexpected it was. "And we can love God together, can't we, Matthew?"

He thought at once of Bunyan's comment: *She will not be happy with a man who is less of a Christian than she is.* He might have given thought to that if he had not been so in love, but he merely smiled and said, "Yes, of course we will!"

They turned and walked back toward the church with a choir of small birds singing an echo of the joy that had filled their hearts.

CHAPTER FOUR

HE THAT FINDETH A WIFE ...

★ ★ ★ ★

Edward Winslow felt the weight of his years as he climbed heavily out of the dusty coach in front of the Mote Hall. He moved stiffly down the narrow lane that led to Pastor Gifford's cottage, speaking briefly to those who greeted him. The brilliant May sunshine painted the thatched roofs of the village with gold, but he had no eye for the beauty of the lush countryside that day.

I'm like an old dog looking for a place to die, he thought wearily, then paused abruptly, for he had been a man of great zest, and the discovery that he had given up swept over him. He stood stock-still in the middle of the street, unaware of the white-washed houses of Bedford or the noisy flock of geese crossing the village green like a snowy cloud. He suddenly remembered the day he had stood on the deck of the *Mayflower*, just off Southampton, with Pastor Robinson—now dead. That day with the small band of believers, they had looked their last at England and turned to face the unseen land across the sea. A lump rose in his throat as thoughts of them—Standish, Alden, Mullins, Bradford, and Captain Christopher Jones! *All gone now—and I'm not far behind.*

"Mr. Winslow!" A voice caught at him, interrupting his reminiscing. As he turned he saw Pastor Gifford approaching from the square with his nephew. "You're two days late," Gifford said as he came to take Winslow's hand. "We've been concerned."

"Every coach was full for two days after the King arrived from France." He shook his head sadly. "I'd have been most happy to leave earlier."

"Come, Uncle," Matthew said quickly, noting his evident fatigue. "These coach rides are enough to make a man take to his bed. I'll accompany you to Pastor Gifford's house. You can tell us the news on the way."

"I think I will take a little rest, Matthew," his uncle nodded. He allowed himself to be led along the street by Matthew's gentle pressure. He said little as they made their way past the first group of cottages north of the Mote Hall, but gave a sigh of relief as they came to the small cottage of the pastor.

"Wife!" Gifford called out as they crossed the threshold, "We have a guest."

Gifford's wife Sarah, a short, heavy-set woman of fifty, turned from the massive fireplace, her face lighting up at the sight of the older man. "Ah now, I've been cooking for you for two days! Sit you down, and you can have these meat pies I've had to fight my husband and your nephew for!"

"Yes, sit down, Edward," Gifford urged, pulling a heavy chair back from the table. "Sit you down, too," he said to the younger Winslow. "You can lie down after you've eaten, Edward, but first, tell us about the event."

"Charles is king of England—and that's the whole of it," Winslow said heavily. He reached into his inner pocket, fumbled around briefly, then pulled a letter out. "A letter from your father."

As Matthew opened the letter, he heard Pastor Gifford saying, "Well, we knew it was coming, didn't we?"

"Yes, we knew it." Winslow leaned forward, placed his brow on his fist and closed his eyes. "Aye, we *knew* it, John—but I don't think any of us really have any idea of what it's going to be like."

"In that you are probably right," Gifford said slowly. "It'll be a dark night of the soul for our people."

As the two older men spoke of the new order and the problems it would bring to their small world, Matthew read the brief lines:

4 March 1660

My son Matthew,

Your request that we travel to England to meet your new bride is, of course, quite out of the question. I fear you do not yet understand how ill your mother is. She is almost completely bedfast now, and I must stay at home to take care of her, except for those times when the neighbors sit with her.

I do not even dare go to preach overnight at any of the churches, for fear she will be gone when I return. She is quite ready to go home to the Lord. This morning when one of the good ladies asked her if she had any fear, she roused up, and her eyes had the same fire they had when I first saw her, and she said right smartly, "Afraid? How could I be afraid to go to Him whom I have loved and longed for these fifty years!"

She had memorized your letters word for word and only wishes that she might have seen your bride. But what has meant the most to her—and to me, my son!—is the portion of the last letter where you indicated your intention to pursue the Lord. That, along with the word from your uncle in which he speaks of your interest in preaching along with good Master Bunyan, have been the joy of her heart, and mine also.

When we parted, Matthew, I said, "Be true to God and to yourself." I can add nothing to that, except that your mother and I have great faith now in you, and that if we do not meet again on this earth, we will be reunited in a better Kingdom!

Gilbert Winslow

Matthew blinked rapidly, his eyes burning as he read the lines, and he bit his lip as he folded the letter and stored it in his pocket. He had been over-hasty in his marriage, he knew, and the guilt of it bore heavily on him. The original plan had been for a trip to Plymouth with Lydia so she might meet his parents, then marry there. But there had been such objections from Martha Smith over Lydia making such a voyage in an unmarried state that they had given up on the idea. "We'll go to America soon, dear," Lydia had said, knowing something of the pain he felt. But the trip was long and expensive. So the five months of their marriage had served only to increase the pain Matthew felt over his parents.

He shook off the thought and heard his uncle speaking of the restoration of Charles to the throne. "The whole country is one big ball, John. You should have seen the excitement when Charles came ashore day before last! He came in a barge with two dukes. Mr. Pepys was with him, and the captain of the brigantine steered. There was also Mr. Mansell and a dog the king loves—and many others from his nest in France. A large crowd was there to meet him, including General Monk, who fell on him with all imaginable love and respect, thousands of horsemen it seemed, and noblemen of all sorts. The mayor of the town presented him his white staff, the badge of his place, which the King gave him again." He gave a short laugh and a sardonic light came into his eyes. "You'll like this, John, the mayor gave him a very rich Bible, which he took and said, holding it up, 'This is what I love more than anything else in the world!' "

"You don't think he meant it?" Matthew asked.

"Meant it? Him, with his fancy French whores in his cabin on the ship he'd just left?" Winslow shook his head violently and struck the table with a clenched fist. "The man's an actor, I tell you! Now it pleases him to play the benevolent monarch, forgiving his enemies—but mark my word, within months the gallows in England will bear the weight of those who were closest to Cromwell."

"What about you, Edward?" Gifford asked quickly.

"I would not be at all surprised to find myself among those pinpointed by Charles."

"But—you won't stay here, will you, Uncle?" Matthew asked.

"Stay here? Of course I'll stay here! I've not so much life in front of me that I'd sell out what I've lived for just to have a few more hours on this earth!"

"That's very well for you, Edward," Gifford nodded. "But I think for your nephew it might be best to return to Plymouth."

"I agree," the old man said.

"Well, I don't!" The face of young Winslow flushed and there was a stubbornness in the set of his chin that brought a sudden image of Gilbert Winslow to the older man. He watched as Matthew got to his feet and paced the confines of the small room in agitation, his trim figure alive with nervous energy. "What sort of man do you take me for? A coward?"

"Now, Matthew, there's no question of that," Gifford soothed. He had grown accustomed to the quick, impulsive shifts in the young man's behavior, so now he reasoned with him carefully. "First of all, this isn't your home. What happens here isn't your battle—except perhaps in prayer. Secondly, you are not alone now. If you were single, that might be a different story, but as Mr. Bacon has said, 'He that hath wife and children hath given hostages to fortune.' You must consider Lydia. And thirdly, you must have been under constant burden concerning your mother. You must see that going back to Plymouth would be the wise thing to do."

"Perhaps so, but you forget one thing," Matthew responded quickly. "You and I have had long talks, have we not, about my preaching? Am I to leave that, too? And don't tell me there's preaching to be done at Plymouth, Pastor Gifford! I will quote you one scripture, and you tell me how I may without peril to my soul ignore it: 'He that putteth his hand to the plow and turneth back, is not fit for the kingdom of God!' "

Pastor Gifford gaped open-mouthed at the fiery ardor of young Winslow. Then he gave a short laugh and threw up his hands. "I leave him to you, Edward!"

"Well, that's no good, either," Edward smiled, and for that moment the lines of his face softened and he looked much like the young man before him. "The Winslows have always been fool-stubborn, and I see this one is no different. His father is that way himself—and so am I, I suppose."

Matthew stood there, so tall that his head almost brushed the rough beam over his head. He smiled down at Gifford. "It would be so much easier if it were a real war with swords and pikes, wouldn't it? Just go out slashing and hacking—then you either killed or got killed. But this isn't like that, is it?"

"No, our weapons are not carnal, but mighty to God to the pulling down of strongholds," Gifford stated emphatically. "And it's a mighty stronghold that lies before us—the realm of England will be set to crush every Puritan and Separatist to powder, and very soon."

There was a silence as Gifford's wife came to the table with trenchers full of meat. "Well," the younger man said, "Lydia is expecting me." He took his uncle's hand. "You'll come to our house for supper tomorrow night, will you, sir?"

"Done!"

"Good day, then. I'll read the book by Mr. Hooker before our study tomorrow, Pastor."

He left the room hurriedly, and as the two men began to eat, Edward asked, "What's your judgment, John, on that young man?"

Gifford chewed a morsel of meat slowly, swallowed, then said, "He's either going to be a great man—" He paused, then with a shrug of his narrow shoulders, finished by saying, "He's got the raw material, Edward, but the crucible we're all going to be in soon will test him out."

"It would kill Gilbert and Humility if he failed," Edward remarked with sadness in his old eyes. "He's all that's left of the House of Winslow, isn't he? If he goes down, it'll be like there never were any of us."

"No! He won't go down!" Pastor Gifford said suddenly, his usually mild expression twisted to an explosive anger. "This king may think to wipe us out, but he shall not do it, not by all that's holy! You and I have fought, but we are old. It'll be young men like your nephew who'll have to stand in the gap this time!"

"Amen!" Edward Winslow agreed loudly. Then he looked at the door and said in a prayerful whisper, "Amen!"

The tiny house on the edge of town was like a doll's house, having only one room for cooking, dining, eating, and studying, and one small room no more than eight feet square for sleeping. It had been used by one of the deacons, Matthew Prince, as a storage shed for his blacksmithing equipment, but he had agreed to rent it to the newlyweds very cheaply.

It had been a delightful game for the pair, cleaning out the rooms, finding a few pieces of furniture and fitting them into every possible location. They set up housekeeping with a wedding gift from Edward Winslow, a small bag of gold sovereigns. "If it hadn't been for your uncle Edward, we'd be roosting on a tree!" Lydia had laughed once as they tried to put a sideboard along a wall that was only two inches longer than the massive piece of oak furniture.

He had dropped the end he was struggling with, picked her up in his arms and covered her face with kisses, crying out, "I'd rather have a woman like you roosting in a tree than any other in a castle!"

"Matthew!" she had cried, but there was a look of intense

satisfaction in her dark eyes as she pretended to pout. She had always been a romantic girl—far too much so for her aunt's tastes. Perhaps it was the French blood. In any case, she had somehow been able to maintain a balance between an inner life alive with imagination and the rigid creed and austere practices of the Pilgrim way. She had learned while very young to act out little dramas she made up only when alone, but even when she ceased to pantomime such things, she kept up a lively imagination.

Those little dramas had been buried deep inside, but she had learned almost at once that the man she had married was at *least* as romantic as she, although he denied it vehemently.

To outsiders, Matthew and Lydia seemed a rather conventional young married couple. She tended her tiny house, sewed, cooked, and sat demurely by her tall, handsome husband through the four-hour sermons, and he went faithfully to work with the dusty books of Asa Goodman, looking as solemn as a deacon.

But when they were alone in their snug cottage, their behavior would have been a scandal to the neighbors, not to mention the deacons and pastors! They both had playful minds, and their verbal give-and-take, puns and jokes that would have been meaningless to anyone else, was a source of constant delight to both of them.

Even now as he walked to the door and stepped inside, his heart beat a little faster at the thought of her. She met him at once, throwing her arms around him and pulling his head down for a kiss. They stood there for a long moment, savoring each other. Then he stepped back and pulled the letter from his pocket. "Uncle Edward is back. He brought a letter from Father."

She read it quickly, then looked up with apprehension. "It sounds very serious."

"I think it is. Father isn't given to idle words."

She bit her lower lip, then said quietly, "You feel very bad, don't you?"

"I . . . wish we could have gone home." Then seeing her face grow tense, he took her in his arms and added, "Now, don't you fret, Princess. It just couldn't be."

"Do you think we should go now?"

He released her and sat down on the single bench in the room. "Uncle Edward and Pastor Gifford say we should go. Not just because of Mother's illness, but they think there's going to be hard times for all of us."

She nodded and sat down next to him. Taking his hand in hers, she spoke softly. "And what do you say, dear?"

He shook his head stubbornly, an expression she had learned to recognize. "I say we stay here. Where in America is there a man like Pastor Gifford or John Bunyan to sit under?"

"All right, we stay!" she cried out; then she jumped up and ran to the fireplace. "Oh, I've burned the potatoes!"

He laughed and rose to go to her side. "Forget the potatoes! Here I'm trying to make the most important decision of our lives, and you're worried about burned potatoes!"

"And you'll be screaming like a madman when I put them in front of you for supper!" she laughed.

"Madman I may be, but not over burned potatoes—just you," he returned, grabbing her and whirling her around the room.

"Oh, Princess," he said, holding her tightly, "I didn't know love could be so wonderful." He looked into her glowing face and kissed her tenderly. "My love, I—"

"Good day, Brother Winslow."

Matthew loosed his grip on Lydia so suddenly that she almost slipped to the floor, then both of them stood there with their faces flaming, staring at John Bunyan and Elizabeth, who had come up to the front door.

"Oh—" Matthew stammered. "Why, Brother Bunyan, come in—we were just—just—"

Lydia pushed at the mass of ringlets that had fallen wildly over her shoulders and moved toward Elizabeth. "Come in. Matthew and I were just discussing our future!"

"It's a joy to see young love. I hope you're enjoying each other like this when you've been married as long as some of us!" He put his arm around his wife and smiled down at her. Then he asked, "Well, Matthew, will you be going with me tomorrow to preach at Hinton?"

"Of course."

"Good!" Bunyan gave the young man a smile. "I think you

might say a few words this time, Matthew."

"You mean—preach?"

Bunyan smiled at his expression. "You have to begin, don't you? We all do. Come, Elizabeth, we must go."

"He's a wonderful man," Lydia murmured, watching them walk away. "So simple."

"Yes, but he's a deep one," Matthew mused. He stared after the departing pair. "Four children! And expecting another! Elizabeth's first—and he may be in jail or deported. How can he face up to that?"

Lydia took his arm and said quietly, "We must pray, Matthew. And we must cling very close together. You know what I fear most?"

"What?"

"Not jail or persecution, but that we'll be somehow divided."

"How could that be, Princess?" he asked gently. "I would never leave you."

She stood there staring out at the disappearing forms of the Bunyans and seemed to be struck by something in their figures. "I don't know how, but it's what I fear. Don't let it happen, Matthew!" she cried, throwing herself into his arms.

"Never!" Matthew stated, smoothing her hair. "Let the world fall, you and I will stay together."

She put her head back and looked up at him with a tremulous smile. "That's all I want, Matthew. It's not too much to ask, is it? We may miss out on the world, but we can ask God to give us that one thing, can't we? Is that too selfish to ask Him for—to let us stay together as long as we're on this earth?"

"No, not too much."

He led her back inside the small, dark cottage and pulled the door, shutting out the outside world with all its clamor and demands. And as it closed with a firm sound, he found himself wishing that it could be as easy as this always—just leave the world, find a snug hiding place with the one you love, and shut the door.

But as he turned to her uplifted face, he felt a wave of fatalism grip him. A cloud crossed the sun, cutting off the bright rays and leaving her a vague and indistinct shadow as she stood before him.

CHAPTER FIVE

THE SKY IS FALLING!

★　★　★　★

Justice Twisten lived in the largest house in Bedford, a sprawling two-story half-timbered affair, with five large chimneys rising high above the eaves. Plumes of white smoke rolled out of them, caught by the sharp September wind and twisted into a braided column against the iron-gray sky. Summer's emerald green lay buried under a dull covering of dead leaves that crunched briskly under the feet of the three men marching down the long lane from the main road.

John Bunyan glanced at his companions, then lifted his gaze to the house which lay in the circle of a serpentine drive. "I wish your uncle were here with us, Matthew. He's used to talking with lawyers and government people."

"There's not much even he could do this time, John, even if he were able to come," Pastor Gifford responded. "I have no hope of any mercy from Twisten. He's always hated our faith."

Bunyan scraped the mud off his feet on the brick steps and grimaced as he gave the brass knocker a loud blow. "No, I suppose that's true. How is he, do you know, Matthew?"

"Very poorly." Anger flew across Matthew's face as he thought of his uncle jammed into a common jail in London. "He has weak lungs and that cold cell could be the death of him." The Winslow blood flared up and he struck the moss-covered bricks with a clenched fist. "Curse them! An old man like that who's served his country all his life!"

"But they'll never forget he served Cromwell," Pastor Gifford reminded them. "I hear the jails are packed with Fifth-Monarchy men and Separatists, but—" He broke off as the door opened and he announced, "We are called to see Justice Twisten."

"He's waiting for you," the tall, thin man who answered the door said. He led them across a large open room, down a broad corridor lined with a series of portraits of stern-faced men. "In here, please."

The three men stepped into a large book-lined study, dominated by a massive desk behind which sat Justice Simon Twisten. He was a large, portly man with a neck of a bull, his small eyes buried in the folds of fat lining his face. He offered no greeting.

Pastor Gifford waited for a moment, then seeing that the man was not going to speak, said, "You sent for us, Justice Twisten?"

Still he waited, the antagonism in his piggish eyes gleaming; then he said abruptly, "You know why you've been sent for, Gifford. We'll have no discussion!" His high voice rose, incongruous in such a bulky form, and his fat face flushed as he added, "You are lawbreakers, and I'll have none of it in this country."

"Sir, if I might—"

"None of your smooth talk, I said! You have been told of the Conventicle Act, and you can spare me your pleas for mercy. The law is plain; it forbids the assembly of more than five people for any religious gathering." He glared at Bunyan and spat out maliciously, "You, John Bunyan, are a known felon!"

"I am no felon!"

"Quiet!" Twisten roared. He heaved his bulk out of the chair and stood there, massive and dangerous, "You have been preaching at night to groups of people—we have information on this. And I warn you, Bunyan, if you are apprehended, you are subject to the full weight of the law!"

"Surely, Justice Twisten," Gifford objected, "you would not classify a few simple preachers with murderers and thieves!"

"The law, Gifford, the law does the classifying!" Twisten shot back as he leaned forward like a huge bear, resting his fists on the desk and glaring at the three of them.

"The same law that throws an old man like my uncle in jail with common murderers?" Matthew raised his voice and took a step toward the justice in a move so unexpected that Twisten straightened up and stepped backward, alarm on his face. "You call that *law*? I call it cowardly tyranny!"

"Matthew!" Gifford warned, taking a firm grip on the young man's arm, but he was too late.

Twisten wheeled and moved across the room surprisingly fast for such a big man. He threw open the door and shouted, "Matthew Winslow, is it? You will join your famous uncle the moment I hear one word of your defying the Act! Now get out, all of you! I called you here to tell you that I am set against you! You had your way with the true servants of the King while that traitor Cromwell lived—now we'll see who will bend their necks to the Royal Monarch, King Charles the Second! Get out!"

Matthew made to move toward the justice, but his arms were pinned at once by Gifford and Bunyan. As they struggled to get him outside the door, he cried out with a ringing voice, "You godless dog! Put me in the jail! I'll stay there until the moss grows up to my eyes before I'll give in to you!"

He was still raging as they cleared the front door.

"You young fool! What good did that do?" Bunyan said roughly as he jerked the young man so hard his neck popped.

"You expect me to stand there and listen to that—!"

"Shut your mouth!" Bunyan interrupted fiercely. As soon as they were clear of the drive and back on the main road, he released Matthew and turned to walk rapidly toward the center of town, Gifford joining him.

Matthew stood transfixed, then hurried to catch up with the two men who ignored him, speaking quietly only to each other.

"No hope for mercy from Twisten, just as I said," Pastor Gifford said despondently. He gave a quick sideways glance at the burly tinker beside him. "What will you do, John?"

"What God tells me to do!"

"But you know the end of that—I mean, if you are appre- hended preaching, you'll be deported, maybe for life!"

Bunyan did not look at Gifford. His eyes were fixed on the horizon where small groups of scudding clouds broke the monotony of the gray sky. He seemed to be lost in thought and it was not until they were abreast the field where the lane turned to his cottage that he stopped and turned his eyes on Gifford and Winslow.

"I'm afraid, Pastor."

"*You*—afraid?" Matthew asked in surprise. Never had a man seemed so filled with total dedication as John Bunyan, and he could not believe what the tall preacher was saying.

"Yes, I'm afraid," Bunyan said simply. He smiled slightly, and his eyes were fixed on Winslow. "You've often told me what a good imagination I have, Matthew."

"Yes?"

"Well, I do have more of that than most men, but it's a curse—at least in this case." He brushed his hand across his face in an odd gesture, as if he were attempting to brush away invisible cobwebs. When he lowered his hand there was a vulnerability in his strong face that Matthew had never seen before. "Every night I have this dream—always the same. I'm in a cell, a dirty, dank cell with filth everywhere. And in the dream I've been there so long I can't remember when I came there, and there's no end to it! Every night is an eternity stretching out to the crack of doom—but that's not the worst!"

"What is it, John?" Gifford asked quietly.

"It's my family—my wife and children." Bunyan brushed his hand across his eyes, and when he looked up Matthew saw they were filled with tears. "I hear them outside the cell, crying— especially Mary—oh, the thought of my blind one, what she may endure, breaks my heart to pieces!"

His companions stood there helplessly. Gifford glanced quickly at Matthew as if to say, *I've never seen this side of John Bunyan.* Then he said gently, "It's asking too much—for a man with a family. Let the younger men do the front-line fighting, John."

"Stop preaching?"

"Just for a while."

"No! Never. I spoke too quickly against you, Matthew," he said with a faint smile. "I like what you told the justice! What was it you said?" He searched for it, then said, " *'I'll stay there until moss grows up to my eyes.'* " He smiled and clapped Winslow on the back with a hearty blow. "That's what you said—and it's what I feel."

"But your family?" Gifford protested. "What about them?"

"God will be the father of the fatherless!" Bunyan exclaimed. He seemed to have shaken off the weight that had fallen on him. Squaring his shoulders, he looked fearlessly back toward Twisten's house. "God will not forsake us. We are in His hand, and if it will be to His glory to be put in a cell, then by the grace of God that is what I will do!"

"Amen!" Matthew cried. "And we will go to lower Samsell tomorrow just as we planned?"

"Yes! Meet me at five. The people there will gather at the river, and we'll preach in the dark if we have to!"

"I would not go if I were you, John," Gifford spoke up. "Twisten is no fool. He'll have you watched."

"Well—perhaps that's so." He thought of it, then said, "Scripture says that a wise man looketh well to his going. We will leave after dark, Matthew. That way we can be sure no one is following us. I'm sure no one in the congregation will betray us."

"I'll be there!" Matthew exclaimed, afire with excitement. He waved quickly and ran off to tell Lydia.

"He's a firebrand, isn't he, John?" Gifford said with a fond glance at the young man.

"He's that. We could have used him in the Model Army. But this is going to be a different kind of war. If it were a matter of swords and gunpowder, Matthew would be the ideal warrior. That kind of hardship he could take. There'd be plenty of danger and excitement—which is what he's after. But his zeal is for adventures not for God. And this struggle is going to be different. Can he take persecution of another sort—jail, deportment, malice from high places?"

Gifford shook his head. "That would not be his strength, John. Until he truly comes to a personal faith, he won't be able to stand under it. We must try to keep him clear of it."

"We can try, but he's young—and he's got a cause. A holy war." Bunyan turned and said, "All of us are going to bear scars from this, Pastor! I pray young Winslow finds faith enough to support him!" The two men fell into silence and made their separate ways home.

Lydia was caught off guard when Matthew came rushing in, his eyes blazing with excitement. She had been scrubbing the tiny floor of their single room when he burst through the door, crying out, "Lydia! Come here!"

He seated her at the table and began pacing back and forth as he told her of the encounter with Justice Twisten and of the determination he had formed to join in the struggle against the tyranny of the crown. She smiled briefly, amused at the boyish quality of his excitement, but when he repeated Bunyan's words, she sobered and raised a hand to interrupt him.

"But, Matthew, you really aren't a preacher—not yet."

"Oh, I will be soon enough," he said carelessly. "Sooner or later I'll be accepted, and until that happens I can go with Bunyan. Oh, we're going tomorrow to Lower Samsell. I forgot to tell you. And we'll have to go after dark—to shake off the sheriff's men." His eyes glowed at the thought, and he laughed aloud and pulled her to her feet.

Lydia hesitated, then asked quietly, "Matthew, why are you doing this?"

He paused, arrested by the question, "Why—for honor, I suppose. Someone must stand against the tyranny of the King!"

"And for God?"

"Yes, I suppose; for God as well!" Catching her in his strong arms, he whirled her like a child. "Come on, you King's men! Try and catch us!"

She had sensed this reckless spirit in him from the first, and it had been part of his charm. There was something of the wild hawk in this spirit, something daring, and she loved that part of him.

But a cloud fell over her face, and she said as he lowered her to the floor, "But, it's very dangerous! Sooner or later. . . ?"

He caught her hand up and kissed the palm. He looked so young as he stood there smiling down into her face. There was no cloud in his bright blue eyes. He was excited with the sheer adventure—much like at a game of chance or a closely fought contest with swords.

Suddenly a fear shot through her, and she caught at him blindly, throwing her arms around his waist and holding on so tightly that he stopped short in surprise.

"Why—what's this?" he asked. "You're not afraid, are you, Princess?"

"For you I am," she whispered, her voice trembling.

"Why, you mustn't be afraid," he soothed, holding her close. "I can take care of myself."

He sounded so sure, so happy, and she drew back, dashing the tears away that had risen to her eyes. "God will have to do that," she said with a serious look. She knew that his commitment to God was not as strong as her own, and this troubled her. Always when she had thought about marriage she had thought of a man stronger than she, and in some ways he was. But his experience with God was superficial; despite the capacity she sensed in him for a devout life of service, he had never been tested, never given himself to the arduous struggle of finding God in anything other than the ordinary ways.

But she had. Bunyan's analysis had been accurate, for despite her appearance (her beauty caused some to think she was not at all spiritual!) and her rather flighty behavior at times, she had gone through a time that had brought her close to God. When her parents had died, she had been distraught, almost slipping off into derangement. No one knew how close she had come to losing her mind, but in that time of crisis, she had learned to pray—and to be obedient to the still small voice of the Holy Spirit.

The strange people called the "Quakers" had risen about this time, led by George Fox, and all over England they had suffered persecution for their outlandish behavior. John Bunyan felt called to speak out against them, and was writing a book exposing what he perceived as doctrinal errors—one of them being a doctrine of "The Inner Light."

Although Lydia had no deep theological views, she had experienced something of the "inner light." It had come suddenly, but only after long periods of desperate prayer. She had eaten little and would not have consciously called it "fasting," but the experience came after several days of eating nothing.

She had been alone in her room, lying across her bed, exhausted by weeping and fear, and she cried out aloud, "Oh, God, I'm so afraid! Help me, please help me!"

And then she experienced something so different from anything she had ever known. She never forgot it, and it controlled much of her life from that moment on.

Her poor, exhausted body suddenly seemed to be filled with light, accompanied by a sense of warmth that ran along her entire frame! The fatigue and the stomachache that had plagued her immediately faded, and she felt warm and safe. Mostly *safe*, for that was her need. She had felt so alone!

For a long time—she never knew how long—she lay there resting in the warmth and sense of security. Then there came something into her mind that she could not understand. It was not a voice, and she heard nothing with her ears, but the words were there—deep inside, as if carved into her mind.

Child, do you love me? Would you let me into your heart? Would you let me be in you forever?

With all her heart, Lydia yearned for love, for comfort and safety. She stretched her hands up as if reaching for her lost father's comforting arms and cried out, "Yes! Oh, yes, come into my heart!"

And at that moment someone came in. She could never explain it, nor did she ever try to. But it was like a door opened and someone came into the room, bringing health, joy, and peace inside!

She began to thank this Guest whose name she didn't know, lifting her small voice in praise. As she prayed, the presence of a mighty power filled her spirit, and she whispered, "Jesus, is it you?"

And in her heart there came an answer that swelled and grew until she could hardly bear it.

Yes! I am now in you, child!

She had lain there for a long time, knowing she was now different. Though she didn't immediately share this experience with anyone, one thing she quickly discovered: when she had troubles or fears, she could pray, and almost at once she was conscious of the presence of the Lord Jesus!

She longed to tell Matthew of this experience, but had not been able to do it. Now, looking into his bright-blue eyes, loving him with all her heart, she knew that he knew nothing of this kind of walk with God—and that frightened her.

"Let's pray, Matthew," she said quietly.

He looked at her in surprise. "You do the praying, Princess," he laughed, "and I'll do the rest." Then he began talking excit-

edly of the coming trip to Samsell, but failed to see the disappointment on her face.

He left the next night at dusk, and as he grabbed her in his
arms and kissed her, his eyes gleamed with excitement. "Wait
up for me, Princess!" he whispered, kissing her fervently. "I'll
play the hare to these hounds of Twisten, and when I return,
we'll celebrate!"

"I'll pray for you," she said, fighting the fear that threatened
to fill her.

"Yes, you pray," he said with a broad grin. Then he was gone.

She went back and sat down, her heart heavy. She knew it
would be hours before he came back, perhaps near dawn, but
she was so burdened she fell on her knees and began praying
with all her heart for him.

She prayed until she was worn out, then fell asleep on the
hard floor, one arm under her in a cramped position. When the
loud knock came at daybreak, she aroused slowly, confused and
heavy-eyed from sleep.

"Lydia! Lydia, wake up!"

She struggled to her feet, almost falling because of her
numbed legs, and threw open the door. There stood Pastor Gifford—alone. She took one look at his face, then said quickly,
"They've been taken, haven't they?"

"Yes, both of them."

"I'll get my cloak."

As she went slowly toward the small jail that sat perched
on a bridge over the small stream, she listened quietly as Gifford
told her how Bunyan and Matthew had been arrested and
charged with breaking the law.

She heard little of what he said, but she knew that never
again would life be as simple as it had been when the sun had
touched her face through the window that morning. The jail,
which she had seen so often, suddenly seemed ominous, and a
quick fear shot through her as they approached. But she called
out, "God, be my helper!" And as always, the peace came.

Matthew will have to learn to pray! she thought as she followed
Pastor Gifford inside.

CHAPTER SIX

BEDFORD JAIL

★ ★ ★ ★

"Elizabeth?" Lydia knocked at the door of the Bunyan cottage and stood there shivering in the cutting November wind. She held a steaming iron pot by the handles, her hands almost numb from the icy cold that had fallen like a physical blow on the countryside.

The door swung open and she stumbled stiff-legged into the room toward the small fire that flickered in the fireplace. "Mary, is your mother here?"

The blind eyes of the child swung toward her unerringly, and she said, "Yes, but she's in bed, Mrs. Winslow. She's sick again."

A look of alarm crossed Lydia's face, and she said, "Well, I've brought a pot of good strong beef broth. Why don't you set the table while I go talk to her."

"Oh, that smells good!" Mary shoved by the other children who had swarmed in close, looking like a miniature adult as she began setting the bowls on the table. As Lydia moved to the door that led to the sleeping room, she thought, *Mary's too young for such things. She's never had a childhood.* It disturbed her that the Separatists treated their children like adults. Her French father had been openly affectionate, and her mother had bent to his ways. The result had been a happy life while they lived, and a cruel shock when she had been taken into the strict world of her aunt.

She moved in the dark sleeping chamber to the high bed and found Elizabeth on her back holding her stomach, her back arched rigidly. Leaning over she put her hand on the suffering woman's forehead, whispering gently, "Elizabeth?"

The sick woman's eyes opened slowly, and she moved to get up, saying feebly, "Oh, I—must have dozed off, Lydia." Her face contorted suddenly with pain. "I must take John something to eat."

"No, you rest," Lydia said, pressing her firmly back into the bed. "I've made enough broth for all of us. I'll take a big pot of it to John and Matthew. And I want you to eat all you can when you get up."

Elizabeth caught Lydia's hand and held it to her face, saying softly, "I don't know what I would have done without you, Lydia!" She shook her head slowly, then said, "I want so much to have this baby—but it seems that everything's gone wrong!"

"I know—but we must trust God." Lydia pulled up the covers and tucked Elizabeth in carefully. She turned to leave, then paused and bit her lip. "I want to ask you something—don't answer if you think it's silly."

"It won't be silly, dear!"

"Well, I've thought so much about my marriage," she said slowly. "We were too hasty, Matthew and I. We should have waited at least until we could have seen his parents! I wanted to, but Matthew was so insistent!" She traced the design of the quilt that covered Elizabeth, then asked with some hesitation. "I—I've been wondering, Elizabeth, about you and John, I mean—?"

"Why did I marry a man older than I with four children?"

"Yes!"

The lines of pain that etched Elizabeth's face seemed to grow faint as she smiled, making her look younger. "You wouldn't believe how I fought against it, Lydia! All my life I'd had this dream of marrying some young man with a future; we'd have our own little house, and he'd be successful; then we'd have a baby—and then perhaps one or two more in time." She laughed then, and brushed her hair from her forehead. "Then came John

Bunyan, with all his awkward ways and his four squalling children—one of them blind! What a time I had when I knew God wanted me to marry him and be the mother of his children!"

"How did you know that, Elizabeth?" Lydia interrupted quickly.

"How? Why, I can't say, Lydia. I didn't hear a *voice* or anything like that—but I *knew!*" She smiled and asked, "Do you think I'd have married him in his condition if God hadn't told me to? No, somehow God let me know that my service for Him was to be tied up with John Bunyan, and that's been my life." She looked up at Lydia and asked, "You've been having doubts, haven't you, dear?"

Lydia nodded slowly. "We married so quickly, and I thought that we had the same thoughts—but the last three months that Matthew's been in jail have been—hard!"

"It would be hard for any man to endure that prison."

"Of course, but it's doing something to Matthew!" she said sadly. "Your husband is different. He's been a soldier, and he's had a hard life in many ways. But Matthew—why, he's never had a trial in his whole life, Elizabeth!"

"But he's so young!"

"Yes, that's just *it!*" Lydia shook her head in agitation and the problems she had struggled with overflowed as she said, "Maybe he's *too* young for all this—and maybe we married too fast. I don't know, but I can see him getting—he's becoming bitter, Elizabeth! You must have seen it!"

"Yes, I have. And so has John. We've talked about it many times."

"Last week he got so upset he—he blamed God for all the trouble!" Lydia's voice trembled and Elizabeth reached up and took her hand again. "He cursed and said that God was either asleep or didn't care what happened to men! Oh, he caught himself, apologized to me. But it was his heart speaking—and I'm afraid! What's going to happen to him, Elizabeth? To *us?*"

Elizabeth asked quietly, "What was it you said to me a few moments ago, Lydia? *We must trust God.* You will have to believe for Matthew until he can believe for himself. He must make it through this trial, for if he falls away now, he may never be God's man!"

Elizabeth's voice had grown strong and her grip bit into Lydia's arm. "We must pray that at the trial, they'll be set free."

"Yes, that's been my prayer," Lydia murmured. Then she said, "You *must* rest, Elizabeth—I'll take the food to the prison."

"Come back and tell me how they are—and don't tell John I'm ill. Tell him I'll be in tomorrow."

"All right."

Lydia returned to the large room, filled a smaller pewter pot with broth, wrapped a fresh loaf of brown bread in a cloth, and set out for the prison. It was not a great distance, but the sharp winds stung her unprotected face and hands like needles. There was a bite of sleet or snow in the air, and she shivered violently as she hurried along the frozen ground.

Bedford was not noted for much, but its jail was the equal of any in England for a town that size. It sat beside the small river that touched the edge of town, a large two-story structure— three, counting the lower floor. The third floor held the rooms for Paul Cobb, the jailer, and his family. The first floor had one small compartment immediately inside the door, and was separated from the rest of the space by solid iron bars. The lower floor, or basement, was used for prisoners as well, but it was so damp, being on practically the same level as the river, that only when the first floor was filled was it used.

Fortunately, the number of prisoners had been low since the beginning of winter, so the twenty or so prisoners were kept in the more comfortable section of the prison. "Comfortable" was a relative term, since there was no fire of any sort to take the chill off the prisoners. They wore all the clothing they could get, and moved around like huge, fat bears in the confined space of their common cell.

Two single windows set high in the wall let in light and air as well as snow and rain, and one set of double windows— heavily barred, of course—was set low enough in the wall so that by standing on tiptoe or on one of the few rough benches a prisoner could get a view of town—or from the other side, a view of the river.

In early fall, this was pleasant enough, and there was keen competition for the space. But during the winter the freezing winds piled sleet and snow several inches deep inside the cell.

Everyone slept in every thread they could put on, and under all the bedclothes they could lay hands on. The bare stone floor, covered by a few wisps of straw, grew more evil-smelling day by day.

Paul Cobb, a thick-set, balding man, came down the stairs at Lydia's call, and as he opened the door, he growled, "Ye'd best be sayin' a word to thot hoosband 'o yours, Lydia Winslow." He pulled the massive door open and added as Lydia stepped through, "He had quite a row with old Jamison last night! I had to step in and keep him from wipin' up the floor wif the old man! Ye'd best have a word with him, I thinks." He shut the door and called out, "Winslow, here's yer wife—maybe she can talk some sense into yer head!"

Lydia caught sight of Matthew at once, but he made no move to come to her. He was standing at one of the windows, staring moodily out at the brown river that purled around the town, and after one glance at her, he turned his back.

John Bunyan caught Matthew's action with one quick glance and tried to cover it by approaching her quickly, saying, "Well, well, what have we here? Do I smell beef soup?" He began busily helping her set the small table, keeping up a steady line of small talk. "Elizabeth didn't come? Oh, well, tomorrow, then—my, look at this fresh bread, Matthew!" He broke the loaf open and smelled it eagerly. "Ah! Now *that's* the way bread should be baked, I tell you! And look at this cheese? Where have you been hiding that, I ask you?"

Lydia let him busy himself with the food, and she stepped over to where Matthew was staring stolidly out the window. She took his arm and stood there, saying nothing until he finally turned and said, "Bloody cold today!"

"Yes. I'll bring another blanket tomorrow—or maybe I can bring it later today."

"No matter," he shrugged. "We'll be out of this hole the day after the trial."

Bunyan looked up sharply at that, then shrugged and went back to slicing the bread and cheese. "Come and have a bite of this, Matthew," he said cheerily.

"I'm not hungry."

"Oh, you have to eat!" Lydia urged, and she pulled at his

arm, forcing him to approach the table. "I put some thyme in this broth—just the way you like it." She ladeled out some of the hot stew into his bowl and set it in front of him. He shrugged, took up a spoon and began to eat indifferently.

Bunyan ignored that, and bowed his head. "Thank you, gracious God, for this good food, in the name of our precious Savior. Amen."

Matthew had the grace to look embarrassed, then grinned and said, "I'm losing all my manners in this place. Pardon me, John."

Bunyan smiled and gave him a clap on the shoulder. Then he looked across the room and said quietly, "Maybe you ought to ask Mr. Jamison to have a bit of this fine stew, eh, my boy?"

Matthew gave him a sharp look, anger suddenly scoring his face. "That old buzzard? He's lucky I didn't pound him into the floor last night!"

Bunyan rebuked him at once, saying, "Matthew, he's old and alone in the world. You're young and strong and you have friends. Can't you be a little charitable?"

Matthew bit his lip, then got up and put some stew into an extra bowl. He walked over to where a very tall old man sat hunched up against the wall, his face buried in his arms.

"Here, Jamison," he said, "have a bit of this good stew. It'll warm you up."

The old man looked up, and when he saw who it was, he spat on the floor and buried his face again.

"Well, that's what you get for being a Christian in this place!" Matthew snapped as he came back and sat down. "Can't blame the old man much. I'm about to go batty in this place! Be glad when the trial is over and we can get out of here. When will the trial come, John?"

"No way of telling. I'm hoping Justice Twisten will schedule it in a week or two, but he's vindictive enough to stretch it out till the crack of doom." He bit his lip and shook his head. "I want to be there when Elizabeth has her baby. The first baby is always harder on the mother, I think." He gave a shake of his heavy shoulders, rose and smiled. "I'll let you two have a little privacy, such as there is."

"Have some of this cheese, Matthew," Lydia urged as Bunyan moved across the room to speak to Jamison. "You're so thin!"

He took a piece of the cheese, bit into it and chewed slowly. "I can't stand this place much longer, Lydia." He spoke quietly, but there was a thick despair in his tone and she was appalled at the hollow look in his face, the fear that leaped out of his eyes.

"It's a time of testing," she whispered softly. Putting her arm around him, she moved as close to him as the narrow bench would permit. She yearned to draw his head to her breast and comfort him as she did the smallest Bunyan child, but it would have been improper in view of the prisoners. "We're going to get through this, you and I. Remember the scripture, 'Whom the Lord loveth, he chasteneth'? This will make our marriage stronger than ever!"

He stared at her as if she were speaking a language foreign to him; then a shiver ran through his thin frame. "I could stand anything, Lydia, I think—except these walls." He gave a look that was almost wild at the massive stones that hemmed them in, and again a violent tremor shook his shoulders and she tightened her hold. "It's not the cold or the stench of this place, though God knows it's miserable enough! It's not even being cut off from *you*. Oh, God, I could be happy in poverty—even in sickness, I think—if only I didn't have to be caged up like a dog!"

His voice rose higher so that several of the prisoners looked their way, and Lydia gave him a sudden hard grasp and said fiercely, "I know! I know, dearest! But it's only for a little while!" She hesitated, then drew his head down so that her lips were close to his ear and whispered something so softly that he missed it.

"What's that? I can't hear you."

She pulled his head yet closer, and her breath was warm and soft as she murmured with gladness in her voice, "You must be brave, Husband, because you're going to have a family!"

He sat there stock-still, as though he had not heard her, then slowly he turned and looked down into her eyes, which were brimming with tears—tears of joy.

"A—baby?"

"Yes!"

He moved his lips but no sound came; only his eyes reflected his deep shock. Finally he smiled wanly, put his arm around her and kissed her, ignoring the guffaws from several of the prisoners. "A son!" he said, and there was more life in his voice than she had heard in weeks.

"Or a daughter."

"Of course—it could be a girl!" He sat there, and despite the abysmal surroundings—the stench and the frigid blasts of air that cut to the bone, the stares of the ragged prisoners and the gray, blank walls—Lydia's heart sang, for it was the time she'd prayed for. Never during their short marriage had she felt in perfect harmony with Matthew—not until now. They had laughed much and their minds were equal, and no couple, she was sure, could have been more fulfilled by the vibrant love they had shared.

But she had always known there was a part of him she had not been able to enter—just as there was a part of her she longed to have him know, but he could not find it. Deep down she was aware that it was their walk with God—that private place, like a deeply hidden grotto where the spirit leaves the noisy world and meets with the living Lord—it was that element which she had not been able to share with Matthew. And deep within there was the lurking fear that the two of them, for all their bonds of body and mind, were strangers. Matthew lacked something, and while she dreaded being judgmental, she sensed a shallowness in his walk with God that kept them apart.

But this moment had been one of total intimacy of spirit, and her heart cried out for him as he sat there holding her. *This is marriage*, she thought happily.

But then he suddenly gave a start, looked around the cell with wild eyes, and when he turned to face her, there was something distraught in his eyes—a fear that was mastering the joy that had flashed out when he had heard of her condition.

"I've got to get out of here, Lydia!" he gasped, and with a moan he put his head in his hands. "How can I live with you having a baby—while I'm cooped up like a dog?"

She put her arm around him and whispered fiercely, "We are God's children, dearest—He will never forsake us!"

But it was as if she had not spoken, for he sat there with his face buried in his arms, and nothing she could say would bring him out of it.

Finally she arose and said, "I must go to Elizabeth. She's having a difficult time with this baby."

Matthew raised his head and looked at Bunyan. Suddenly he motioned for the preacher to come, and Bunyan rose and stepped to where they stood. "John, Lydia is going to have a child!"

Bunyan's broad face beamed and he said heartily, "Is she now? Well, that's fine—fine!"

"No—not with me in prison! And Elizabeth—she's having a hard time, Lydia says. John, we've got to get out of this place!"

Bunyan asked quietly, "Elizabeth is worse?"

"She's not well, I'm afraid."

He stood there, a strong shape in the gray light that filtered feebly through the high window. His form seemed to be made of the same material as the walls—enduring, tough, and impervious to time or hard wear. But his face was not so, for as the light caught it, though his eyes, hidden in the hollow sockets of his face, evidenced deep pain, his features held such an expression of pain and sorrow that Lydia wanted to weep.

Matthew stood there waiting for his reply, but when it came, it was not what he expected.

"We must be faithful to God, my boy. 'He that loveth husband or wife more than me is not worthy to be my disciple.' Those are hard words, but our Savior speaks. You and I can bear the suffering to our own bodies, and Satan knows this well enough! He will not attack us there, but where we are weak. And that is—that is our wives and our little ones!"

Matthew stared at him, then shook his head. "He that does not provide for his own is worse than a heathen," he quoted. "Does God expect us to let our loved ones suffer, those whom we've vowed to protect?"

"He is the Father of the fatherless, and we must be faithful to His word. He will care for Elizabeth and my little ones—and He will take care of your dear wife and the little one to come."

Matthew stared at him, then turned with a bitter light in his blue eyes. "God is unfair!" he said through clenched teeth, then wheeled and stalked stiff-legged to the window he'd occupied earlier, staring out at the gray river that rolled heavily by the prison.

"He'll be better," Bunyan whispered to Lydia as she stood there with tears in her eyes. "He's young in the faith, and I was no stronger at his age. Pray! Pray for him!"

Lydia was so full of fear she could not answer, but finally said, "Yes, John, I'll take care of Elizabeth—perhaps she'll be strong enough to come tomorrow."

She went home, walking slowly with her head down, impervious to the icy bite of the wind. A deadly spirit of fear more potent than winter's blast was sweeping through her heart, and the tears that she could not contain rolled down her pale cheeks.

She tried to pray, but the words would not come. So she walked beside the cold river, the dead brown grasses of summer breaking beneath her feet, and her heart rose up to God. She did not know what it was that she brought to God, but as the urgent cries of her soul ascended, somehow the presence of God came down, and the fear that had pierced her fled and she knew a peace in her spirit such as she had never known!

For many days this was her strength. Day after day rolled by, turning into weeks, then months, and there was no trial. Everything in her world was shaken. Elizabeth grew worse, so much worse that Lydia moved into the Bunyan house and with Mary's help did all the housework. She was a comfort to Elizabeth, spending hours reading the Word of God, and the children came to look on her as a second mother.

She made the short journey to the jail daily, for the state did not furnish food for the prisoners. This made the chore even more demanding, for neither she nor John Bunyan could bear to see those prisoners who had no family nor friends starve; therefore, she brought as much extra food as she could.

Matthew's condition worsened almost daily. He lost weight at such an alarming rate that she feared for his life. His lungs were affected by the biting cold, and he developed a cough that disturbed them all. But even worse was the awful depression that gripped him. He spoke little, and seemed not to hear what she said most of the time.

Her walks along the river grew longer, and she prayed fervently; prayer built her up, edified her spirit, and enabled her to carry the heavy burden.

Snow came, and on the second day when the earth was

muffled with white, Lydia left the Bunyan cottage and started for the jail. The heavy pot of soup dragged at her arm, and walking was difficult in the six-inch blanket of snow that covered the earth.

She had turned the corner onto the main road that led to the jail, and as she lifted her eyes, what she saw sent a shock running through her so violent that she almost dropped the heavy iron pot.

"Matthew!" she cried out, struggling to run toward him, crying out his name, filled with wonder that he was free.

Finally she set the pot down and ran toward him, her eyes so blinded with tears that she could barely see the tall figure so familiar to her. She fell into his arms and he caught her with a powerful grip.

"Matthew! Oh, my dear!" she cried out, holding to him as if she would never let him go.

Then she heard the familiar voice—but at the same time strangely different, "Well, daughter, I am here. . . !"

She looked up, drawing back at once from his embrace. She saw a wedge-shaped face with wide lips, cornflower blue eyes such as she loved in Matthew—but it was not her husband!

He said, "I've just come from my son, Lydia. We have much to pray about, you and I." Then he smiled, and she saw the same courage and strength in the father's eyes that she had fallen in love with in Matthew. "But first, will you allow me to have a father's embrace? For you are my daughter now!"

She gave a cry and fell into Gilbert Winslow's strong arms as a battered ship comes out of a wild tearing storm into the peace and safety of a calm harbor!

CHAPTER SEVEN

THE TRIAL

★　★　★　★

"She slipped away with the tide," Gilbert Winslow said slowly. "Just as she had lived trusting in the Lord God, so she endured her going hence." He sat relaxed in front of the cheerful fire that threw leaping figures on the walls of the small cottage. There was a quietness and peace in his voice that took away the sting of the news that Matthew's mother was dead. He leaned forward to pick up the heavy iron poker, and Lydia's eyes stung as she recognized in her father-in-law the easy grace and strength that she loved in Matthew.

"It must have been terribly hard on you, Mr. Winslow."

"Hard?" He looked at her with a starboard twist of his head, just as she'd seen in Matthew a thousand times, then smiled and shook his head. "No, child, not hard. What was hard was watching her in pain from day to day. That last night the pain left, and we both knew it was time. She'd always loved to watch the tide go out, so I picked her up and carried her to a clearing on the hill—the same spot where I'd asked her to marry me forty years ago. It was dawn, and just as the morning light came to turn the sea red, and the tide began ebbing from the shore, she turned to me, put her arms around my neck, and whispered, 'You've been a good husband to me on this earth, Gilbert—but I must go now to my heavenly Bridegroom!' And then she put her head on my shoulder—and she left to be with Him!"

Sitting with her feet tucked beneath her, Lydia could not

keep her eyes off her father-in-law. *He looks far more like Matthew's older brother than his father!* she thought suddenly. As he went on speaking quietly, she drew the brightly colored quilt around her like a cocoon, her eyes never leaving his face. *Matthew is so much like him—but there's something different*, she thought. It was not long until she discovered what that difference was. Gilbert's face was Matthew's, but it had been refined by hardship to a coun-tenance of sharp planes and fine lines that contrasted strongly with the soft, handsome features of the son.

"I—I'm glad you've come, Mr. Winslow," she said when he paused. "Matthew has been a good husband, but he's changed since he went to prison."

Gilbert smiled at the first confession, then shook his head at the second. "He's been like a wild hawk all his life, Lydia. He'll dare anything, but you can't cage a wild creature without killing his spirit, I think."

"It's killing him, that prison." She threw the quilt back, got up and bent to pick up the heavy kettle. As she poured a cup of steaming water for his tea, she said steadily, "What do you think will happen to him?"

"If he stays in prison?" He took the tea, sipped it carefully, then looked at her over the lip of the heavy cup. "He may not survive it. I hardly *knew* him, Lydia!" he exclaimed. "He's very ill, as you know. That cough is bad—down deep in his lungs, and prison fever is quick and deadly as a serpent!"

She stared at him, hesitated, then asked the question aloud that she'd never dared to frame to anyone. "Do you think he should give in to the Crown? You realize he and Brother Bunyan can leave anytime they agree to obey the new law?"

"I know." Gilbert turned the cup in his hands, seeming to find something fascinating in the plain surface. He sat comfort-ably in the chair, a strong figure even in repose. She had heard both from Winslow's son and his brother how he had the daring of a buccaneer in his youth; how he had been forced to choose between a place of prominence as the husband of Cecily North, daughter of Lord North, the beautiful aristocrat who had fol-lowed him across the Atlantic, and the simple Pilgrim maiden, Humility Cooper. He had been a swordsman with few peers, a lover of some repute, and would have risen in the world—but threw it all away to embrace the hard life of a poor minister on the rocky shores of Plymouth.

She saw that strength in his hands, in his face, and in every line of his tall figure, and suddenly she thought, *This is what I want for a husband! This is what I thought Matthew was like!*

He looked at her sharply, and said in answer to her question, "If he gives in to the Crown, he'll live—but what will he have left? A man who lets a king—or anyone else!—direct his soul may be alive physically, but he's dead to the best that's in him!"

"I'm afraid for him. I'm afraid for myself, for Mr. Bunyan, and for his poor wife and children!"

He rose and came to stand by her. Taking her hands in his he looked down on her for a long moment, then said gently, "Never take counsel of your fears, Lydia. I would be afraid, too, for Matthew is the last of his family—the last of the House of Winslow."

She smiled tremulously and said shyly, but with a note of triumph in her voice, "No, this child will have the Winslow name."

"Ah!" A tender smile crossed Gilbert's broad lips, and he embraced her, and the tender kiss he placed on her forehead broke down all restraint. It was as if she had known him all her life, and she leaned against him, clinging to him in her need as she had clung to her own father years ago.

"I'm glad you're here," she said again. "It gives me faith, and I know you can help Matthew."

He shook his head, saying only, "I trust that is so—but in one sense and in some things, a man must make his own way. We will try and we will pray, but my son must choose for himself."

"I know—but he has such faith in you—and so do I!" She laughed awkwardly and added, "Here you are fresh off the ship, and I dump all my care onto you the first time we meet!"

He said at once, "You're not a weak woman, Lydia. No, indeed! You know that thought that came to me, not five minutes after we met? *Here is a woman as strong as my Humility!* I never thought to hear myself say it," he smiled.

She was embarrassed by the compliment, but warmed all the same by his approval. "I must go to Mrs. Bunyan's. Would you go with me, to pray for her?"

"Of course!"

The two of them made their way through the falling snow, and Mr. Winslow became an instant success with the small Bunyans. He knew all sorts of games it seemed, and he thought nothing of roughing with the little ones. Elizabeth felt well enough to sit in a chair by the fireplace, and she watched in amazement while the tall minister got down on his hands and knees with the children. "He's an unusual man, isn't he? He loves children, that's plain," she whispered to Lydia.

When the children were in bed, he spent a long time reading the Bible to Lydia and Elizabeth; the Book of Hebrews, the eleventh chapter, and the ancient promises seemed to fill the small room with warmth. Finally he closed the book and prayed for Elizabeth and for her husband warmly and fervently.

After he had left, the strength of his presence lingered somehow, and Elizabeth smiled at Lydia, saying, "He's got a strength in him, that man has! John will love him!"

"Who wouldn't?" Lydia responded softly. "He's the kind of man—"

She broke off and Elizabeth finished, "The kind of man you saw in Matthew? Yes, and it's there, my dear. Blood will tell, and there's enough of his father's blood in Matthew Winslow to win his battle!"

During the weeks that followed, Lydia thought often of Elizabeth's words. But there seemed to be little to merit hope that Matthew would justify the thought. She saw no improvement in him; indeed, the news of his mother's death came as such a blow to him that even the strong encouragement Gilbert offered was offset.

Gilbert's presence was more of a blessing to John Bunyan, it seemed, than to his own son. The two men became fast friends at once, and Winslow spent most of his time at the prison studying the Scripture with Bunyan. Gilbert was captivated by the man's vivid imagination, and often when Mary came to visit, he sat there listening to Bunyan's stories as intently as she. "You ought to write a book, John!" he often said.

"I'm no book writer!"

"You're the best teller of tales I've ever heard," Winslow insisted. "That one about the chap named Pilgrim—it's almost like reading the Bible, in a way! Think what it would mean if Christian parents had a story about a man who leaves his home and fights his way through difficulties to get to heaven!"

"They have the Bible," Bunyan shrugged.

"But, Father, your stories make the Bible easier to under-stand," Mary protested.

"There you have it, John," Winslow laughed. "Wisdom from the lips of babes, eh, Matthew?"

"Yes, I suppose so." Matthew sat on a pile of straw, picking at it listlessly. There was no life in his voice.

Bunyan and Winslow exchanged glances, but said nothing. They had spoken quietly about the young man when Matthew was out of hearing, and agreed that if he gave in to the Crown's new law, he would live, but would be forever scarred in his spirit.

Bunyan picked up the story of Pilgrim and had gotten the hero into a terrible predicament when Paul Cobb opened the door of the cell and Pastor Gifford rushed in, his eyes filled with excitement.

"Twisten—he's set a date for the trial!"

"*When?*" Matthew wheeled from where he stood and leaped to the pastor's side, showing more animation than they had seen in weeks.

"A month from now, less a day!"

"Thank God!" Matthew cried out, tears gathering in his eyes.

"Yes, thank God," Bunyan said; then he added carefully, "Now we must pray for a verdict in our favor."

Matthew stared at him, then declared defiantly, "God will not leave us here to rot!" He shook his head and laughed for the first time since Gilbert had come to Bedford. "It's going to be all right! You'll see!"

When Lydia came later that day, she was taken off guard by the difference in Matthew. He embraced her, swinging her around in a circle in the old way, crying, "It's over, Lydia! It's over!"

"Matthew, be careful," she cried out breathlessly. "You'll get your cough started again!"

"Devil take the cough!" he grinned. "Let me get a breath of free air and that cough will leave one way or another!" He carried on wildly all the time she was there. The activity did start his cough again, and she had to force him to lie down before he strangled. The two red spots which had shown in his cheeks a week earlier reappeared, and she knew his fever was up.

That night when Gilbert came by to pray for Elizabeth, she said, "He's better, isn't he?"

"Yes, I suppose." There was a caution in Gilbert's voice, and he added soberly, "But it will go hard with him if the verdict isn't favorable."

"Do—do you think that it will be bad—the verdict?"

"It's a bad time, Lydia. The tide is against us. I have to go to London to see my brother in two days. I'll find out something from him. He's in prison, but he still has powerful friends, and some of them may help."

After Gilbert left, Lydia made the mistake of mentioning his words to Matthew, and he grabbed at the chance eagerly. "Why, of course! Uncle Edward will help us!"

"He's unable to help himself, lad," Bunyan said quickly.

"You never have a cheerful word, do you John?" Bunyan's efforts to prepare the young man for the possibility of bad news from the trial had not worked; on the contrary, they had driven a wedge between the two that had given grief to the Bunyans as well as to Lydia.

"John is just—"

"I know what John is doing!" Matthew snapped at her. "You're a fine help, all of you! Where's your faith? We're supposed to believe God, aren't we? Well, that's what I'm doing— and the rest of you are digging my grave with your unbelief—!" He broke off into a paroxysm of coughing and fought Lydia as she attempted to help him. "Leave me alone, you doubters!" he gasped and withdrew into the farthest corner of the cell.

He apologized the following day, but there was a constraint in him, and he had little to say to either of them. The only subject that he cared about was the trial—that and the return of Gilbert with good news.

Lydia was at the jail the afternoon Gilbert came back. Bunyan was standing on a bench, speaking out the window to a small group who had formed the habit of coming from time to time to hear him preach.

Gilbert saw them as he approached, and he paused to listen as the strong voice of Bunyan carried easily on the cold air. The shivering listeners stood there, shifting from one frozen foot to another, beating their hands together to get the cold blood stirring, but none left until he prayed a final prayer and called out a cheery "God bless you!"

Cobb said as he entered, "Well, sir, here you are, ain't you now? I hopes it's good news you be bringin' to the lad. He's lived for little else!"

Matthew saw his father enter and came to him at once. "Father, what did Uncle Edward say? Will he help us?"

Gilbert pulled off his cloak slowly, not taking his eyes from Matthew's face. There was something in his eyes that held the young man speechless. Finally he said, "Your uncle is dead, my boy. Gone to be with his Lord."

Matthew jerked as though he had been struck; his face twisted and he dropped his head, turning blindly toward the wall.

Lydia ran to him, and Bunyan said quietly, "I'm sorry to hear it, Gilbert. He was a godly man."

"Yes." Gilbert sat down and Bunyan joined him. "He's better off, John. He was very ill, and there was little hope of any sort of life for him. I think they would have executed him if he had lived until the next sitting of the court."

"No, surely not!" Bunyan said, shocked at the thought.

Gilbert leaned back against the wall, saying in a tired voice. "They executed Major-General Harrison last Friday. I was there."

"I can't believe it," Bunyan said. "He was such a good man."

"But close to Cromwell—as was Edward. It was Edward who asked me to go. I'll never forget it. He came to his death as cheerful as any man could do in that condition. He made a brief speech giving glory to God, making no reference to the shameful manner in which he was being treated by his enemies. After he was taken down, his head and his heart were removed and shown to the people—amidst great shouts of joy, John! How beastly these people can be! That's why I cannot grieve over Edward. He was spared that. I was with him when he died. He was anxious to go."

The shock of his uncle's death hit hard at Matthew, causing him to speak only of the trial. Two days before the date which Justice Twisten had set, Lydia sat beside her husband, listening as he spoke eagerly of the day he would be set free.

Finally he stooped, and she said, "I found something you might like, Matthew."

"What is it?"

"Oh, it's just a poem. Your father showed it to me last night. A man he knew as a boy wrote it, and it's become famous."

"A poem? What does it say?" Matthew asked listlessly.

"It was written to a young woman by a man named Lovelace. It's just the last verse that I thought you might like." She took out a slip of paper and read it softly:

> "Stone walls do not a prison make,
> Nor iron bars a cage.
> Minds innocent and quiet take
> That for a hermitage.
> If I have freedom in my love
> And in my soul am free,
> Angels alone that soar above
> Enjoy such liberty!"

She smiled up at him, saying with a smile, "Stone walls do not a prison make, nor iron bars a cage."

He stared at her soberly, then shook his head. "That's pretty poetry, but it's not life."

She sat there and for the first time she asked what had been in her heart for weeks, "Matthew, what if—what if things don't go well?"

"What?" he asked angrily. "What are you talking about?"

"I've prayed so *hard*," she said, taking his arm. "But even if you and John *did* have to stay here for a little while longer, it'll be—"

"It's not going to be that way!" he interrupted with a wild look around at the walls. "Lydia, I'll *die* in this place! God won't let it happen!"

She changed the subject quickly, but her heart was filled with foreboding as she went home, and she knew that Gilbert felt the same.

The hours crawled slowly by, but at last the day came for the trial. Every square inch of space was filled in the large hall used for trials, and in spite of the freezing cold, those who could not get inside thronged the outside.

Justice Twisten sat on a raised platform, his beefy face stony as the case proceeded. "What is the charge against these men?"

A reedy-voiced clerk named Jacob Tillage read from a large sheet: "John Bunyan and Matthew Winslow, both of Bedford, are charged with a violation of the King's law, being upholders and maintainers of unlawful assemblies and Conventicles, and for not conforming to the National Worship of the Church of England."

A great hulking fellow named Ryeson was the deputy who had arrested the two, and he gave a long, rambling testimony as to how he had followed the two and found them addressing a group of people.

"Were they armed, any of them?" Justice Twisten demanded.

"Sir?"

"Were they armed, I say!"

"No, sir, they didn't have naught but Bibles!"

"Very well."

The testimony droned on and finally the justice said, "John Bunyan, you may rise and give your defense."

Bunyan was pale from his stay inside, but he spoke firmly and eloquently. A duel soon developed between him and the justice, and it terminated in Twisten shouting, "You will heed the laws of England or I will either see you hanged or you will be harried out of this land!"

"I will in all civil laws be obedient to my king—whom God knows I respect and pray for—but I will obey the voice of that King who is immortal when there is a conflict between the two!"

"You stand convicted by your own mouth!" Twisten cried out, getting to his feet in his anger. "You have not denied that you and Winslow were engaged in breaking the King's law. On the basis of your own testimony and on the evidence presented to this court, I sentence you to perpetual imprisonment!"

A hum went over the court and he looked around the crowded room, adding, "Do not waste your pity on these men. They may leave prison at any moment—at any moment, that is, when they agree to obey the law."

Bunyan suddenly raised his voice and cried out loudly, "I will preach the gospel until the moss grows up to my eyes!"

"Be it on your head then," Twisten said, staring at the two men. "You will stay in Bedford Jail until you promise to do your preaching within the limits set by the King! Bailiff, take these two men back to their cells! This court is dismissed."

CHAPTER EIGHT

END OF A MAN

★   ★   ★   ★

"Will you go tell him, Gilbert?" Lydia asked wearily. She leaned her arm against the wall, placed her forehead on it, and bit her lip to keep back the tears. "It's going to kill him, you know—he's lived for this new baby."

"Too bad! Too bad!" Gilbert shook his head. He picked up his heavy coat and said as he pulled it on, "Yes, I'll go. You'll stay with Elizabeth?"

"Yes." She straightened up and tried to put a little cheer into her voice. "At least Elizabeth is all right. She can have other children, the doctor said. Tell John that."

"All right."

"And tell Matthew—" She broke off suddenly and stared at the tall man so much like her husband. A question leaped to her lips, and she suppressed it, then seemed to be in fear of something. Finally she asked, "I don't know what to tell him. Have you noticed anything—different—about the way he is?"

Winslow nodded slowly. "His mind is troubled. I worry about that more than his health."

"Yesterday he talked so wildly I couldn't make sense of it. He talked about dying. I think he's given up hope."

Gilbert nodded slowly. "He's sick in body, but we must pray even more for his spirit, Lydia."

Winslow left the cottage and made his way along the muddy

road, dodging puddles as he went. The first breath of spring had come, melting the snow and stirring the life that lay buried in the frozen ground. He looked at a tiny crocus shouldering a chip inside, vibrant with color against the dull winter earth, and thought of the dead child that all of them mourned. "Too bad!" he murmured again.

Cobb admitted him into the cell, and he went at once to where Bunyan and Matthew sat together on a bench. Bunyan rose at once, and there was a prophetic look on his heavy features. He waited until Gilbert drew near, then he searched his face, and said quietly, "Elizabeth's lost the baby."

Gilbert nodded. "Yes. I'm sorry, John."

"Is she all right?"

"The doctor says she's fine. She can have other children."

"Praise God!" Bunyan breathed heavily, then went over to stare out of the window, alone in his grief.

Gilbert sat down by Matthew, noting that he looked more worn and haggard than ever. The cough had gotten worse, too, but the mental state troubled Gilbert more. "It's getting warmer, son. Spring is on the way."

Matthew shrugged, saying only, "I suppose I should have known it would happen."

Gilbert did not understand him. "What's that, son?"

"I knew the baby would die."

"It's a shame—but you mustn't worry about Lydia. She's very healthy."

Matthew looked at his father out of haggard eyes, sunk deep in his skull. He bore little resemblance to the vigorous young man he had been before his imprisonment. When he spoke, his voice was dead and lifeless as his eyes. "I can't believe anything anymore."

"You don't mean that, son," Gilbert said quietly. He put his hand on the young man's shoulder and there was an urgency in his eyes and in his voice as he spoke. "You've had a bad knock, but these things will pass . . ."

Matthew listened as his father spoke, but there was a sullen set to his shoulders, and finally he said, "Didn't you hear Justice Twisten? 'Perpetual imprisonment' was the term. You know as well as I that there's no way out of this hole, unless—"

"Don't even *think* that way!" Gilbert said quickly. "I know you're sick and despondent and there's the baby on the way. But if you give up now, you'll never be a man again."

"And if I don't get out of here, I'll be dead!" Matthew snapped, a madness glowing in his eyes. Then he took a deep breath and said, "I've decided what I'm going to do, Father—and I know you and John will disapprove. You think it's terrible for a man to give in, but it's different with me."

"How is it different?"

"Why, you must see that John is a preacher—that's what he's going to do. But I'm not."

"You were preaching the gospel, Bunyan tells me—and you told me yourself that you felt God's hand on your life."

"Well, I did say that, but many young fellows take a try at preaching and find out it's just a notion."

"Matthew, don't—"

"Don't tell me what to do!" Matthew cried, and his voice turned Bunyan from the window. He watched carefully, then came over to stand beside them. "I couldn't help overhearing." His fine eyes were filled with compassion and he said, "Don't make a decision now. Wait until you've had time to pray about it."

Matthew stared at them and a wild look came into his eyes, a look of madness, and Gilbert saw how close his son was to losing his mind. He said at once, "I'll leave now, son. You try to calm yourself and I'll come back tomorrow. We'll think of something."

He bade goodbye to Bunyan, begging him with his eyes to look after Matthew. He did not go to the cottage but walked along a little-traveled road, seeking God with desperation. Bunyan had spoken to him of his son's preoccupation with death, and it frightened him more than anything that had ever come to him. He prayed until finally he looked up and saw that the sun was setting, then turned his steps toward the Bunyan cottage.

Lydia was busy with the children, and he took over some of the chores so she could be with Elizabeth. It was late by the time the children were in bed and Elizabeth was asleep, but he sat beside her, telling her about his visit with Matthew.

She sat there staring at the glowing coals in the fireplace, then said, "I'm so tired of it all, I can't even think."

"I know. I—I'm not sure it's right, Lydia." The strain had etched new lines on Gilbert's face, and he shook his head in despair. "If it were my life, I'd know what to do—but who can decide a thing like this for another?"

That was as far as they got, and he trudged on home wearily. He did not expect to sleep, but he did by some miracle. He had missed much sleep, and slept far past his usual early time for arising. A loud knocking at the door awoke him, and he saw in one startled glance that the sun was high in the sky.

"Gilbert! Wake up!"

He staggered to the door groggy with sleep, threw the door open to find Lydia there with fear in her eyes. "He's gone!" was all she could say. Then sobs rose to her throat and she fell against him, weeping with abandon.

"Matthew?" he demanded.

He had to wait until she could collect herself. Finally she drew back and wiped her eyes. "Yes! He sent for Justice Twisten yesterday and agreed to obey the new law—so the justice released him."

"Did he tell you this—Matthew, I mean?"

"No! I haven't seen him—but when I got home from the Bunyan's yesterday, his clothes were all gone, and I found this note."

Gilbert took the scrap of paper she thrust at him and read it quickly: "Lydia, I'm going away. Please try to forget me—and God forgive me!"

It was written in a wavering hand and was not even signed.

"He was almost mad yesterday," Gilbert said, biting his lip, trying to think what to do. "And I think he was delirious with fever."

"Where could he have gone?" Lydia moaned.

"Well, he can't have gone far," Gilbert said quickly. "Don't worry, we'll find him, Lydia."

But that was not the case, for after getting the word out to all the village, the best they could discover was that he was not in Bedford. Everyone knew him well from his connection with Bunyan, and it was not until the following day, after a sleepless night, that Gilbert came to the Bunyan cottage to meet Lydia.

"You've found him?" Lydia cried, seeing no gloom on Gilbert's face as he had worn since the previous day.

"No—but the coach driver came back through—the one that drives the London stage. He didn't make the trip all the way through this time, but he has said that a man of Matthew's description got on here in Bedford and was still on the coach headed for London yesterday."

"London! Why would he go there?"

"I fear he's making for the coast to get a ship out of the country." Gilbert took her arm and squeezed it tightly. "I'll go at once. Surely I'll be able to find him! All I have to do is check the ships about to depart."

"You must find him, Gilbert! He's out of his mind—I'll go with you . . ."

"No, you stay here in case we're wrong and he comes back," Gilbert said. "I'll not go on a coach; that'd be too slow. I've already bought a fast horse, and I'll be in London almost by the time the coach gets there. God willing, I may even overtake it!"

"Yes, hurry! And I'll pray," Lydia said. She touched her body unconsciously, and he knew she was thinking of the child that was to come. "God is still in control!"

"Amen!" he said; he embraced her, then hurried away, his mind whirling with plans.

The hours crawled by for the next week, and although Lydia knew with her mind that the distance was too great for Gilbert to go and return in such a short time, she spent hours looking south down the Great Road. She ate nothing, but fasted and prayed until her face grew pale with strain. Bunyan urged her to eat: "God knows the intent of your heart," he said gently. "You must think of the child."

On the sixth day, Pastor Gifford brought a note direct from the coach. It was from Gilbert: "I have looked day and night with no success. But do not despair. It may be that he left the coach and went on to a coastal town. I go to Southampton, which is the most likely place for a man to take a ship for other lands." He urged Lydia to keep her trust in God, and promised to write as soon as he found any trace of Matthew.

Three weeks later Lydia looked up the lane and saw Gilbert walking slowly toward her cottage. There was something in his air that brought a great fear into her heart, and she rose to her feet slowly. His face was very thin, and it bore the unmistakable marks of grief as he walked up to her side and said at once, "Lydia, my dear . . ."

She saw that he could not finish, and she said dully, "He's dead, isn't he?"

"Yes." Gilbert's lips tightened, and he took her in his arms. "You must be mother and father now to the little one." He drew back and there was a fierce intensity scored across his strong features.

"What happened, Gilbert?" she asked quietly. "I want to know all of it."

"There's little to tell, child," he said wearily. "I found no trace of him until a week ago. I had gone to Southampton first and found nothing. One of the men I met there was a ship's carpenter named Lyle. He was waiting for his ship to be refitted. It took longer than he thought, and he came to Portsmouth where his family lives. I ran into him by accident, and he remembered me at once."

"Had he seen Matthew?" Lydia asked eagerly.

Gilbert nodded slowly. "Yes. Lyle knew him from my description, and he told Matthew about my inquiry."

"What?"

Gilbert shook his head, his eyes cloudy with grief. "Lyle reported that Matthew said, 'There's no one in this world who'd want to find me now!' "

"But what happened?"

"Lyle told me he took passage on a trading schooner *Intrepid*, Captain George Milton's ship." He took Lydia's hand and said softly, "My dear, the *Intrepid* went down with all hands in a hurricane two weeks ago."

"Could—could there be a mistake?" Lydia's eyes pleaded with him, but Gilbert shook his head firmly.

"I went to Southampton and talked to the owners. Another ship, *West Wind*, was in the same storm. She saw the *Intrepid* go down, but there was no way they could help. He's gone, my dear!"

She looked up at him with horror and pain in her dark eyes. "Are you certain?"

"It would be torment to live on false hope, Lydia, much as I would like to offer some hope. I questioned the quartermaster who fitted out the ship, and he remembered Matthew well. He signed on and left with the ship."

Lydia shut her eyes and suddenly began to sway. Gilbert helped her to a bench in front of the cottage and sat down beside her, waiting until she had wept her heart out. Then he said, "I want to tell you what I think God has said, Lydia, concerning you and the child . . ."

The salt spray bit Lydia's lips as she stood on the deck of the *New Hope*, a two-masted schooner, watching England fade as the ship plowed into the green-gray seas.

"I know, child," Gilbert said quickly. "It's hard on the heart, leaving your home—but the New World will be a better place for you—and for my grandson."

That had been his plan, and Lydia was anxious to go—to find a new life for herself and her baby. The only relative she had in England was her aunt, and she had grown to love Gilbert Winslow as a father. He had no blood kin of his own, and this loss drew them together more than anything else.

Now she expressed one flickering moment of doubt. "Gilbert, is it right—my going to Plymouth?"

He looked down at her, and she thought with a sharp pain in her heart, *I'll never forget Matthew—not as long as his father is alive!*

He put his strong arm around her and smiled. "It's only a little while before we *really* go home, Lydia. But until that day comes, you and my grandchild need a place and a people." He paused and looked westward, almost as if he could see Plymouth with his keen blue eyes.

Then he looked down at her and said quietly, "The last of the House of Winslow, Lydia—that's the precious burden you're carrying!"

And then he led her to the jutting prow of the *New Hope*, where they looked out to the open seas to the future together.

PART TWO

PLYMOUTH

★ ★ ★ ★

1675

CHAPTER NINE

RACHEL

★ ★ ★ ★

The wedding day was clear and bright on the morning of April 2, 1675. Rachel Winslow smiled to herself as she peered into the polished mirror, murmuring, "Fourteen years old this day—an old woman you're getting to be!"

She tossed the mirror on the bed with a typical careless gesture, and left her small upstairs bedroom in a rush. Her mother looked up from the table where she was kneading dough, saying, "One would think you were the bride, the trouble you take prettying yourself up!"

The words sounded harsh, but there was little of that quality in Lydia Winslow. Plymouth folks had come to take almost for granted her numerous charities, and the daughter who came over to smile at her did not seem in the least alarmed. She reached out and tucked a raven black tress of her mother's hair under the kerchief she wore and said carelessly, "I want to look nice for Joshua, Mother. He's probably going to come by and ask me to marry him again." Lydia did not miss the saucy look in Rachel's hazel eyes, and she shook her head.

"And you'll turn him away as usual. You may be sorry for that one day, Rachel. He'd be a good husband."

"Country's full of good husband material," Rachel responded cheerfully. "Full of groundhogs and all kinds of other pesky varmints, too, but I don't have to take up with any of them."

Lydia stared at her, knowing she ought to be outraged and shocked, but as usual she threw up her hands and laughed. "You are a silly girl!" she said with affection.

"Grandfather says I've got more brains than the whole New England Confederation," Rachel stated with a demure look.

"Your grandfather is a wise man—except where you're concerned, and in that area he hasn't a grain of sense!"

"He says you're the most beautiful woman in the Colonies. I guess he's just prejudiced about you, too, Mother."

"Indeed he is. Now, get out of here, you goose! Go help that poor girl who's going to look as plain as an old shoe when she stands up next to you!" Then she flung one last comment at Rachel as the girl was leaving: "But homely as she is, she's marrying today—and that's more than I can say for you!"

Rachel laughed and ran lightly down the road that sloped past Governor Bradford's house toward the harbor, and took a right. She found Mercy Doolittle, the bride, inside the bungalow where she lived with her parents and five other children.

"Oh, it's you, Rachel!" Mercy's mother exclaimed. She handed the comb to Rachel, saying, "See if you can do anything with Mercy's hair—I'll go help with the cooking!"

"Well, the big day is here, girl," she said, pulling the comb through Mercy's hair with such force that the poor girl cried out. "Be still, now! This is your last day of freedom, and that husband of yours will give you worse if you don't mind him."

"Oh, Praise God and me, we'll do fine."

Rachel smiled at the name of the bridegroom—Praise God Pittman. "It'll be hard for you to have a fight with him, won't it, Mercy? I mean, how can you scream with anger and yell 'Praise God!' at the same time?"

Mercy was a tall, homely girl, rawboned and awkward, but her good humor and kindness redeemed her for everyone—especially Praise God, who could not be convinced that she was not as lovely as a rose. The stocky, muscular man of twenty-two was a blacksmith and a tinker, had been known to drink a little too much on occasion, and his reputation as somewhat of a la-dies' man persisted in spite of his denials. In any case, the two were satisfied with one another and as Mercy put it, "So long as we suit each other, why, let others keep their noses out!"

Her one beauty was her hair, and as Lydia combed it into a shining fall of reddish gold, she asked curiously, "Mercy, are you afraid?"

"Afraid? Of what?"

"Why, of marriage," Rachel answered. "Won't it be hard to do everything Praise God tells you?"

Mercy pulled away, turned and stared at her friend, and a smile touched her lips. "Why, it would be for *you*, I'm thinking, you bein' so smart and all. But most women don't have a very strong mind." This was commonly believed among most of the colonists, and Mercy elaborated on the doctrine. "Why, I heard tell of a lass once, and her father taught her all sorts of readin' and writin'. Well, one day she goes mad and strangles her daughter, she did! Them at court said 'twas the learnin' of readin' and writin' as done it, destroyed the brain, it not bein' so strong as a man's brain."

"I see," Rachel smiled wryly.

Mercy reached out and touched the cheek of the dark-haired girl, saying with a smile, "You'll not take to a man orderin' you around, will you, Rachel Winslow. Lord help the poor fellow who tries to get *that* job done!"

"No hurry about me," Rachel said; then she laughed and urged, "You'd better get your finery on, Mercy, or Praise God will have to wait for his bride—and he's not a man to wait for a woman long, is he now?"

She had just finished helping Mercy put on her wedding dress, a bodice dyed blue for constancy and an orange skirt. Some who came from England had the idea that the Separatists at Plymouth wore only black or gray, but that was only for meetings on Sabbath; most of them loved bright colors and decked themselves out with finery on every other occasion.

They heard the sound of singing and Rachel cried, "There they come!" Soon the air was filled with the sound of song, and they went outside to be greeted by the marriage party. There were at least forty of them, every young person who could get free, for marriage was not a church matter to the Separatists, just as Christmas was not recognized as a religious holiday.

They proceeded to the large open space in front of the Common House, where the civil wedding was performed by Judge Haskell. A long prayer by Gilbert Winslow completed the ceremony.

"Now, for the cake!" Judge Haskell cried out, and he took up a large plain cake in his hands, and parted it by breaking it gently over Mercy's head. He tossed it out to the crowd in fragments, and there was a wild scramble, for it was considered a fine thing to gather up a piece of bridecake and put it under your pillow and dream of whom you were to wed.

As Rachel picked up a small piece, she heard a voice in her ear say, "Why settle for a dream, Rachel, when you can have the real man?"

She turned with a smile to face a tall fair-faced man with dark blue eyes in his large round face. "Why, David, is this a proposal?"

He laughed at her and there was admiration in his face, but caution, too. "Well, you've got enough poor devils wandering around moonstruck without adding me to the bedlamites."

"I thought you'd back out, David Morris! You're no man!"

He stood there laughing at her, drinking in her fresh beauty and her wit, but like others, he wondered if it was quite *right* for a woman to be so witty. *Well enough for a man to have sharp wit, but would it be wearing to have a wife who was so sharp?* He admired her, but she saw the same reservation she'd seen in other men, and since she had no idea of marrying David Morris, it gave her pleasure to keep him off balance.

Noticing her grandfather standing close, listening to their conversation, she left young Morris to take his arm. She pulled him away, saying, "Let's go eat while the food's hot."

"You give these young men a time, Rachel," he said with a smile.

"You've spoiled me, Grandfather," she laughed up at him. "When I find a man as handsome and as witty as you, I'll submit at once!" She looked at him with a smile, half-serious, for he was still a fine-looking man at the age of 75. The auburn hair had some silver in it, but was still thick and smooth over his neck, and the lines in his angular face only made it look stronger than ever. His wide-set bright blue eyes, undimmed by age, gleamed from under bushy brows. He moved easily, his tall frame still strong enough to walk most young men into the ground.

"You'll have to settle for what you can get, girl," he jibed with a sudden smile that made him look much younger. "You're pretty enough, but you've scared most of the suitors off with your pert tongue."

"If they're afraid of a woman's tongue, they won't do for me!" she retorted.

He could never argue with her for long, this beautiful granddaughter of his. He had been the first to hold her after she was born, the only grandchild he'd have on this earth, and although he'd hoped for a grandson to carry on the family name, he had lost his heart to the red, squalling bit of humanity—part French, part English, and for fourteen years he had made her his chief interest in life, taking second place only to his loyalty to God.

They came to the great table laden with roast venison, roast turkey, fricasse of chicken, beef hash, boiled fish, stuffed cod, pigeons, boiled eels, Indian pudding, succotash, roast goose stuffed with chestnuts, pumpkin pies, apple tarts and to wash it all down, beer, cider, claret, flip, brandy, and sack posset.

As they ate Gilbert said, "I'm going to the Indian camp tomorrow."

"Oh, take me with you!"

He grinned at her and said, "Who wants to make a hard journey to a dirty old Indian camp filled with fleas?" He laughed at the color which had risen to her cheeks. "You couldn't intend to stop by and see Jude Alden, I don't suppose?"

"Why, I suppose, since it's on the way . . ."

He smiled at her, knowing her as well in some ways as he knew himself. "You little minx! Think I don't read that devious little head of yours?"

"Can I go, Grandfather?"

"I suppose. Someday you're going to ask me for something I won't give you!"

She smiled up at him, and he said impulsively, "You're very much like your father—when you smile, I see him in my mind's eye as clearly as I see you."

Her eyes opened wide, and she stared at the old man, for

he almost never mentioned her father. "Do I really look like him, Grandfather?"

"Not so much as you look like your mother—which is God's blessing!" he added, and as always Rachel marveled that the only bitterness she had ever seen in Gilbert Winslow found its object in his son, Matthew. She had heard the whole story of his short marriage to her mother and his death. When her mother had first told her of her father's sad end, she had cried for days, then ended up hating him. She never reasoned it out that she despised him for being a coward, or for depriving her of a normal family. Inside she kept her feelings buried, but it always shocked her to see her grandfather subject to any fault, and now she stood there marveling at this one flaw in his otherwise perfect character.

He said hastily, "Be ready early, child, it's a long trip."

He left, and all afternoon during the dances and festivities, Rachel could not help thinking of her father—even as Praise God carried Mercy over the threshold as the sun was going down. As the custom was, the rosy-faced couple sat in bed dressed in their shifts, and the young people took turns standing at the foot of the bed throwing socks over their shoulders. The belief was that if a sock thrown by a girl hit the bride, or one thrown by a boy hit the groom, it was a sign of a speedy marriage.

When Rachel threw a sock that hit Mercy square in the face, a scream went up, and she ran from the room with her hands over her ears to shut out the rather crude jokes that always accompanied such a feat.

She made her escape from the crowd and walked along the rocky beach. Soon she passed beyond the large rock where it was said the first of the Pilgrims set foot when alighting from the *Mayflower*.

Weary of the wild singing and loud merry-making, she let the quiet of the isolated beach flow over her. The crashing of the surf punctuated the silence and the cry of the gulls melded with them. She loved this coast, this beach, and for a long time she made her way aimlessly, picking up a shell to examine its intricate whorls, then tossing it back to the sandy beach.

You're very like your father sometimes. The words of her grandfather came back to her, and she tried again to imagine what he

had been like. There was no portrait at all, of course. Few people
had such things, for they were expensive. The one portrait her
grandfather had was a beautiful oil painting of his brother Edward, the older brother he'd been so close to. Rachel's mother
had told her once that her father had looked very much like
Gilbert and his brother. "All Winslow men look alike, they say.
But you take after me."

She thought then of her mother, who spoke of her father in
a general way, but Rachel could never get beneath the impene-
trable surface of Lydia Winslow's manner—in this one matter.
Once Rachel remembered saying in exasperation, "Mother, you
never tell me anything *important* about my father. Just little
things!"

She thought of that conversation as she climbed the hill that
led to the house she shared with her mother and grandfather,
and her powerful gift of imagination brought it back to her as
clearly as if it were painted on a canvas before her. She saw her
mother's smooth face suddenly break in some minute way, and
her eyes dropped. Finally she said with just a suggestion of a
tremor in her voice, "We had so *little* time, Rachel! Just a few
months, and then he was—gone."

"Did he love you?" Rachel heard her young voice piping
back to the present.

Her mother looked up, her eyes moist as she whispered,
"Oh, yes, child, yes! He loved me at first—but later . . ." She
had suddenly straightened up and said in a tone almost harsh,
"He's gone Rachel, and it grieves me to speak of it."

Rachel reached the house, a new "salt box" that Gilbert
Winslow built when a chimney fire destroyed the tiny house he
had built in 1622, when he and Humility had first been married.
She passed through the front door into a short entrance hall; to
the left was a combined kitchen and dining room, but she turned
right into the common room where she found her mother en-
tertaining Mr. Oliver Bradford, the grandson of the famous governor, John Bradford.

"Well, did you get the young folks married, Rachel?" he
asked, getting up as she entered. He was a robust man of 46,
slightly less than medium height, with brown hair cut short and
warm brown eyes. He had always been partial to Rachel, and

since the death of his wife, her willingness to spend time with his young children had made him value her even more.

"Oh, they're tied together forever, Mr. Bradford," she smiled. "Happy as larks and poor as church mice!"

"Ah, but Praise God is so much in love, he'd never notice a thing," Lydia laughed. She was dressed in black, as she always was, but the sober garb only seemed to set off her beauty. Her cheeks were as rosy as a girl's, as were her full lips. Many young women were put to despair when they took in her slender, rounded figure, for at the age of 32, time seemed not to have touched her. Her grandfather had said once, "Rachel, if I didn't know better, I'd think your mother was a witch! It's *unearthly* how she simply refuses to get old—why, she looks exactly the same as she did before you were born!"

Indeed, the dark beauty of Lydia Winslow had drawn men to her for years, but she had never shown the slightest interest in marriage. When Deacon Charles Milton had courted her in vain, Gilbert had said, "Well, Charles has looks, money, charm, and is a godly man, Lydia. If *he* won't do, who will?"

His daughter-in-law had only smiled at him, and gone to carry food to a hungry family. The church had become her life, and though many had said that an unmarried man like Gilbert Winslow would have trouble with her, she had spiked those guns by being a handmaiden of the Lord in a way that nobody could fault.

"Did you manage to give the bride a touch with the sock?" Bradford asked with a smile.

"Yes, but I'm waiting for a man like you or my grandfather to come along," Rachel shot back. Glancing slyly at her mother, she asked innocently, "Did you two settle anything?"

Oliver Bradford had been slow in making his decision. It had been over a year since his wife died, but his sudden frequent calls on Lydia Winslow had been a little too obvious. Everyone in the settlement knew he had made up his mind to marry Lydia Winslow.

His sharp-featured face flushed, and he answered, "We—have talked somewhat, but your mother is reluctant." He rose, suddenly uncomfortable, and took his leave. Lydia followed him to the door, and they said a few words that Rachel could not catch.

When Lydia returned, she said, "You shouldn't tease people, Rachel."

"Why don't you marry him, Mother?" Rachel asked suddenly. She came to look closely into Lydia's face, and then, seeing a trace of confusion, she added a question she had wondered about for years. "I've wondered why you never married—but then, everybody has. Is it because you're still in love with my father?"

"No!" Lydia answered brusquely. "No, that would be foolish, Rachel. I shall never marry because I believe that God has called me to live a single life."

"Don't you need a man, Mother?" she asked, then flushed suddenly and stammered, "I—I mean . . ."

Lydia threw back her head and laughed, and it made a merry sound in the room. "That's one of the few times I've ever seen you blush, Rachel!" She put her arm around the young woman, a younger edition of herself, and laughing, added, "I thought you were much too grown up and 'advanced' to be embarrassed by a reference to what the deacons call 'the intimacies of the connubial bed'!" Then she saw that the girl was really stricken, and she stopped laughing, saying softly, "Most women do need a man, just as a man needs a woman, Rachel. But Paul says, 'The unmarried woman careth for the things of the Lord, that she may be holy in body and spirit.' That is what I will do, Rachel—and it is not hard, for we have such a loving Bridegroom!"

Her mother had always had such a close and intimate walk with God that Rachel had learned more from just being around her than from all the sermons she'd heard in church. Lydia Winslow could pray and God would answer. Rachel had learned when she was just toddling that when she scraped her knee or injured herself, she could run to her mother, and as she prayed and rubbed the injury, the pain went away. She never called it "healing"; indeed, she never called it anything; she just did it. Rachel had come to take her mother's faith for granted, and never questioned her about it.

"Well, Mother, what about me?" Rachel asked suddenly. "I'm going with Grandfather to the Indian Village, and you know I don't give a pin about that. I'm thinking a lot of Jude."

She had always been an honest girl, and as Lydia looked into her eyes, she was thankful that her daughter had confidence enough in her to speak her heart.

"He's getting to be quite prosperous, I hear. How much land does he own now?"

"I don't know. I told him once he just wanted *all* the land that joins his, and he got embarrassed. But I don't care about land, Mother."

"What *do* you care about, Rachel?" Lydia asked quietly.

Rachel stood there in surprise. The question had caught her off guard and it went through her quick mind. Finally she said, "I don't know, but I want to do *something*!"

Lydia Winslow bit her lip, then said slowly, "That's your father, Rachel. He was exactly like that."

"Am I like him, Mother?"

"You have some of my French impulsiveness, but it's not that I fear."

"What then?"

Lydia gazed at her daughter steadily. "It's the Winslow blood. Your grandfather may seem to you the most steady man in the world, but when he was your age, he was *wild*! And my Matthew had the same restlessness. It sometimes skips a generation, Gilbert tells me, but you have it, Rachel—and that's why I've wanted to see you marry early."

"So I'll have a husband to keep me from running wild?"

"You laugh at that, but I've seen it happen. Your father was for me all that I could ever desire—but the Winslow blood was strong, and—I lost him. I can't lose you, Rachel! Not you, too!"

Rachel suddenly found her mother's arms around her, holding to her fiercely as if to protect her from some sudden danger.

Finally Lydia drew back and said gently, "Well, I've wanted to say these things to you for a long time. Now you think I'm just a nervous old woman worried about her only chick."

"No." Rachel stared at her mother, and for the first time in her life, she saw her as a woman—not a mother, just as a woman, and it saddened her.

CHAPTER TEN

KING PHILIP

★ ★ ★ ★

Rachel left the house when the east was barely tinged with the red light of dawn, and was delighted to discover John Sassamon standing beside her grandfather, his bronzed Indian features a welcome sight. "John! You're back!" She ran to greet him, and in an uncharacteristic move he embraced her. It was a rare gesture; women and men who were not related never embraced, but it was even more unusual for an Indian to show such feeling for a white woman.

But John Sassamon was not a typical Indian by any means. He had been reared in a community of Christian Indians at Natick, fifteen miles west of Boston, and had studied at Harvard. Then in a crisis of identity, perhaps, he had rejoined his native Indians in the wilderness. He served as an aide to Philip Metacomet, the son of Massasoit.

Philip had treasured the young man, and had broken into one of his legendary fits of fury when John had been led by the Spirit of God to return to Natick, where he was given the task of instructing young Indian converts.

Rachel had practically grown up with him, for he had been assigned to study under Gilbert Winslow, and the two of them had been a sturdy pair, accompanying the tall minister as he made his pastoral calls. They had sat together through the eternity-long sermons and studied the same books together, but her fondest memories were their times in the woods. He had made an Indian out of her, teaching her the forest arts of tracking, hunting, and a thousand other facts of the wilderness. She had cried for days when he left to go to Harvard, and beneath his stolid features she had seen that he was saddened, too.

Now he stood there, embarrassed at their embrace, but with a glow of joy in his ebony eyes as he said, "You are a woman, *Nahteeah*." She laughed as she heard his pet name for her, "little deer."

Gilbert said, "You two can renew your acquaintance as we travel. We've got a long day's journey." The road to Middleborough, some fifteen miles southwest of Plymouth, was good enough for the cart pulled by one of Gilbert's two horses, but past there they would have to ride or walk through Indian trails too narrow for any vehicle.

Rachel walked behind with John as Gilbert drove the cart, and after giving him all the news on what his old friends at Plymouth had been doing, she asked, "What are you going to do now that you're through at Harvard, John?"

"My people at Nemasket have prospered in the Lord, Nahteeah," he smiled. "I go to be their pastor."

"How wonderful!" Rachel exclaimed. "That's not so far. We'll get to see each other often."

"That will be good, Nahteeah. I have missed you." He laughed and said, "Do you remember when you were twelve years old and fell in love with me?"

Rachel laughed in delight at the reference. "I tried to get you to run off with me, didn't I? And you said, 'I can't marry you because I'm going to be a preacher!' "

"What a pompous boy I was!" The memory warmed them; then John gave her a look and said with a peculiar tone in his voice, "You haven't chosen a husband yet, Mr. Winslow tells me. You are fourteen now, and one of our maids would be disgraced if she got to be so old without getting a husband."

Rachel looked away from him, glancing up at a squirrel chattering angrily at the travelers for disturbing his peace. Then she said with a trace of embarrassment, "There's plenty of time."

"Is Jude Alden still courting you?"

The question disturbed her, and she said shortly, "I see him sometimes."

"He does not love my people, Nahteeah," John said quietly. "If you marry him, we could never speak to each other like this."

"He's a good man! If I did marry him, I would change his mind."

John gave her a sardonic smile, saying briefly, "That is the talk of a foolish woman, Nahteeah. If a woman cannot change a man's ways before marriage when he is warm and eager to please her, how can she do it when he has captured her and has no need to satisfy her any longer?"

The statement troubled Rachel, and she changed the subject, but all the way to Middleborough she had turbulent thoughts about what John Sassamon had said. She had long been aware of Jude's hatred for the Indians, but, despite her close friendship with Sassamon, had tried to ignore his attitude. His prejudice left no room for distinction between friendly and hostile Indians—all red men were "savages" to him. Such a perception was not rare on the frontier, although there had not been an Indian war since the war against the Pequots in 1637. But three tribes—the Nipmuck of Massachusetts, the Narragansett in the Bay area, and the Wampanoag led by Philip in Plymouth— were growing restive under the increasing pressure of white civilization. Living on the frontier was like living on a powder keg, for if war with the Indians did come, there was no protection, no militia or army to keep the tribes at bay.

All morning they kept to a steady pace, stopping only briefly at noon to eat a simple meal of cold beef and bread washed down with cold water from a clear brook. They rested for less than an hour, then continued their journey, but this time Rachel rode in the cart and the two men walked in front. She listened as they talked over the matters of the ministry, and presently they spoke of the low spiritual state of Plymouth.

"You young people must get tired of hearing old men say that the church here isn't what it was in our day," Gilbert said. "But it's true. Oh, there are little fires of true godliness breaking out in places, but I can't help remembering the first years here."

"Why is it so, Brother Winslow? Why has the fire died down in the people?"

Winslow thought about the question, and finally said, "It's partly the easy living, John. People are born in town situations instead of having to wrest a life out of the wilderness. This generation has never known desperate need. They grow up never knowing what it means to be imprisoned merely because they love God enough to put Him first—like John Bunyan. They don't know what it's like to have no land and no work and no say in how they are governed. It did something to us, John—the first-comers, I mean—to live for weeks in wet misery on the open seas, then living in tents or holes in the ground, while cold and sickness ticked us off one by one. I remember one month that first year when we had to bury our dead by night so Indians wouldn't know how our ranks had thinned! We ate ground nuts or grubbed for mussels to stay alive—and all for the sake of a vision of a Promised Land!"

John nodded. "I have often heard you say, Mister Winslow, 'God hears only desperate men!' "

Winslow shrugged, and his step was as strong as it had been at dawn, causing Rachel to marvel again at her grandfather's youthful body. "I fear the only way God will get the attention of our people, John, is for them to become desperate—as we were at the first."

"You think good times ruin the church?"

"Rev. Cotton Mather believes that. He said in a sermon last month, 'Religion begat prosperity, and the daughter devoured the mother.' And he's not alone, for Daniel Gookin showed me a letter from Judge Sewall, and the wise judge said, 'Prosperity is too fulsome a diet for any man—unless seasoned with some grains of adversity.' "

They passed through Middleborough that afternoon, and leaving the cart with a friend, proceeded on foot to Philip's camp. It was growing late in the day when they walked into the collection of rude huts, made for the most part of saplings tied together with vines. The smell of cooking fires was in the air, and they were greeted at once by Philip, sachem of the Wampanoags.

"You have come," he said, advancing to meet them. He held his hands palms up in the traditional Indian greeting, showing that he had no weapons. "We eat first, then talk."

They sat down in a circle inside his tent, which smelled strongly of fish, dog, and unwashed bodies, and Rachel made a show of eating. The food was some sort of stew in a great iron pot, and the guest simply reached in, pulled out a piece of meat or vegetable and ate it with the fingers. She avoided the meat, knowing the Indians' weakness for young dog. She had many times seen a squaw knock a puppy on the head, dress it in a few deft movements and throw it into just such a pot; although she had eaten such food, it never appealed to her.

Philip was not physically impressive. He was small, and his slight frame was covered with stringy muscles. A large nose dominated his face, and he had a small mouth which he kept tightly shut. But he had not risen to be sachem over his tribe because of his appearance, but simply because he was by far the most intelligent of all his people. Perhaps *crafty* was a better word; as Rachel studied the small Indian who was talking to her grandfather, she was struck again with the glittering eyes that illumined his face. She had always been somewhat afraid of the man, and now she felt a chill as he spoke angrily, making violent gestures with his hands.

"You come like locusts, you white men," he said staring hypnotically at the visitors. "Soon the People will have no place to put their feet. You talk about Great God in the sky, but is He only the white man's God? Does He not make the People as well?"

"He is the God of all men, King Philip," Winslow answered quietly.

"Then does He let one of His children rob the other? The Wampanoag fathers are not so cruel to their sons! He is cruel, this Jesus God!"

John Sassamon spoke up then in his clear baritone voice. "No, Jesus is not unjust. He died for the sins of all men, red and white. He longs for all His children to walk in love with one another."

Philip shot a malevolent glance at the young man, and fairly spat out his next words: "The white man robs us, takes our land and pushes us into the sea! How can you call this love? You have forsaken the People, and can see only the white man's way!"

Philip's thinly veiled hatred of Christianity, especially of the Christian missionaries who were pulling away some of his best warriors, was no secret. To Philip, John Sassamon was a turncoat of the vilest sort, and from that moment, he turned from the young Indian, ignoring him completely.

"You have been paid for your land, King Philip," Winslow said, but he knew the words were meaningless to the man. Indians never understood ownership of land in the English sense. Their idea of signing a deed to real estate, usually in return for a specified number of axes, kettles, matchcoats, or mackinaws, was to share it with the palefaces, not to move out; they regarded the price as rent, to be repeated every so often.

Philip listened sullenly as Winslow pleaded with him, stating the case for the white man in the fairest terms, but finally when all was said, it was obvious that the smoldering hatred in Philip was not quenched.

"We must go before it gets too dark to travel," Winslow said, and they took their leave of the surly chief, to hurry along the trail.

"We'll not get back to Middleborough by dark," John remarked.

"No, but we can stay the night with Alden," Winslow said.

They walked as fast as Rachel could go for two hours, but the sun was behind the low range of hills to the south when they turned off the trail to Jude Alden's farm. He was not expecting them, but when they came into the clearing cut out of the large oaks where his snug house was set, he came out at Winslow's hail.

"Mr. Winslow—" he said, then peering behind caught sight of the two behind him. "Well, Rachel, this is a surprise."

He did not acknowledge John. Rachel went up to him and said, "Hello, Jude. Can you take in three tired travelers tonight? You remember John Sassamon."

Alden hesitated, glaring at the Indian, then nodded. "Of course! Come in and we'll have some tea and a little bite of food."

They filed into the small house, and he put his musket down and busied himself with the food. He talked steadily, mostly with Winslow, but he was very conscious of his other two guests.

He could not disguise his suspicion of Sassamon, and Rachel was grieved to see the covert glance of distrust he gave the Indian who stood silently with his back against the wall.

But he was most aware, she saw with some pleasure, of her.

He listened to her grandfather, even made replies, but he could not keep his eyes off her. Rachel was accustomed to attention from young men, but as he poured the tea and they sat down to eat, she felt a sudden pride that he was so captivated by her.

"God, we thank you for this food—Amen!" Jude said quickly, and they were all caught off guard by the brevity of it.

Gilbert laughed and said as he cut a slice of beef from the large portion in the platter, "That's your grandfather speaking there, Jude." He referred to John Alden who had courted and won Priscilla Mullins on board the *Mayflower*. "He was a devout man, but had no time for long prayers—or sermons, either! I recall he said once to Governor Bradford's face after a three-hour sermon, which was not one of the governor's *best*: 'Yer pardon, Governor, fer goin' to sleep, but yer should take note of the oyster.' Well, Bradford stared at him, completely mystified, and finally he asked, 'The oyster? Why the oyster?' And John looked him right in the eye and said, 'Because, sir, the beast knows when to open—and *when to shut!*' "

Jude laughed louder than the others and said, "I believe it of him, Mr. Winslow. I miss him very much."

"So do I, Jude," Winslow said quietly. He traced a figure on the table with his finger, then looked up and said, "They were a goodly people, the Firstcomers."

"Yourself, too, Mr. Winslow," Alden nodded at once.

"No, I was the black sheep, John." Gilbert Winslow shook his head sadly. "I could tell you some of my sinful past that would curl your hair, if I so chose."

"I've always wanted curly hair, Grandfather," Rachel piped up suddenly. "Please tell us about those times."

Winslow seldom spoke of his part in the settlement of Plymouth, but he did that night. He did not spare himself, for he had not been aboard the *Mayflower* voluntarily, but was fleeing from the King's Justice. He told them how he had entered the service of Lord North, fleeing the life of a ministerial student at Cambridge to pursue fame and fortune with one of England's most powerful lords. He told of Lady Cecily North, the beautiful aristocrat he had fallen in love with, and Rachel longed to ask him more about her, but was afraid to interrupt.

"I joined Bradford and the Pilgrims in Holland with one idea in my mind," Gilbert said with a sad look in his fine eyes. "I was to ferret out William Brewster, one of the founders of the congregation, so I became a spy."

"A spy, sir? I can hardly believe it!" Alden exclaimed.

"Then you do not know the depravity of the human heart," Winslow smiled. "But there is a worse thing; I gained the love of a pure young woman in the group in order to get myself into the inner circle."

He went on to tell how when the choice had to be made, he had fought a duel with Lady North's admirer, Lord Roth, and had killed him in a duel to protect the young woman and the congregation.

"So I fled England on the same ship with the congregation, but I hated God!"

"What happened then, Grandfather?"

Winslow spoke slowly, seeming to live over the days when they had fought for survival, with what they called simply the general sickness, killing over half their number the first winter. He told how he had been profoundly influenced by the sacrificial lives of Bradford and others, and how he had finally found Jesus Christ as his Savior in a blinding blizzard, as God revealed himself.

"Tell about the young woman, about Grandmother," Rachel insisted.

Gilbert Winslow leaned forward, put his chin on his folded hands, and thought. Finally he said, "She was the loveliest thing on God's earth." Then he turned his head and there were tears in his eyes as he said, "You are very much like her, Rachel. Very much. Oh, you don't *look* like her at all, but her spirit has come to you." He hesitated so long they thought he was finished; then he said quietly, "All that was good about your father came from her—his generosity, his sympathy with the downtrodden, his wit—and all that was wrong came from me—from the Winslow blood!"

"No! I don't believe that!" Rachel reached over and took his hands in hers, gripping them fiercely. "You mustn't say that!"

The candle was guttering in the pewter holder as he finished, and he looked around in shock. "I can't believe it! I've never told some of this to a soul!"

"I'm glad you did!" Rachel said, putting her arms around him. "It's wonderful to have a hero for a grandfather!"

He laughed in embarrassment and got up, "Well the 'hero' is dead on his feet. Shall I sleep in the loft, Jude?"

"Yes. Rachel can have the bedroom. But there's only room for two in the loft—" he turned a hostile eye toward Sassamon.

"I will sleep in the barn," the Indian replied impassively.

Jude hesitated, then continued blandly, "I've got to see to the new calf first. Just a few hours old, and can hardly eat."

Rachel glanced from Jude to Sassamon, whose face betrayed no hint of anger at Jude's rudeness. She hesitated, as if making a decision, then turned back to Jude.

"Let me go with you, Jude!" she pleaded, just as he'd known she would. She loved all animals, especially baby ones, and she skipped over to go outside the door, calling back, "You sleep well, Gilbert Winslow; I want to hear more about this Lady Cecily North!"

She heard her grandfather's loud laugh as they stepped outside and took the path that led to the small hay shed fifty feet from the house. He opened the door and held the candle high so that she could see.

"Oh, what a darling!" she cried, and ran at once to stroke the tiny calf wobbling across the straw. "How beautiful!"

Jude Alden put the candle on a stool, and came to stand over her. "Yes," he said with a smile. "A darling—and very beautiful."

She felt her cheeks grow warm, and confusion swept her. Alden reached down and pulled her to her feet, and she felt his strong arms go around her. As he pulled her close, she whispered, "No—Jude!"

But he said again, "You are very beautiful, Rachel—more so all the time!" She was intensely aware of his male strength as he tightened his arms, pressing her even more closely to his chest. "I think about you all the time, you know. Stuck out here by myself in this wilderness! Every night I go to sleep thinking of you."

She began to tremble, filled with a fear of wrongdoing, but at the same time dizzy with the raging emotion that had suddenly risen in her. She lifted her head, and in the flickering light of the candle, he saw her lips frame his name: *Jude!* She felt her arms go around his neck, and she wondered at her boldness, but it was almost as if it were another, and not she herself, who was responding to his kiss.

He released her slowly, and as she slipped from his arms, he said, "I've never known a woman like you, Rachel."

She waited for him to say more, but he did not. Suddenly she remembered what she had heard said of him, that he was something of a ladies' man, and the thought shamed her. "I'd better go inside, Jude," she said quietly.

Then he said, "Have you ever thought of marrying, Rachel?"

She stared at him, then said, "Every girl thinks of that." Then the quick sense of humor came to her and she quipped, "You'd better ask Betsy Small, Jude. Her father's got a big farm he's going to give for her dowry—big enough that you won't mind her being so thin!"

He smiled but said at once, "I've got a bad reputation, haven't I, Rachel? About women and about being ambitious."

"There is talk—about both."

"About the first," Alden said easily, "I must confess that I've been lax—but that's over. About the second, I plead guilty. I see nothing wrong in having things. What's wrong with that?"

"It depends on how you prosper—and what you do with the money when you get it."

"I'll spend it," he smiled. "You think I'd enjoy sitting around *counting* it? No, I'll work hard for a few more years, then I'll live the good life—travel, go places, meet people!"

He had touched on a longing that she had never let another soul know of—her desire to travel, but she did not let a flicker of this yearning show in her eyes.

Then he said, "What about you, Rachel? What do you want?"

She bit her lip, then shrugged and said, "I don't know, Jude. I suppose I'm trying to find out."

He looked at her in the darkness and said, "Maybe we can help each other to find our way, Rachel."

"Maybe, Jude." She turned and they walked out into the night; then she went to her room and tossed fitfully on the straw mattress.

117

The next morning they left early and on the way home, Gilbert said to her out of John's hearing, "You decide on Jude?"

She stared at him, then laughed. "I wouldn't put it past you to climb out of the upstairs window and creep on your hands and knees to eavesdrop on us."

"I would if I thought it would help you," he said simply.

She took his hand and squeezed it, saying, "Tell me about Cecily North." Then she added with an odd smile, "I don't know about Jude. I'll tell you as soon as I know."

CHAPTER ELEVEN

OUT OF THE PAST

★ ★ ★ ★

Lydia said nothing to Rachel, but for several days after her return from the Indian village, she was aware that something was troubling the girl. Finally when she and Gilbert were alone in the church after a service, she approached him about it.

"You haven't said much about your trip to see King Philip," she said as they sat down on one of the benches. "Were you discouraged about him?"

"Yes. He's sour, and sooner or later he's going to give trouble."

"Rachel's been very quiet since you came back."

"Oh, that's a different matter," he said. "She's all tangled up about what to do with young Alden. They had some sort of meeting out in the barn, and she's been all het up ever since."

"In the barn!"

He laughed and patted her shoulder. "Now, don't get your feathers ruffled, Lydia. She told me some of it, and there's nothing to worry about. They're just circling around trying to decide whether to make a match of it or not."

She shook her head. "I wish she would marry him, Gilbert."

He shrugged and bit his lip. "I'm not so sure I agree. He's a good match, I suppose—he's got land, and he's a hard worker, but his walk with God isn't much. Pretty much of a Sunday man. And he's got a rather unchristian attitude about this Indian issue.

Snubs John Sassamon dreadfully. I'd like to see Rachel get a man who puts God first."

They talked for a long time that night, and it was on the following Wednesday that Sassamon came by. It was late afternoon, and they did not hear his step. A knock at the door startled them all as they sat reading in the front room.

"Who can that be?" Gilbert muttered, as he went to answer it. "Well, John, come in!"

Sassamon entered and said, "Hello, Mr. Winslow—and how are you, Mrs. Winslow?"

"Hello, John," Lydia smiled. "Come in, come in."

"No, I have to go see the governor right away." He hesitated, then said, "I would like for you to go with me, Mr. Winslow. He may not believe what I have to tell him."

Gilbert looked hard at him, then at Lydia and Rachel. "What's the trouble, John?"

He shifted his weight from one foot to the other, then burst out, "It's Philip, sir!"

"What about him?"

"He's organizing for war against you!"

"I knew it!" Winslow cried. "The fool! He'll set the frontier on fire!"

"Will you come with me to see Governor Bradford?"

"Yes, of course, but is it certain, John?" He pulled his coat from a peg and was shrugging into it. "How did you find out?"

"My brother, Matthew, has been to see me. He says that he was there when Philip came to his village. Philip promises that if the tribes all rise up together, the settlers will be wiped out and the land will be back in the hands of the People!"

"Come along!" Gilbert barked, plunging out the door. "I don't know if we can convince the governor or not, but we'd better!"

Rachel and Lydia stayed up until midnight, waiting for them to come back. They had talked fearfully about the possibilities of a war, but it was late and they were sitting quietly, busy with their thoughts, when Rachel suddenly said, "I kissed Jude Alden in the barn, Mother."

Lydia almost laughed out loud at the confession; it was much like those times when as a small child Rachel would think over some small misdeed for a long time, then come marching in to look her straight in the eye and announce it boldly.

"Did you now?"

"Are you angry?"

"No, I don't think so," Lydia said with a smile. "Did you think I would be?"

"Oh, I suppose not. But it made me feel a little wicked, Mother." She turned her clear hazel eyes on Lydia. "How do you know you're in love with a man?"

"Why . . ." Lydia was caught off guard. She finally cleared her throat and said, "I don't think there's any rule about that, Rachel. You just have to be sure you want to spend your life with him and that you respect him."

But that was not enough for Rachel, and she asked insistently, "But how did you know you were in love with my father?"

Lydia was trapped, and the pulse in her throat beat more rapidly as she said at last, "I can't put it into words, Rachel. You'll just have to—to—"

Rachel was staring at her mother, disappointed that there was no simple answer coming. Just as she was about to pursue the subject, they heard voices, and they got up as Gilbert and John entered.

"What did he say?" Lydia asked at once.

"The governor can't believe that it's so serious as John says," Gilbert shrugged. "He wants John to keep an eye on the situation and let us know if there's any danger."

John was angry, and Rachel saw it. "There's danger right now!" he said grimly. "When Philip attacks, he won't send any announcement, I tell you!"

"I'll work on it, John," Gilbert said, and he put a restraining hand on the young man's shoulder. "Governor Bradford is getting on, but I may be able to bring him around."

John shrugged. "It will have to be that way, I suppose. But be quick, Mr. Winslow."

"You'll stay the night," Lydia said and she went to get some cover for John. She gave it to him, and she went to bed, saying, "I'll make you a big breakfast before you go home tomorrow."

"We will pray about it, won't we, John?" Gilbert said, and

gave the young man a firm embrace before he went to his own room.

Before she left, Rachel said, "Be careful, John. Philip hates you. If he thought for one second that you were talking to us about this, he'd cut your throat."

"You're right about that. I'll be very careful." He turned to go with the blanket in his arms, then paused and said, "You're very special in my heart, Nahteeah. I treasure the memory of our childhood days here more than anything else."

She stared at him, for he had always been reticent about his feelings. "I feel that way, too, John. But there'll be more good days to come."

"I hope so, Nahteeah," he said, then turned and left silently as a shadow.

He was gone when they got up the next day, and Gilbert said ruefully, "He's in a bad place, Lydia. I fear for the Praying Indians, converted to Christianity. They're going to be in the middle if a war breaks out. Both sides will hate them."

"We'll have to see that they don't," Lydia said, and as they spoke, Rachel felt a chill of fear, for there had been something fatalistic in John's eyes as he had left her the previous night.

Then she felt the two watching her, and Gilbert said, "It'll be bad for Jude, too. He's right in the middle of Philip's territory." He said nothing more, and the weight on her heart kept her subdued for the next few weeks.

Lydia awoke and glanced carelessly at the calendar, little thinking that the date—April 10—would be any different from another day. She rose, dressed, and spent the first hour with her Bible, praying quietly while kneeling beside her bed. Then she hurried to the kitchen and put some bread in glowing coals left from the night's baking, and by the time she had sliced the loaf, Gilbert and Rachel entered and sat down.

When the simple fare was on the table, Gilbert said, "I must go to see Mrs. Hewitt over at Langley. She's not doing well. Would you like to go with me, Lydia?"

"No, I'll go later in the week, Gilbert. You tell her I'll make her some of that good strong rabbit broth she likes so well."

"All right. I think I'll stay overnight. Be back by noon tomorrow." They bowed their heads and ate quickly. "What are you going to do today, Rachel?"

"I'll help Mother this morning. Maybe I'll go to see Mercy this afternoon."

Winslow gave her a sharp look, for she had been subdued, but he said nothing. After the meal he left, and the two women spent all morning cleaning house.

It was almost noon when Rachel glanced out the window and said, "Why, there's Grandfather! I wonder why he came back?"

Lydia looked up in surprise from where she sat at the table sewing. "I can't imagine. Maybe he changed his mind."

Rachel stepped to the door and opened it. "What brought you back—?"

The words were cut off as if a noose had tightened around her neck. The man who stood there was not her grandfather— but so like him she was speechless!

He stood there, his bright blue eyes searching her face calmly, and he had the same wedge-shaped face, the same broad cheekbones and wide mouth as Gilbert Winslow—only this man was in the prime of life.

Lydia looked up to see why Rachel had broken off, and when she saw the two standing there, a fear ran through her. She rose and went quickly to the door. "What's wrong, Gilbert?"

She had no doubt that it was her father-in-law, for he had the same tall frame, and the shape of his head was so like Gilbert's that it never entered her mind as she stepped forward that it was anyone but him.

Rachel stepped to one side, her eyes fixed on the man. He took one step forward and said, "Hello, Lydia."

He stepped out of the brilliant sunshine and Lydia saw his features clearly for the first time. Her hand flew to her mouth and she felt terribly sick. She heard her heart pounding fast and hard, and the room seemed to sway. She closed her eyes and almost fell, but Rachel caught her, crying out, "Mother!" and she backed away from the door until the edge of the table caught her.

There was a sudden silence, and the three of them seemed to be frozen in place—or like a picture painted on a canvas. Lydia knew that as long as she lived she would see that scene: the brilliant

April sun streaming through the windows highlighting myriads of dust motes that swarmed madly as if to escape the shaft of light— Rachel, pale as old ivory, staring at the tall man who had stepped inside and stood looking at her across the small room.

"I've—come back. Lydia."

She tried to speak, but her mouth was so dry she had to lick her lips. When she finally found her voice, the sound was harsh and brittle, cutting the intense silence.

"I—we thought—you were—dead!"

Rachel gave a small cry, and Lydia saw the fear scoring her pale face. She moved quickly to stand beside the girl. Rachel placed an arm around her mother as if to steady her, but she herself was faint and dizzy with shock.

Matthew, too, was trembling, his ruddy face, burned with the sun, gray with strain. But he swallowed hard, his words coming slowly. "You need to sit down, both of you." He grabbed a chair in each hand and shoved them toward the two women, saying, "Please—sit down, Lydia!"

Lydia sat down heavily, for the shock of his appearance had robbed her of strength. She had seen a man almost sever his foot with an ax, and she had had the same lightheaded feeling as the scarlet blood had pumped out on the white snow. She closed her eyes and tried to pray, but nothing came. Her thoughts rolled wildly through her mind, but as she sat there, her breathing became more even, and she could feel her racing pulse slow to a normal rate.

She opened her eyes, took a deep breath, and carefully looked at her husband's face, repeating, "We thought you were dead."

"I thought of sending you word that I was coming, but I had no one to send."

Lydia stared at him; then she looked up at Rachel. "This is your father, Rachel."

The two looked at each other, and neither spoke. Finally he said, "You are beautiful—" He broke off, bit his lip and said, "I'd like to sit down myself, if you don't mind."

He stood there, and for all the strength he radiated, a vulnerability filled his face—a slight movement in his broad lips, just a trace of uncertainty in his clear blue eyes. Certainly not the brash Matthew Winslow Lydia had known. He did not move, but stood there as if he expected to be ordered out of the house.

Lydia nodded. "Of course." She watched as he pulled the third chair from the table and sat down. There was something eerie about him, for he was not the eighteen-year-old she had pictured in her mind for years, but a heavier man, stronger, with an assurance and steadiness in his gaze that was foreign to her memories of him as a youth. There was an air of authority in him, as if he were accustomed to being obeyed, yet his face bore a look of simple humility. His hands were brown and corded with muscle, and as he moved there was a suggestion of tremendous power, ready to leap into action at an instant's notice. He had a white scar that began over his right eyebrow and disappeared into his thick hair, and another on the side of his neck shaped like a fishhook.

He was dressed in knee breeches and boots, a waistcoat of dark red velvet, and a dark-brown coat of fustian with silver buttons. His shirt was of white linen; he held a felt hat with a wide brim and high crown. There was nothing to mark him as to profession, but the clothes, though not new, had been expensive.

He let the silence run on as the women stared at him, enduring it quietly, and not taking his own eyes off them.

"I know it's a shock, my walking in like this." He hesitated then said very quietly, "You can't know how I've longed to see you all these years, Lydia."

"But—we thought you were dead!"

He stared at her, then nodded. "I suppose that would be natural enough, not hearing from me all this time. But I couldn't write!"

Lydia twisted her hands together, trying to conceal the trembling, but the anger in her voice betrayed her as she said, "You let me think all these years that you were lost at sea!"

"Lost at sea?" he exclaimed, lifting his head. "Why would you think that?"

She stared at him in disbelief, and her lips grew pale as she pressed them together. "You left on that whaling ship—I've forgotten its name—but it went down with all hands!"

His mouth dropped open, and he tried to speak, but the words would not come. Finally he swallowed and said, "As God is my witness, Lydia! I never once *thought*! Why, I was signed to go on the *Intrepid*—but at the last moment I changed my mind and took a berth aboard a schooner headed for Africa. I never knew—not until this minute—that the whaling vessel sank!" He got to his feet and began to pace nervously back and forth, twisting his head to one side in a familiar motion that Rachel had seen in Gilbert Winslow a thousand times.

"By all that's holy, I never thought of such a thing—not once!" He shook his head, then said, "I was almost mad, Lydia, in that prison, you must remember how my mind was going."

"I—remember," she said slowly, her eyes cold as steel.

"That day, the day I sent for the justice, I was in a fever, maybe you remember that, too? It seemed to burn what little will I had out of my soul! So when I signed the paper promising to never preach again, I was numb. I think I went mad. I remember Bunyan trying to talk to me, but it was like—it was like I was under water, in a way. I was moving slowly, and I couldn't see through the haze."

"Why didn't you come home?" Lydia demanded, and such pain filled her eyes that he bit his lip and looked away. "Oh, why didn't you just come home, Matthew?"

"I wanted to, Lydia—and that was where I started. But I was out of my mind. I—I knew you and Father would never understand what I had done! I suppose if I had been rational, I might have done it, but all I could think of was the shame of it! So I wandered around for a while, and then the idea just came to me—to leave the country and get away from it all."

He stopped, finding it difficult to explain. Pulling a handkerchief from his pocket, he wiped the perspiration from his brow. "That's what I did, Lydia," he began again in a hoarse voice. "I went to the house, got my clothes and some money—then I got on the coach and left Bedford. Couldn't bear seeing you."

Breathing heavily, Lydia waited for him to continue, but he said nothing more. Finally she asked, "And then? Where have you been all these years?"

As he turned to face her, she saw something in his eyes she did not recognize. He hesitated, then answered quietly, "I can't tell you now. You would not be proud of my life for the past fourteen years, Lydia."

Anger suddenly coursed through her and she got to her feet.

"And that's your explanation for deserting your wife and child?"

He flinched, but faced her blazing eyes steadily. "If there were a reason for my behavior, Lydia, don't you suppose I'd give it? But I have none." He straightened his heavy shoulders and implored, "I've come to ask for your forgiveness, Lydia—and for yours, daughter—but don't ask me to account for my life! Forgive me—that's my only request."

Lydia stared at him for several minutes, and then she began to tremble violently. Rachel watched, dumbfounded, for she had never seen her mother lose control.

"Forgive you!" Lydia spat out. "Just like that, Matthew Winslow, you expect to walk back into our lives and take up where you left off fourteen years ago?"

Winslow's head jerked as if he had been physically struck. "I can understand, Lydia—"

"Understand? You understand nothing!" she interrupted. "Once I thought you dead, I was free from the anguish of your desertion. I could go on with life, forgive your memory, give myself to God. But here you are again, and—"

Lydia stopped short, her face flushed. She breathed deeply once or twice, fought for control, then finished in a whisper, "Sin it may be, Matthew, but I cannot pretend to forgive you when my heart cannot accept you. I—I can't think clearly—"

He got up at once. "I don't wonder." He picked up his hat and stood, a tall shape against the sun that caught him in a yellow beam. He started to speak, then shrugged. Rachel saw a dark look of fatalism cloud his eyes. He looked at the two women and asked, "Where is my father?"

"He's gone to Langley," Rachel said. "He'll be back tomorrow at noon."

"I'll be on board the *Carrington*, just offshore," he stated. "If he will see me, tell him to send word."

"I'll tell him . . ." She paused, not knowing how to address him.

He gave her a slight smile and said, "You are indeed lovely, Rachel."

Then he wheeled and left without another word. Rachel watched him walk rapidly down the street until he was out of sight. She turned to look at Lydia, and said, "Mother—I can't believe it!"

Lydia whispered, "Nor I, child." She walked over to the door and stood looking down the street. Then she turned, her shoulders sagging, and she began to weep.

"Mother! Are you all right?" Rachel ran to her mother and held her close. For a long time great sobs racked her mother's body. Finally she took a deep breath, wiped her eyes, and pulled away.

"I must go to Gilbert," she said numbly.

"I'll go with you!"

"Rachel—would you mind if I went alone?"

Rachel sensed that there was a need in her mother that only Gilbert Winslow could meet, so she said, "Of course. You'll have to hurry to get there before dark."

Ten minutes later Lydia stood at the door and in an unexpected move embraced Rachel, then said, "How do you feel, Rachel? I won't leave you if . . . ."

"I'm fine, Mother, really. It's just so strange—to have a father."

Lydia glared at Rachel. "You don't have a father. Matthew Winslow gave up all rights to that name when he ran away fourteen years ago!"

"I suppose so—but it's different." Rachel shook her head. "No matter *what* he's done, he's *real*."

Lydia bit her lip and said gently, "Rachel, I have done my grieving over your father. To me he died before you were born. Now he comes back and begs for forgiveness. I hardly know how to forgive him. But I will not let him hurt me again—nor *you!*"

"Yes, Mother," Rachel said quietly. "You must hurry; it'll be dark by the time you get there."

"We'll be home early in the morning."

Rachel watched her mother until she was out of sight, then stood there, uncertain and filled with such emotion that she could not be still. She threw on a coat, and all afternoon she walked the shore, looking often at the ship that lay offshore, thinking of the tall man who had appeared out of the past.

"My father." She said the title aloud as she continued to look at the vessel until darkness began to descend. The fog soon swallowed the ship, making it invisible, so she turned and walked slowly back to the cottage, filled with an emotion she could not identify—a mixture of hope, joy—and fear!

CHAPTER TWELVE

A NEW MAN

★ ★ ★ ★

Rachel slept no more than the barn owl that kept calling all night. For three hours she tossed about on her bed, then finally rose and dressed. Her mind was confused, filled with wild thoughts and an emotion she could not define. She had long ago accepted the fact that she had no father, but for him suddenly to appear made her somehow angry. *He could have come home before this!* she thought as she waited for Gilbert and Lydia to arrive. *If he had loved me and my mother, he would have come!*

By the time she heard the footsteps approaching the house, the hurt and bitterness had taken a firm hold of her mind. She opened the door, and saw at a glance that neither of them had slept. Gilbert's face was pinched in a way she had never seen it, for he was a cheerful man, never gloomy; but now he looked old and worn as he came to embrace her. "You look tired, Rachel," he said quietly.

"I didn't sleep much. You two didn't either, from the looks of you. I've got some tea ready." She sat them down and as she poured the tea, she said, "It's hard for me—but much worse for both of you."

Gilbert took the tea, stirred it slowly with his spoon, then tried to smile. "I feel very guilty, you know. Here is my only son come back from the grave, and I've not been giving God the glory."

Lydia sat down wearily, looked out the window where the morning sun was beginning to warm the earth. She shook her head and said, "Matthew is alive—not dead, and I feel so—so . . ."

Gilbert gazed at her steadily and said, "It will take a while, my dear." He sipped his tea, adding, "I've sent word for him to come as soon as he can."

"But—what are you going to say to him?" Rachel asked, frustration mirroring her usually cheery face. Her full lips narrowed under the pressure, as she continued. "He can't expect to just step back into our lives as if nothing happened! I can't just smile at him and say, 'Father, I'm so glad you're home,' can I?"

Gilbert stared at his cup, then looked up at her. "I hardly think he expects that, Rachel. But I know what you mean." Nervously he bit his lip, then added, "Let's wait until we talk to him before we try to make any decisions or form any judgments."

The next hour was a strain as each tried to occupy himself. But none mentioned Matthew's name. Then as Lydia looked out the window she cried, "Here he comes!" They all stiffened. Following the knock at the door, Gilbert moved stiffly forward, then pulled it open and stepped back.

Matthew took two steps into the room, paused, then meeting Gilbert's gaze, said quietly, "Hello, Father."

The two women did not move nor speak, for they were caught by the tension that filled the room. Both of them looked at Gilbert's face, now masking his emotions.

Gilbert Winslow was not a man to hide his feelings; that was one of his charms. His expressive features reflected his moods, for he had not formed the habit of concealing his emotions. When he was angry, his bright eyes blazed with a fury that most men could not match, and when he was filled with joy, the light on his face made all who saw him glad.

But now his impassive face revealed no emotion. "Matthew," he began, "this is a glad day for me. Welcome home." The words were cordial, perhaps, but they were spoken in a careful, guarded tone, with little warmth.

Matthew's face, bronzed with an eastern sun, had been tense, but Lydia had seen the sudden light of expectancy that had lurked in his eyes and on his lips. At his father's words, his face had gone still, and he bit his lip, nodding slightly. "Thank you, sir."

It was all so formal, painfully so, that Lydia said quickly, "Come in and sit down."

"Thank you." He moved toward the table, sat down and folded his hands on the table. Gilbert sat down opposite him, but the two women remained standing.

Gilbert looked his son in the face and said, "You're looking well." Then he suddenly struck the table and cried, "Matthew, why—!"

"Father, wait!" Matthew implored, twisting his head to one side. The memory of that mannerism raked hard across Gilbert's nerves, and he knew for a long time he would be seeing and hearing things he had forgotten.

Matthew suddenly smiled, and though it was a bitter-sweet expression, his tone revealed no malice. "Let me put your minds at ease—all three of you. You're all in a state of shock—and you're all angry with me—" He held up his hand as Gilbert started to speak, and raised his voice as he said, "How could it be otherwise? You are angry, Father, because I ran away from duty. Lydia, how could you not be bitter with a man who deserted you? And you, Rachel, how can you possibly accept a stranger as a father—a man who's never done one thing for you that a real father would have done?"

The words struck all three of them like musket balls. Gilbert finally spoke, his voice edged with agitation and a trace of wonder. "You have picked up some discernment along the way." This time a smile touched the corners of his mouth and he said, "In my case you are correct—but I will expect that as we spend time together, I will be able to overcome this attitude."

Looking intently at each one, Matthew said quietly, "You need have no fear that I've come to move into your lives." At his words a look of surprise swept across Lydia's face, but he did not see it. "It took me two years to convince myself even to come back. I was ashamed, of course, and I had decided that whatever else I did, the one thing I would not be guilty of was inflicting *more* pain on you."

"What changed your mind—Matthew?" Lydia asked. She

seemed to have trouble pronouncing his name, but the shock of his presence was lessening, and the tense lines on her face had softened.

He hesitated, then gave a smile tinged with embarrassment. "I'll tell you—but it sounds so weak, I'd not expect you to believe it."

"I'd like to hear whatever part of your life you will tell us, Matthew," Gilbert encouraged him. "Lydia informs me it's your opinion we would be shocked by some of it—but I think we deserve to know *something*! You owe us that, I think."

Matthew bit his lip, then shrugged, saying, "Certainly. Father, if you want to know, I'll tell you." He got up and began to pace the floor, and his gait, his every movement brought back to Lydia and Gilbert the young man they had last seen fourteen years earlier.

"As I told Lydia, I was delirious when I left the jail, and you remember that my mind was in bad shape at that time. The ship was bound for Africa, but for most of that long voyage, I was so ill they kept me in the hold, pretty much expecting me to die. Perhaps you don't know this, but England and Spain are in stiff competition with one sort of merchandise—black slaves from Africa. Well, the *Eagle* made a good haul, but she was overtaken by a Spanish man-of-war and impounded as contraband. They kept the ship and the slaves, and every man on board was tried and found guilty of smuggling!"

Matthew gave them a curious look, then said, "I was in a Spanish prison for nearly six years—which is as close to hell on earth as you'll find on this planet!"

"I've heard something of it," Gilbert responded. "It's a miracle you're alive at all, from what's said of such places."

"I wouldn't be if I hadn't escaped. There was a prisoner named Rolfe, Isaac Rolfe. He'd been a soldier, a pirate, and just about everything else—but he got us out of that prison!"

"What did you do then?" Rachel asked suddenly. She had been watching her father pace the floor, and there was a burning desire to know all about him.

"Why, I joined with Rolfe," he shrugged. "And for the next six years we did all manner of things that men in our condition do to stay alive. We called ourselves 'soldiers of fortune'—which was a fancy way of saying we would fight on any side for any cause if there was enough gold in it for us." He paused and his brow furrowed as he thought; then he added, "I must have been in half a dozen armies, and most of the time I didn't even ask what the war was about."

"There are worse things than being a soldier," Lydia said.

"Yes, there are, and I managed to discover one," Matthew said bitterly. "Trading in human flesh—that was my next fine profession! I joined with Rolfe to buy a schooner and we made the trip to Africa time after time, but it never failed to make me sick. We packed them in so thickly on the ship they had to sleep hugging each other, like spoons pressed together. And when the plague would break out in the hold, they'd die like flies! We've thrown them over the side by the dozens—women, nursing mothers, babies—!"

He walked to the window and leaned on the sill, staring out at the green grass and the swaying hills. He stood there so long that he seemed to have forgotten them. Finally Gilbert gave a quick glance at Lydia and cleared his throat. "What happened then?"

"What? Oh, I took it as long as I could—" Matthew turned and looked at them with an odd light in his blue eyes. "Finally I sold my share of the ship to Rolfe and cleared out. I had enough money so that I could go anywhere, and for a few months I just wandered around, looking for something—but I couldn't find any peace."

He smiled at Gilbert and said, "Here's the part you won't believe. It sounds too much like a bad story. You see, ever since those days in that Spanish prison, something you told me once kept coming back. You may not remember it—but I've never forgotten. On the day that Uncle Edward and I were leaving for England, you and mother were there. It was the last time I ever saw her."

"I remember very well," Gilbert said quietly.

"Do you remember that you started down the ladder, and you called out to me: 'Be faithful to God, Matthew—never fail Him! Be true to God—and to yourself'?"

"Yes, I said that."

"Well, those words came to me all the years I was in prison, and even while I was serving the devil in the wars and in the slave trade. But when I finally cut all my ties with Rolfe and was alone with nothing to do, those words got even stronger. I tell you, it was like losing my mind—the way they kept ringing in my ears! So then—and here's what I find hard to say to you . . ."

He seemed so embarrassed that Gilbert said, "Go on. Let us hear it, son!"

Matthew nodded, then continued in a quiet voice charged with emotion. "I went back to England with no purpose, but one day I suddenly decided to go back to Bedford. It was like a dream when I got there, seeing the little house where we lived, Lydia—and the jail, of course! I found out Pastor Gifford had gone on, but you know about John Bunyan?"

"Yes." Gilbert smiled for the first time. "He's become quite a famous preacher since his release three years ago. In great demand all over England. And he and Elizabeth have two children of their own now!"

"Yes, I know," Matthew said. "I stayed with them for six months. He hasn't changed, John hasn't. The years in prison just made him pure gold! But now I have to tell you both—I was a lost sinner when I went to stay with the Bunyans, but through their love and kindness—I found Christ as my Savior." The confession seemed very difficult for him, and he laughed shortly. "I told you it would sound like a bad piece of fiction. Sinner gets converted and runs for his father's house—after ruining the lives of the three people he loves most." Matthew got up, wheeled and started for the door. He paused, turned and added roughly, "I won't trouble you, you may be sure of that!"

His departure was so sudden that they were stunned. Gilbert called out, "Wait—!" But he was gone.

"I—I don't understand, Gilbert," Lydia said in bewilderment. "Why should he be so—so *ashamed* to tell us he's become a Christian?"

"It sounds too easy for him, I think," Gilbert said slowly, rubbing his chin thoughtfully. "I can see how he feels, can't you? He behaved shamefully, and now his pride won't let him believe that all he has to do is ask forgiveness."

"But—is it real? His conversion, I mean?"

Gilbert turned to look at Rachel, then answered, "I don't

know, but in a way, it's just as well he feels this way. It will give us all time to think, to try and sort this out."

"But, what will he do?" Lydia asked.

"I think," Gilbert murmured softly, "he'll spend a lot of time *showing* us that he's found God—instead of *telling* us!"

Matthew's words on leaving—*I won't trouble you, you may be sure of that!*—were followed so strictly that for the next month it was almost as if his sudden appearance had been a dream! He did not return to the Winslow house, and they had to learn of his movements from others.

"The gentleman with your name, Pastor Winslow, he's your relation, is he?" Martin Tillotson asked one day as Gilbert stopped by the single inn in Plymouth. Tillotson was new to the town, a small, polite man, very regular in his church attendance. He smiled and said, "I could see the resemblance between the two of you—a fine looking man he is, too, like yourself, if I may say so."

"Yes, Brother Tillotson," Gilbert said quickly. "He's my son. How did you happen to meet him?"

"Why, he took a room here last week, Pastor—but he's been gone since that first day. Said he'd not be in much. He didn't mention his business."

Gilbert didn't take the broad hint, for not knowing himself what Matthew was doing, he could not very well answer the innkeeper. He repeated the conversation to Lydia and Rachel. They too were perplexed.

"Why did he come here if he was intending to leave so soon?" Rachel asked sharply. "Everyone knows about it. Mercy asked me right out, 'Is that *really* your father living at the inn?' And what was I to say? The whole thing makes me feel so—awkward!"

All three of them felt that way the next Sabbath Day, when Matthew walked in and took a back seat in the small church. It was a small town, and every stranger was subjected to minute examination, but Matthew's appearance sent a hum of whispering around the congregation, and several members were in danger of dislocating their necks trying to swivel around and catch a glimpse of the visitor.

Lydia's cheeks burned. Rachel turned to her mother and

whispered, "We can't *bear* this, Mother!"

Gilbert took in the avid interest, noting the embarrassment on the faces of Rachel and Lydia. His own face was paler than usual, but he rose and called the congregation to order as if nothing had happened. They sang and several members gave interpretations of scriptures; then Gilbert preached for an hour.

No one dared to turn and stare at Matthew during the sermon, except Mrs. Lawson, who would have stared at the archangel Michael. But if the eyes of the congregation were not directed at their visitor, their interest surely was.

Gilbert concluded the sermon, but instead of closing with a final prayer, he said in a steady voice, "We have a guest in our congregation this morning, my son, Matthew. Some of you who have been here for a long time will remember him. He was presumed to be dead for many years—but God in His mercy preserved him. I ask you to welcome him back, and to join his wife and his daughter in thanking God for His tender mercies."

Then he prayed, and afterward several of Matthew's old friends approached him eagerly. Matthew's teacher, in his eighties, but with eyes as sharp as a bird's, greeted the tall man, so unlike the small boy he had known. "Thank God, my boy! I thank God!" he exclaimed, giving him a hearty grip of the hand. "I've never forgotten you, never! It cut me like a knife when the word of your death came, and for all these years I've had fond memories of those days when you came to my house—such a bright little chap!" Then he suddenly reached out and embraced Matthew, weeping and patting him on the arm.

Matthew looked over the old man's head at Gilbert, his eyes misty as he said, "Why, that's good of you, Mr. Morrison—and just like you! I've thought of you often."

Others came, and those who had moved to Plymouth after his presumed death came to be introduced.

It was a strange moment for Matthew, who stood there receiving the greetings of old friends and others, feeling like an imposter. But it would not have been quite so difficult if Mrs. Lawson had not raised her voice, saying loudly, "Well, now, Lydia Winslow! What will it be like to have a husband again after all these years?"

Lydia flinched slightly at the impertinent question, but she managed to smile. "I rejoice with all of you," she said noncommittally, "that God has seen fit to preserve my husband."

Then the awkward moment passed, and the crowd began to leave. Gilbert walked over immediately and said, "I'm glad you came, son."

"We—expected you to come back," Lydia said with some hesitation.

Matthew gave her a direct look, then shook his head. "As I said, Lydia, I'll not be a trouble to you."

Rachel had moved to stand beside Lydia. "Well, you can't just *ignore* us!" she said sharply.

Matthew smiled at her. "Rachel, I realize how awkward it is—especially for your mother—but I'm leaving Plymouth today, so people will have to just *wonder* about our family."

"Leaving!" Lydia said quickly. "But—where are you going?"

"I was going to stop by and tell you about it before I left, but—"

"Come and have a bite with us," Gilbert said quickly. "It will look odd if you don't—and besides, I want to hear your plans."

They ate cold beef and bread, their usual Sabbath noonday meal, and Matthew related his plan. "There's a big market for beaver in England. I'm going into the trading business. As a matter of fact, I brought a wagon load of trade goods with me from England. I'll be gone for a few weeks; then when I get a shipment, I'll come back and put them on a ship here at Plymouth."

All three of them realized it was more than a business venture; he was taking himself out of Plymouth to remove some of the pressure from the three of them. "Matthew," Gilbert said, "you don't have to do this on our account—"

"It will be best, I think," Matthew broke in, "if I'm gone for a time. Give people time to get used to the idea of my being back." Then he added simply, "I'll have to go permanently, sooner or later, you know. There's no other way."

These weeks since Matthew's sudden appearance had not been easy on anyone. All three had wondered how he could fit into their lives. It would not do for him to remain at the inn, separated from his wife and daughter. In Plymouth that was

simply not done, and in any case, it would have put an intol-
erable strain on all of them.

Breaking the awkward silence, Matthew stated, "I'll call
when I get back in a few weeks."

He left, and although the village had not stopped speculat-
ing about the strange and sudden appearance, by the middle of
June most of them had given up trying to ferret the truth of the
affair from the family.

Lydia lost weight, Rachel noted, and was much quieter than
usual as she went about her work at home and tended to the
many charities she pursued. Rachel wanted to speak about her
father to Gilbert and her mother, but they seemed engaged in
some sort of inner journey and would only say, "We must continue to pray about it," when she brought the subject up.

On the last of June John Sassamon suddenly appeared, full
of news. Arriving at the cottage, his first words to Rachel were,
"I've been with your father!"

Rachel eagerly pumped the young Indian for information,
and discovered that her father had gone to John's village. The
two had met and become fast friends; Sassamon could not speak
highly enough of Matthew.

"He is a good man, Nahteeah! As good as his father!" That
was high praise, indeed, from the Indian! He went on to add,
"He is the most honest trader my people have ever met, but the
other traders are very angry with Mr. Matthew because he gives
a fair price and does not rob the People! And he is as good as an
Indian in the woods, Nahteeah! I have traveled with him and he
can stalk the deer better than I!"

Rachel hung on his words, and Sassamon asked suddenly,
"What is wrong between Mr. Matthew and you, Rachel?"

"Why, nothing, John!"

"That is the first lie you have told me in a long time!"

She bit her lip, ashamed to be dishonest with him, then said,
"It is an old thing, John. My father did a bad thing years ago,
and it still lies between us, I suppose."

"That is bad—for he is a good Christian," Sassamon said
vigorously. "I am disappointed for the first time with Pastor
Winslow. He should thank God he has such a good son—and
you and your mother—you have a good husband and father."

Rachel had no answer, and John said, "I must go to Governor Bradford now."

"Is it bad news again, John?"

"Not good! Philip is trying to get the other tribes more unhappy with white men. And he is having success." Sassamon shifted his feet. "I think it will come soon," he added.

"You must be very careful, John," Rachel continued. "He will kill you if he even suspects you are talking to the authorities."

He shrugged, "Do not worry about me, Nahteeah." Then he smiled, saying earnestly, "You must learn to love your father."

Then he was gone as quickly as he had come. His visit left Rachel so shaken she could not concentrate on her work. She went to the beach, walking the rocky shores and thinking, wondering if John was right. "But I don't hate my father," she protested to herself. Even as she spoke the words, she knew she was being dishonest. *I've never forgiven him for deserting me and mother!* she admitted.

She walked home slowly, unhappy with herself. When she arrived, her mother had come back, so she went to where she was sitting outside in the sun. "Mother, I've got to tell you something."

"What is it, Rachel?"

Rachel hesitated, then said with a vigorous gesture of her head, "I—I can't feel right about my father!" she said. "No matter how hard I try, I still can't—can't—"

"You can't forgive him, Rachel, is that it?"

"Yes—but I *want* to, Mother! Why is it so hard?"

Lydia shook her head, and looked out at the sea before she said with bitterness in her voice, "I'm having the same trouble, Rachel. And it's pride—nothing more. We've been hurt, and we won't be satisfied until *he* suffers as we have!"

Rachel looked at her mother in amazement, for she had never known of Lydia bearing a grudge. "But, Mother—surely *you* don't feel that way!"

Lydia suddenly put her fist to her mouth, pressing hard, and Rachel knew that she was stemming a sob that had risen to her throat. "Yes! I feel that way—and God forgive me! But He won't, Rachel, because the Bible says that if we won't forgive those who've wronged us, God will not forgive us!"

Rachel said slowly, "I want to forgive him—but I just *can't!*"

Lydia stared at her daughter and then before she rose to go into the house, she said slowly, "We're finding out something about ourselves, aren't we, Rachel? God blesses us with a miracle—and we throw it back in His face! I wonder how we will pray when we need God? And I wonder if He'll say, 'I gave you a blessing and you rejected it—now you provide your own miracles!' "

Rachel watched her mother go inside. The rest of the afternoon she went slowly about her work, mechanically and duly, unable to forget her mother's words. *Whom would I call on if I needed a miracle?*, she wondered.

And there was no answer except the slight breeze that stirred the trees and the far-off cry of a curlew.

CHAPTER THIRTEEN

DEATH IN THE WINTER

★ ★ ★ ★

Jude Alden was a contented man. He leaned against the rail fence and gazed off into the distance, savoring the knowledge that every blade of grass and every tree as far as the eye could see belonged to him. He glanced down at Rachel, then raised his arm and indicated a low rise of hills off in the distance. "There's where the new plot begins—see? There—by that line of timber off to the left."

"How many acres did you say?"

"Over three hundred in the whole tract." Jude chuckled deep in his chest, and a broad smile crossed his lips as he said, "Old Taylor thought he'd do me in on the swap—but I knew if I held out, he'd get greedy and make a snatch for that worthless piece I traded for this. I let word get out that the new road to the north was going to go through my place—and I made sure that Taylor thought I *didn't* know it. Why, it was enough to make a dog laugh, Rachel, the way he came up so innocent and offered to trade me this place! It was like taking candy away from a baby, I tell you!"

Rachel looked up with an uneasy smile at Alden as they walked back along the trail to his house. She was sure her grandfather would never approve of his methods. Besides, she could never understand the pleasure he got in trading, and now she asked curiously, "Doesn't your conscience ever hurt, Jude? I mean, you traded the old man a worthless piece of rocky ground for one of the best farms in the area."

He stared at her in surprise, and the blank look on his face showed that he had never once considered such a thing a moral issue. He studied how to explain it to her, his sharp-featured face expressive. "Why, I'd not treat a widow or an orphan this way—but if a man wants to do some trading with me, he'd best watch out for himself. It's just a game, you see, Rachel? I try to best him and he tries to best me—and that's the fun of it!"

She thought about it, but her own sense of right and wrong was too limited to render judgment, so she shrugged and said, "Well, you own it, Jude—all this land. But I can enjoy the trees— and the birds sound just as sweet to me with their singing as they do to you."

He said little more as they made their way back to the cabin. Finally he smiled and said, "Now, you're a woman, Rachel, and not able to think about business like a man. And that's all right with me. I don't want a wife to do the trading in the family."

"What do you want from a wife, Jude?" she asked mischievously. She was amused to see his jaw drop and a look of confusion sweep across his regular features.

He suddenly stopped, pulled her around and kissed her resoundingly. His lips were cold in the December chill, and the bulky clothes they both wore hindered him. "I guess I want a wife for *that* for one thing!" he laughed, then kissed her again, holding her soft form tightly until she pulled away.

"Come on, I'll race you back to the house!" She took off running, and was so light and fleet of foot that he did not catch up to her until they turned into the clearing where his house sat. She stopped suddenly and was not even breathing hard as she said, "You've got company." She lifted her hand to shield her eyes from the bright winter sun and bit her lip, adding, "It's my father and John Sassamon."

He gave her an odd look. Then as they walked across the open field he said, "Nobody in Plymouth understands about your family, Rachel." She didn't answer and he went on, "Your father came out of nowhere eight months ago. He doesn't live with you and your mother. He runs all over the country with those savages, and I suppose he's made a fortune in beaver by this time. But—you never say a word about him."

"It's a family problem, Jude." Rachel shrugged and added only, "There was a falling out years ago, between him and my mother."

Jude shook his head. "I don't like to say anything about your family, Rachel, but it'd be a tragedy if your mother took him back."

"Why do you say that?" She lowered her voice, for they were less than a hundred feet away from the house. "My grandfather says he's a changed man."

"Changed from *what?*" Jude asked instantly. "This country is on the verge of an Indian war, Rachel. Philip is a madman! And your father spends all his time with the Indians."

"It's the Praying Indians he's with most, Jude. He's working with Reverend Eliot a great deal."

"Praying Indians!" Jude muttered. "When the trouble comes, there'll just be one kind of Indian! You'll see. And your friend Sassamon will be right with them!"

Rachel had argued this with Jude many times, but it was hopeless; Alden, like many of the settlers who lived in the wilderness areas, had no confidence in any Indian.

Sassamon stepped forward, saying, "Hello, Rachel."

She took his hand and gave him a warm smile. "This is a surprise, John. Hello, Father. You're looking thin." She took his hand also, and thought about the many months it had taken for her to do a simple thing like calling Matthew Winslow "father." He had been to their house exactly four times over the past eight months, never staying the night anywhere except in the inn. It was always something like an armed truce, and none of them had been able to feel very comfortable, though outwardly they appeared to be.

"We're like a bunch of porcupines!" Gilbert had exclaimed in disgust one evening after Matthew left the house. "We just seem to be full of spines that keep poking somebody else in tender places!"

"Well," Lydia said, "it's not as bad as it was. We can sit down and talk now, at least."

"That's just, *wonderful*, isn't it?" Gilbert had growled. "I'm actually able to sit down and *talk* with my own son!"

For the first time in her life, Rachel had flared up at her grandfather. "Well, you're as bad as she is! He comes here and sits and you talk about nothing but some idiotic sermon! It wouldn't kill you to *bend* a little and say a kind word to the poor man, would it?"

Gilbert and Lydia had stared at her, and finally Gilbert had said resentfully, "Maybe you're right, Rachel, but there's some deep wounds in our past. Scars that don't heal all at once. But what about you? I don't notice as how you're sitting on his lap, and if you said one warm kind thing to Matthew tonight, I missed it!"

Lydia had stopped the quarrel, saying, "We're all guilty, Gilbert. The next time he comes, I—I'll be more—gentle."

Now, standing there in the cold air, that scene flashed back to Rachel, and she made herself smile at Matthew. "We've been disappointed that you've not been back to the house."

Matthew's face changed suddenly, and a warmth appeared in his bright blue eyes. "Why, thank you, Rachel. I've thought of you every day."

Jude said, "Where you headed, Mr. Winslow?"

"John and I thought we'd make a sweep around the north country. Maybe find a few beaver streams we can trap in, in the spring."

Jude frowned. "I'd be careful if I were you. You know how jealous Philip is of his territory."

"Philip won't mind if we take a few beaver, Alden," Matthew said easily. "Indians don't mind sharing things."

Jude grew defensive then, for Winslow was actually saying that settlers such as himself made the Indians go on the warpath. "Well, I been hearing that the tribes are restless. You hear about the attack on that farm in Bennington?"

"Bunch of wild young boys drunk on whiskey," John Sassamon answered. "They weren't Wampanoags, either." He turned and said, "I'll be back this way in three days, Mr. Winslow. Where can we meet?"

"Why, right here, if Alden doesn't mind."

"Of course." There was not a great deal of warmth in Jude's voice, but he could not refuse with Rachel standing there.

"Rachel and her grandfather are here for a visit. You'll be welcome."

"Lydia didn't come?" Matthew asked Rachel.

"Oh, yes. She and Grandfather are over at Pageville. There's a little church there having a struggle and they visit when they can to try to help out."

"You'll stay for supper, Mr. Winslow?" Jude asked.

"Yes, please do, Father," Rachel said quickly. There had been a cold formality in Jude's voice, and she had seen Matthew start to shake his head. He was surprised at her insistence. "Why, I think I will."

John was not included in the invitation, but as he left, he whispered to Rachel. "That's my good girl! You honor your father and you'll live a long time, like the scripture says!" He started to leave, then paused and said so softly she almost missed it, "God love you, Nahteeah—you've been a good sister to this Indian!" Then he left on silent steps and disappeared into the line of trees to the east of the house.

Rachel spent most of the afternoon cooking, and to her surprise, Jude and her father walked around the farm talking, apparently content with each other's company. Jude was making an attempt, she saw, to get to know her father, and it gave her a warm feeling to see it.

Gilbert and Lydia got back just as the sun, white as if frozen by the raw winter wind, slipped behind the tall oaks. They came inside the house and as they took off their heavy coats, Rachel said, "Did you know Father is here?"

Lydia stopped abruptly, turned and said quickly, "No, where is he?"

"Jude's been running him all over the farm." She laughed ruefully, adding, "You'd think Father was interested in *buying* it, the way he's looked at it."

Gilbert came to stand before the fireplace, holding his hands out to the flickering blaze. There was a wry light in his eyes and he said, "Matthew wouldn't be interested in this farm—maybe in the man who owns it?"

Rachel flushed slightly, then said, "Mother, will you help me set the food out? They went up to see a tract of land that Jude is interested in. Said he wanted to know what Father thought of it."

By the time the table was set, the two men walked in. Rachel did not miss the way her father's face changed at the sight of Lydia and his father. She could not say exactly what it was, but there was a certain sadness in his face that she had gradually come to notice. It was not gloom or despair, and few would even discern it, but now as she watched him enter, she saw his whole expression subtly alter. As his eyes fell on Lydia, she saw a longing in his face and a soft smile on his lips. *He still loves her*, she thought. Then her attention turned to Jude.

Jude's face was flushed from the long walk, and he spoke briskly, saying, "Look at that food!" He moved to the table, shook his head and said, "I haven't had a home-cooked meal like this since the last time you were here."

"Hello, Matthew," Gilbert said, coming to take his hand. "You've been away for a long time."

"Yes," Lydia said quickly, coming to stand beside Gilbert. "We expected you back before this."

"I've been on some pretty far trails since I was in Plymouth." He hesitated, then added, "You're both looking well."

Rachel interrupted, "We can talk while we eat—everything's getting cold."

They all sat down and spent the most relaxed time any of them had had since Matthew's return. Time had blunted the initial shock, so they were not constantly ill at ease just being with him. It helped to have the presence of Jude, making it necessary to speak of ordinary things in a normal fashion.

Jude kept the conversation going, and as the two women kept the food coming and the cups filled, he told Gilbert how he'd been increasing his holdings. "Land will never be so cheap as it is now, Rev. Winslow!" he exclaimed. "Now's the time to buy up every inch of ground you can, because this country will be worth a great deal of money in the years to come."

The rest of them listened, saying little, and finally the meal ended. As the women cleaned the table and put the dishes away, the men sat around talking idly of local matters. Rachel came and sat off to one side, joined by her mother.

Gilbert had been telling of the church close by. Then he turned to Matthew. "Deacon Lattimore tells me you've been quite an encouragement to him, son."

"Why, I've done little enough," Matthew protested.

"Lattimore would disagree," his father smiled. "He thinks you're quite a Bible scholar. Told us over and over how much he's appreciated your visits. And I didn't know how much you'd done to help with the Indian mission schools."

"Oh, John is responsible for most of that. I've just been able to help a bit with the cost."

Gilbert saw that his son was embarrassed, so he merely smiled and said, "God will bless your work, I'm sure."

At last Matthew went to sleep in the barn, and Gilbert and Lydia retired. Jude and Rachel sat before the fire talking for a while.

Jude had been put in a mellow mood by the quiet evening, and he talked of things he hoped to do—not business matters, but of things he'd never shared with her. His face grew dreamy, more relaxed than she'd ever seen him, and he moved his hands expansively as he spoke of travel, of going to England, even to Germany, someday. For a long time she sat there, her feet curled under her, her head resting on her palms as she listened intently. Several times he said *we* when speaking of journeys and plans, and she smiled quietly, thinking of how carefully he'd avoided any direct talk such as that for a long time.

He got up to poke up the fire, then came to sit beside her; she said in a whisper, "I love it when you talk like that, Jude!"

She made a lovely picture as she sat there, the golden firelight catching fire in her eyes, her lips slightly parted. His blood was stirred, and he lowered his head and kissed her, then put his arms around her, holding her close.

She allowed this, even went so far as to put her hand on his neck, her heart beating faster. Then just as she was drawing back from the increasing pressure of his lips, whispering, "Jude, we mustn't—" the front door suddenly opened, and Matthew entered, saying, "Alden—there's some kind of—"

Jude and Rachel pulled away so rapidly that she nearly fell off the bench. Her hair fell in disarray and there was a look of guilt in the way they came to their feet, staring at Matthew who stopped suddenly, the words broken off abruptly.

He stared at them, and for the first time in her life, Rachel saw the Winslow anger she'd heard about since she was a child.

Her father's light eyes blazed like blue fire, and he actually took a step forward so suddenly that Jude stepped backward and raised his hands!

"Don't!" Rachel cried, taking a step forward, and it was well she did, for it brought her father's eyes to her, and she saw his wrath turn to sorrow as he looked at her. Then he pulled himself together and said, "There's some sort of animal after the stock, Alden—a bear, I think."

Jude, welcoming the break in Matthew's mood, leaped to pull a musket from the wall, crying, "I'll take care of him."

He left the room at a dead run, and Matthew turned without a word to leave, but Rachel said sharply, "Wait!"

"Yes, Rachel?"

She was suddenly angry through and through, and she did not realize it was at herself instead of her father. She threw her head back and it was his turn to see some of the Winslow wrath, this time in the French blackness of his daughter's eyes!

"I resent what you think!" she said in a tense voice that quivered with rage.

"I—said nothing," Matthew answered. He stood there, a tall shape in the flickering light of the candle, the sharp planes of his face bolder in relief.

She struck out at him; it was not the embarrassment of the moment that drove her to a rage, but the buried resentment and anger at what she had felt from the moment of his return. His act of betrayal fourteen years ago struck the fire that blazed out at Matthew as she stood there.

"You're so *holy*, aren't you?" she cried. "The father looking so offended that his precious daughter is kissing a man!" Tears then flooded her eyes, and she dashed them away angrily, saying bitterly, "Well, what gives you the right to think *anything*? Where were you when I was growing up—when all the other children had fathers—and I—didn't!" Her voice began to break as sobs rose to her lips, and she took two steps that brought her up to him, staring up into his face with an anger she had never shown to a living soul. "Why did you have to come back?" she cried. Then she raised her hand and struck him in the face twice, each time crying out as if he had struck her!

He stood there, the burning imprint of her hand on his

cheeks. His eyes held no anger—only a deep, profound sadness. He let the silence run on, so that the sound of a log breaking in the fire sounded very loud. Then he said so quietly that she almost missed it for her sobbing.

"I can't blame you for feeling that way, Rachel," he said. He hesitated, then added, "I never should have come to this place."

She turned blindly and ran to her room, not hearing the door close. For a long time she cried bitterly, until there was nothing in her but emptiness. Finally she got up and undressed and went to bed. As she pulled the covers over her, she thought of the sadness in his face—that face so much like Gilbert's from whom she'd never had an unkind word, and her throat ached with the pain of it all.

Tomorrow! Tomorrow I'll make it right with him, she thought. All night she lay there, longing for the dawn.

But he was gone, and Jude, not meeting her eyes, said, "He just left."

Rachel waited until she had a chance to speak with Lydia alone, and when she had told the whole story, her eyes filling with tears, Lydia took her in her arms. "You'll have a chance to tell him you were wrong." She hesitated, then added, "I have to tell him some things, too—many things."

Rachel and Lydia waited anxiously for Matthew to make one of his rare visits, but he did not come back to Plymouth. Two weeks passed, and the winter scored the land, closing the trails to travel. They did not speak of him, but he was not far from their thoughts. Lydia vacillated between a longing to recapture those lost years and feelings of bitterness that would spring up, locking her in a vise of unforgiveness.

The weeks ran on into February. Then the settlement was shaken with a violence such as it had not known in years.

Rachel and Gilbert were on their way to take food to a widow with three small children. They had just turned to go past the cannon on the square when they saw a crowd milling around near the Common House, making so much noise that Gilbert said, "Must be trouble."

He led her in that direction, and they were met by Jake Mason, whose face was blazing with anger, red despite the freezing wind. "They killed 'im, they did!"

"Killed who, Mason?" Gilbert demanded quickly.

"Why, that young Indian—" Mason stopped at once, cast a quick look at Rachel, and said in embarrassment, "It's bad news fer you, Miss Rachel!"

"For me?" Rachel thought with a blinding stab of fear that it might be her father.

"It's the young Indian lad, you know? John Sassamon. Murdered, he is!"

Rachel gave a sharp cry and followed Gilbert, who pushed his way through the crowd until they came to stand before a sled drawn by two large horses. The driver was a man he knew slightly, Samuel Holt, a deacon of the church at Lenton, one of the magistrates of the town. He said at once, "We have much trouble, Pastor Winslow!"

"What happened, Mr. Holt?" Gilbert asked.

"Why, one of our young men found the body of Sassamon nigh onto a week ago. John Wingfield found him, and it was strange! John and two others was passing by a frozen pond near Middleborough and they noticed something out on the surface of the pond. It looked like a man's hat, and they found a musket close by. Well, a man's not likely to leave them things in the dead of winter, so John took another look. And then he saw it!" Holt shivered a little, and went on, his words being devoured by the crowd.

"Right there under the ice was a face! They ran to get an ax, and they chopped the body out, and it was John Sassamon!"

Gilbert felt the shock run through Rachel, and he held her with one arm, asking, "He drowned, then, and the pond froze over him?"

"Well, so we thought, but Sassamon was an Indian. He wouldn't have been fool enough to cross the ice before it was hard. We took a look and seen a swelling on the side of his head, which could have come from a blow—but then we found out his neck was broken! Now a man falling into a pond, he's not likely to do that, is he now, Pastor?"

"Not likely."

"No, indeed!" Holt said vigorously. "We began to think the lad had been murdered, and it made to look like an accident."

"No way to prove that, is there, Mr. Holt?"

The magistrate had the audience in his hand, and he savored the moment. "Not for most, I'm thinking. Be sure your sin will find you out.' " He nodded as a few of his hearers muttered *amens*.

"What? You did discover something?" Gilbert asked.

"Yes, Reverend, we did—and it was like this: An Indian who'd been on the outs with King Philip seen the whole thing! And he come to me and when he told his story, we arrested three men for the murder. And we had a trial—well, we had *two* trials, as a matter of fact, to be sure. One was made up of settlers and the other of Indians as can be trusted."

"What was your finding?"

"Guilty as charged—and sentenced to be hung, all three of them!" Holt stared at the crowd and said solemnly, "And hear this, if you please—Philip was in a rage, and all three of the men denied it. They stood on the gallows and swore they was innocent." Holt again paused, and despite the cold, his brow was beaded with sweat, and he pulled out a large handkerchief and mopped his forehead with a trembling hand before he went on.

"We hung two of them, but the rope broke under the last one, and he came to himself! He confessed that all three of them had done the deed, and he swore Philip put 'em all up to it! Well, we hung him again and the rope *didn't* break that time!"

A babble of questions rose up, but Gilbert's voice rang strong and clear. "What about Philip?"

Holt stared at him, licked his lips, then shook his head.

"That's what I've come to tell you," he said. "Philip is on the warpath, and we got to organize—because when that red devil breaks loose, there's not a man, woman, or helpless child in this part of the world who's got a chance to live!"

CHAPTER FOURTEEN

THE WINTER IS PAST

★ ★ ★ ★

Spring melted the icy covering of the land early, freeing the rivers by early March. It was one of the fairest springs that Rachel remembered, but she could not rejoice in it. The memory of her last words to her father came to her day and night: *Why did you come back?* She avoided his presence whenever possible.

Lydia observed Rachel's reaction. In turn she saw what Rachel's rejection was doing to Matthew. It made her ashamed of her own resistance to him, suppressing the happy memories of their life together, but she could not seem to break out of her resentment. As long as she had thought him dead, she could manage to forgive him. But he was alive! And no matter what changes had come about in his life, she could not get past her own deep bitterness. She longed to speak to her strong-willed daughter, but could not find a way. How could she help Rachel forgive when she herself could not?

June came, and Rachel grew restless. She walked the shores of the sea and followed the nearby paths through the woods, and she threw herself into the work of the church with an energy that both Gilbert and Lydia recognized.

Relief at last offered itself in the form of a trip to Swansea, a village only a few miles from Jude's farm. Mercy and Praise God Pittman had moved from Plymouth in the fall, and the stocky young husband dropped by unexpectedly to ask a favor.

"It's time for the baby—and Mercy is asking for you to come and be with her," he said to Rachel. " 'Course there's some older married women there—but she's partial to you, Miss Rachel."

Rachel said instantly, "Of course, I'll come."

"But there's talk about the Indians, Praise God," Lydia said. "Why don't you bring Mercy here to have her baby?"

"I tried, but she says she wants me around. I told her I'd beat her into submission," he joked, grinning, broadly, "but she knows she's safe enough 'till the little 'un comes!"

Lydia resisted the idea, for the settlement swarmed with talk about the possibility of Indian raids, but Rachel got around her by getting Gilbert to agree. She had always been able to sway him, and when she put the request in the form of an opportunity to perform a Christian charity, he could hardly refuse.

"You're a fool where that girl is concerned, Gilbert!" Lydia said angrily. "War could break out at any time, and you know it!"

Gilbert felt the rebuke keenly, but he had given his word, so when he and Lydia said goodbye to Rachel as she left with Praise God, he could only make one last plea. "Wait until next week, Rachel, and I'll go with you myself."

She laughed and kissed him, her eyes bright with excitement. "Where's your faith, Reverend Winslow? God's still in control, isn't He?" She ran to Lydia, gave her a tremendous hug, whispering, "Don't you worry now, Mother. Who knows, maybe you'll get a son-in-law out of this trip!"

She left with Pittman, and when they were out of sight, Lydia stood there staring, her dark eyes filled with apprehension. "She's been very unhappy lately, Gilbert."

"And so have you, Lydia," he answered, looking intently down into her face. He made a restless movement with his shoulders, then said tightly, "The Lord has been very quiet to me lately—and after all these years of sweet harmony with Him, that's very painful. I—I feel rebuked by the way I've treated Matthew, Lydia. I had a dream about it last week."

"A dream?"

"Yes, I dreamed I was going into a beautiful house, and somehow I knew it was the house of God. I went through a door and there was a beautiful light, so powerful I couldn't bear to look at it, but I yearned to go closer, for I knew it was my Beloved! So I tried to go closer, but out of the light came a voice, and it said, 'You are my son, but I will not accept you until you have been made pure!' " Gilbert stared at her, and there was such pain in his honest eyes that she wanted to weep. Then he added, "It doesn't take a Daniel to give the interpretation, Lydia. I've been saying that to my own son ever since he came back."

"You haven't been unkind, Gilbert—"

"Not *unkind*!" he cried out. "God in heaven! *Not unkind*—is that all I can be to my son who comes back from the dead? What if the father in the story of the Prodigal had been only that—*not unkind*! Lydia, I should have brought forth the best robe and put a ring on his finger! I should have shouted from the rooftop, *This my son was dead, and is alive again—he was lost, and is found!*"

Gilbert's eyes were blinded with tears, and he wheeled, stumbling away, his shoulders shaking with grief.

Lydia was overwhelmed, and she sought the quiet of her bedroom, fell on her knees, and prayed as she had never prayed before. All day she stayed there, unconscious of the passage of time. The sun reached its zenith, then began its fall; and still she called out to God. Sometimes her cries were out of the Bible, "Help, Lord, for thy servant perisheth!" Her grief often struck her dumb and she simply lay on her face saying nothing; then a prayer would rise up in her very innermost being, as she called out, the absolute certainty that she was in the presence of God flooded her spirit.

Darkness came, and still she prayed. On into the night as the stars came out to make icy dots of light on a velvety sky, she waited for something. She seemed to be tied to the diurnal movement of the earth itself, and as the night covered the earth, so her spirit seemed to be covered by a terrible darkness. She remembered when her child was born, the pain and grief, and all night long she struggled to give birth to something in her spirit.

By dawn her strength was gone. She lay spent and drained on the floor, her hair wet with perspiration and her limbs trembling with weakness. She could not cry any longer, and as the ebony sky outside blushed into pale crimson, the room suddenly seemed to catch some of that light. Lydia did not lift her head, but she felt her heart strangely warmed, and her spirit became calm.

She felt as the disciples must have felt as the stormy, raging seas that filled their ears with blasts of sound suddenly fell silent and only a hush remained.

For a long time she lay there, drinking in the silence, knowing that she was in the presence of the Lord God of all the earth. Then a message came, beginning as a whisper far away, but swelling louder until it filled her heart:

> Rise up, my love, my fair one, and come away. For, lo, the winter is past, the rain is over and gone; the flowers appear on the earth; the time of the singing of birds is come, and the voice of the turtle is heard again in our land.

Never did Lydia forget that voice, nor did she forget the commandment that followed, for after the words of Solomon's Song echoed sweetly in her heart, there followed a time which she knew she could never speak of on earth. Some things are too sacred for words. When she finally rose from the floor, her limbs were cramped with pain, but her heart was filled with a peace such as she had not known existed.

All week long she walked with God, shut in with a holy presence, and the light on her face told Gilbert that she had passed out of her crucible.

He was made sure of this when on Wednesday of the following week, he came home late in the afternoon to say, "Matthew came in today with a load of beaver pelts."

She looked up suddenly from the garment she was sewing, and said quietly, "Gilbert, I want you to go to Matthew. Tell him I want to see him."

He stared at her, caught off guard by her sudden announcement. "You mean—now?"

"Yes."

He slowly got to his feet, a question in his eyes, but he said nothing. He had learned over the years that when his dark-eyed daughter-in-law made up her mind, there was nothing to do but stand aside.

"I'll go at once, Lydia," he said, and left at a fast gait. She sat there holding the cloth for a while, her eyes fixed on nothing. Then she took a deep breath and said, "Amen."

Thirty minutes later she heard his footsteps on the walk.

Her heart quickened and she stood up. Then he was at the door knocking.

"Come in, Matthew," she said quietly, trying to suppress her emotions.

He opened the door to see her standing beside the table, and as always, her dark loveliness caught at him powerfully. He stepped inside, closing the door, then stood there waiting for her word. "You wanted to see me, Lydia?"

Her oval face was framed by a halo of dark curls, and the smooth planes of her features made her dark eyes seem enormous. Her full red lips trembled slightly, then she nodded. "Matthew, I want to ask you—to forgive me."

He stared at her, noting that she was trying to maintain her composure. "Why, Lydia, I don't think—"

"Please—" she whispered softly, "don't say anything! Ever since you came back, I've been—terrible!" Tears welled up in her eyes and she let them run down her cheeks unheeded. "I've been so filled up with bitterness and hurt pride that God has had to break me! And it's not only that I've been unjust, but I've made Rachel feel the same—and that's what's breaking my heart!"

Matthew stood there quietly enough, but his emotions were chaotic. He shook his head, and wonder touched his eyes as he said, "Lydia, you have nothing to reproach yourself for."

"But I do!" she cried out, and she raised her hands and came to him so suddenly that he caught her in his strong arms. She looked up into his face, and slowly she said, "I am your wife, Matthew—if you want me!"

A great roaring seemed to fill his head, stirring memories he thought had died long ago. She put her hands on his neck, and as she drew his head down, she suddenly cried out, "I love you, Matthew!"

He kissed her gently at first; then exulting in her courageous offer of herself, he finally lifted his head and whispered huskily, "I've never stopped loving you—Princess!"

The use of the old name ran through Lydia, and she laughed softly. "You haven't forgotten?"

"Forgotten?" he said with a smile. "I've lived on those scraps of memories from our love."

She pulled closer to him, and pressing her face against his chest, she said, "No more! Thank God, we can start over—and we'll make better memories than any you've ever dreamed, Husband!"

Gilbert had waited at the inn for Matthew to come back, but when nine o'clock came, he gave an odd smile and glanced toward the hill where his house stood. Getting to his feet, he said to the innkeeper, "Brother Tillotson, I have a strong impression that my son will not be using his room tonight, so I believe I'll use his bed." He started up the stairs, then paused and called back with a gleeful note in his voice, "I don't think my son will be requiring the use of this room anymore. I believe he's found more suitable accommodations!"

CHAPTER FIFTEEN

CAPTIVE!

★   ★   ★   ★

For two days after Rachel arrived at Swansea, she managed to forget her woes, giving all her time to Mercy, who was having a difficult time of it. The baby was not due for three months, but as healthy as Mercy had been, she was so ill she could eat little and had grown so weak that Rachel had to attend to her constantly.

Praise God left to go back to Plymouth for a load of tools, and Jude came the next day. He found Rachel churning butter, and came to her at once.

"Jude, I was hoping you'd come!" she said, and rose to greet him. He embraced her and gave her a quick kiss. Then she pushed him away with a smile, saying, "That will have to wait. How long can you stay?"

"Just until tomorrow," he said, and then a worried look crossed his face. "You shouldn't be here, Rachel—and neither should Mercy. The savages around here are stirring up trouble, and when it comes, nobody will be safe—not man, woman, or child."

She laughed and squeezed his arm playfully, "Oh, you're getting to be a regular prophet of doom! Besides, all Indians aren't 'savages,' as you call them. Sit down and tell me what you've been doing."

They had a pleasant day together, and that night they sat

up long after Mercy went to bed, talking and laughing. He finally got up, and as she walked with him to the door, he suddenly stopped, turned and said earnestly, "I want to marry you, Rachel."

She stopped, taken aback by the suddenness of it. For one moment she stood there, then she said quietly, "All right, Jude."

He took her in his arms, kissed her more gently than ever, and said, "I love you very much, Rachel! Very much!"

Then he released her and walked out of the room quickly, as if he did not trust himself. Rachel stood there, leaning against the wall, thinking how different life would be shortly, then she went to bed and slept a dreamless sleep.

The next morning she arose and was fixing some gruel for Mercy when she heard the first cries. Puzzled by the voices, she put the skillet down and started for the door. When she opened it she saw a wagon loaded with women and small children careen wildly around the big oak tree in the yard. A bearded man leaped from the driver's seat, and seeing Rachel, yelled at her, "Get these women into the house!"

"Indians are coming!" a young woman carrying a baby answered, looking over her shoulder. "They're killing everything in their path!"

Rachel's heart turned to ice, and she deposited the child in the house. Running back to get another, she saw Jude running from the barn with his musket. "Is it Indians, Isaac?" he yelled.

"They'll be here in thirty minutes, Jude," the man answered, his face grim. "They wiped out the Hendersons and the Potters and God knows how many more! My boys is coming—there they are now—but we'll be hard put to it, Jude!"

"We'll have to fort up in the house," Jude nodded. He turned and saw Rachel, then came to her. His face was pale and set as he said, "Do what you can to help the women and children!"

"I can shoot, Jude!" Rachel cried. "Grandfather taught me that."

"Good," the older man nodded. "We'll need everyone who can fire a gun. I got a load of ammunition and some extra muskets in the wagon!"

Two boys aged about fifteen came running up, completely

winded, and their father, whose name was Trowbridge, said, "John, I want you and Luke to load every musket we got. Come on, now, we got precious little time!"

They all began hauling the muskets and ammunition inside the house, and for the next fifteen minutes Jude and Trowbridge organized their little force as well as they could. There were four women, all of whom could load a musket, each situated so the shooters could reach the freshly loaded firearms easily.

"They'll be here soon," Trowbridge said. He looked around at his wife and children, then said, "Let us give ourselves into the hands of God." They all bowed their heads and he prayed a short prayer, then said urgently, "Me and my boys will take the downstairs, Jude. You two take the upstairs. You ought to be able to keep 'em off up there, but they'll be trying to pot you first."

"Come on, Rachel!" Jude said, climbing up the ladder leading to the loft, when he placed her at one of the small windows. "They'll have to cross that clearing to get to the house, and we can stop that—at least until it's dark."

"Do we have any chance at all, Jude?" she asked quietly.

He came to her, put his arm around her and they stood there in the quiet. "I don't know, Rachel," he said softly. "I been told all my life that God is able to do anything. Maybe He can get us out of this but I have to tell you, it's a mighty small chance."

"I thought so."

"I—I'm glad I asked you to marry me last night, Rachel," he said. "You know what I thought about all night?"

"What, Jude?"

"I thought, *That Rachel—she'll make a better man out of me!*"

He kissed her quickly, and she said, "I hope we have a life together, but if we don't—at least we found each other."

Just then a shot rang out; he wheeled and, picking up his musket, laid it on the sill and aimed carefully, then fired. "That's *one* redskin who won't do us any harm!"

Rachel picked up a musket and laid it carefully on the sill. Her heart was pounding, and she wondered if she could send a man to death. Just then she saw an Indian painted in various hues running for the house, a rifle in one hand and a hatchet in the other. At his belt were several bloody scalps, and without hesitation she drew a bead on his chest and felled him with one carefully placed shot.

Before she had a chance to feel sick, another Indian approached from the far side, and she snatched up another loaded musket and hurried her shot. His leg was knocked from under him as he fell, badly wounded.

A loud volley of shots erupted from the first floor, and both Rachel and Jude emptied their muskets, then loaded them quickly as the Indians withdrew. But they were not gone, and their hideous screams of rage cut through the morning air.

For over an hour there was no sign of an attack, but then a sudden burst of musket fire riddled the house, sounding like gravel as it struck. Every pane of glass was shattered; a sliver of it sliced Rachel's cheek, but she was unaware of it until she felt the blood running down her face, and even then had no time to do more than wipe it with her sleeve.

As the shots continued to rake the house, driving them away from the windows, there was another rush, and this time three of the Indians managed to reach the house. They threw their weight against the stout oak door; when it refused to budge they moved to try the windows, but were cut down at once by Trowbridge and his sons.

Again there was a lull. Rachel eased her head around the facing of the window. From a shelter of gum trees, a blazing arrow flew in an arc and fell to the ground a few feet from the house. "Get ready to run for it! They'll get the roof sure!" Jude shouted.

He was right, for despite their attempts to drive the archers back and disturb their aim, an arrow sailed high, and landed with a *thud* in the roof.

The dry thatch caught at once, and within minutes Rachel and Jude were forced to climb down the ladder, blinded by the thick smoke.

"We'll have to take the fight outside, Jude!" Trowbridge shouted over the roar of the blaze. "We'll burn to death in this cabin!"

Suddenly the roof began to collapse, and wisps of blazing thatch fell past them to the floor.

"I'll go first and you come after me, Jude!"

Trowbridge threw the door open and started to run out, but an arrow hit him in the chest. He dropped his musket to pull at the shaft, but another caught him in the throat and he fell to the floor lifeless.

"Everybody out!" Jude shouted, and they all made a rush at the door. Rachel ran to Mercy who was struggling to get to her feet, and by the time she helped her to the door and stepped outside, the butchery was in full sway.

One burly Indian had seized John Trowbridge with one hand and even as Rachel watched, he drew his war club up and killed the boy with one blow to the head. The other boy was trying to protect his mother from two warriors who were pulling at her, and one of them slashed him across the throat with a long knife, leaving him dead.

The other Indian then turned to the woman who was on her knees clutching a small baby to her breast. She turned her face up, and cried out, "Please—don't kill my baby!" But the Indian gave a howl and killed them both.

Screams of agony and fear scored the air. Suddenly a shout louder than the rest rang out: "Rachel! Look out!"

Rachel whirled to see a tall, muscular Indian with red paint smeared all over his body running for her, a hatchet raised high.

Jude came through the surging bodies to her right, and the Indian took his eyes off Rachel and Mercy. He swerved to meet Jude's charge, making a wild sweeping blow with his hatchet. Jude parried it on the barrel of his musket, then swung the heavy butt around, catching the Indian with a blow that crushed his skull.

"Rachel!" Jude yelled and turned to her; even as he turned, a bulky form on his left appeared—a short Indian with a heavy war club raised high. Jude caught a glimpse of him, but he was too late. The heavy head of the club struck him in the temple, and he dropped to the earth dead.

As the short Indian swung around and raised his club to strike Mercy, Rachel instinctively did what she would never have dreamed of. She leaped in front of the woman who had fallen to the ground and faced the savage without a sign of fear.

"In the name of Jesus Christ!" she cried out in a voice that carried like a trumpet over the bloody yard, "I command you to leave this woman alone!"

The Indians stopped short, looking around to see who was calling out. They saw a young white woman standing over her friend. The most fierce warrior of their tribe held a club over her—and she was not afraid.

But it was more than that. She had called on the name of her God, and although none of them were Christians, they were superstitious, and there was magic in what they were seeing.

The short brave who had killed Jude was called Fox. He was not only the most valiant warrior among them, he was also as shrewd as his name suggested. He stood there, aware that the others were watching, and his Indian sense of drama overtook him. He gave a scream and raised his club, whirling it over his head and giving every impression of a man intent on killing.

But the white girl did not move—did not even blink. She said again more quietly this time, "In the name of Jesus, I *command* you to leave us alone!"

Fox let the club fall to his side, and stood there staring at the girl. He was not as impressed with her God as he was with her courage. He had a contempt for most Christians, having seen enough greed in some of them to convince him that their religion was a sham. But one or two had been different, and he was curious.

The blood lust had died down, and he suddenly said in broken English, "We take this one."

A heavy-set Indian leaped forward to grab her arm, but Rachel drew back and knelt beside Mercy. She looked straight at Fox and said, "You are a *woman* if you hurt this mother!" The word she used was one that John Sassamon had taught her when they were children. It meant a womanish man, one who would rather be with squaws than with warriors, and it was a deadly insult. "If you ever want to rile an Indian," John had said, "just call him that!"

She had heard that Indians conceal a peculiar sense of humor under their impassive faces, and now she saw it. Something about the young girl telling Fox he was womanish tickled their fancy. They began to laugh wildly, like small boys, and it was a sight that Rachel would carry to her grave—those brutal killers smeared with the gore of children and women slapping their hands on their sides and screaming with laughter, taking up the word that she had used on Fox.

Fox himself would have killed a man instantly for such an insult, but the very weakness of Rachel, and the absolute fearlessness of her demeanor somehow cooled his blood; it was the kind of joke an Indian could understand.

He said something she didn't understand, and two Indians, still laughing, came forward. *They are going to kill both of us*, she thought, but they did not. They helped Mercy to her feet, and then marched both women toward their camp, being especially careful with the pregnant woman. Fox came back to the rear of the war party and walked along with Rachel, looking at her from time to time with curiosity. Finally he said, "You not afraid to die?"

"No." For the first time in her life, Rachel realized it was true. Something had happened back there when she had called upon the name of Christ. Suddenly she was aware of a presence with her—perhaps the presence her mother had so often spoken of, the peace that settled on her when she prayed. Rachel had scarcely had time to pray, but she knew—amazingly—that she was not afraid.

"Fox not afraid either." He looked back toward the light from the burning house. "The man I kill—your man?"

She almost broke down then, thinking of Jude's broken body lying on the ground, but drew herself up straight and said calmly, "He was going to be." Then she looked at Fox and said, "Now he is with Jesus Christ."

He met her gaze for a moment, then said, "Your God, Jesus Christ, he not save your people."

She replied at once, "He saved me, Fox."

He nodded, admiration lighting his black eyes. But he said only, "Yes—for now His medicine is strong for you. We will see."

He looked ahead, saying, "We camp here. You take care of woman."

Mercy was almost unconscious, but she was alive. Rachel washed her face with water from the river, and later they ate some of the half-raw meat that one of the Indians didn't want. He tossed it to Rachel as he would have to a dog. Her pride rose up, but she instantly thought, *Do what you have to do to keep Mercy and yourself alive!* She almost forced the meat down Mercy's throat, saying, "Eat! It may be the last for a long time."

They slept a few hours, then Fox prodded Rachel with his foot, saying with a gleam in his beady eyes, "Up—see if you can keep up with Woman." He had taken up her name "Woman" to jibe at her insult. "What is your name?"

She stared at him. "Nahteeah."

He blinked and said, "Who calls you that?"

"My brother—John Sassamon."

He looked at her in a different way, and she had no way of knowing that Fox had hated Sassmon for leaving the old ways for the white man's God, but he had come to admire him for his honesty and willingness to suffer for what he believed.

"We go now," Fox said, but he made the pace easier so that the pregnant woman would not die. In the days that followed, he came often to speak with the two women, and his influence kept them alive.

They arrived the next day at a larger camp, and for several days they rested. Rachel had been afraid that the shock would kill Mercy, but miraculously she seemed to thrive on the scanty diet and the hard conditions. She had one fixed thought in her mind. Every day she would say, "Praise God will find us, Rachel—don't fear!"

Rachel was not at all certain, for the Indians were on the move constantly. Philip was in the camp from time to time, and there were long war talks; then he would ride off again. Soon after, the band would move and raid another group of settlers or a small village, then move as far away from the scene of the raid as possible.

Often Fox would come and sit with Rachel, and in some strange way the two grew into a strange intimacy. He often argued with her about religion, telling her that Jesus was too weak, but she never let him see a doubt. "Jesus has me here for a purpose, Fox," she would say. Once she added to this, "Maybe to show *you* the way to the true God."

He rocked back and forth with silent glee, finally saying, "You want me to be a Woman, like you say first time? Fox a man—Jesus men weak."

She never lost her temper, and he was impressed at the way she accepted the frightful hardships of camp life without a word of complaint. He also was waiting for her to beg for release, but she never said a word.

She worked hard all day, doing her share of the work, and the Indian women, who had been cruel at first, came to marvel at her patience. At first she could do nothing that they did with ease, but by the end of two weeks, she could keep a pace nearly equal with theirs, and they let her alone.

At night she prayed—she and Mercy together; then for long nights she prayed as sleep came and enveloped her. She had dreams of Jude for a while, but she was far too weary to grieve.

She lost track of time, knowing it had been weeks after Jude's death. Then one day Fox came to see her with some news. "We leave this place soon—maybe two days." He waited for her to ask where they would go, but she said nothing. "Maybe you think white men come—take you home? No, we go far away— to Nipmuck people, very far away." He waited for her to speak, then grew angry. "You die with us! Never go home!" She stared at him and said evenly, "Fox, my God has a million angels in His tribe. He could send *one* of them, and you would be helpless against him."

Fox reached out and grabbed her long hair, the first time he had touched her, and said angrily, "No one Jesus man can kill Fox!" He let her go then, and shook his head. "We leave soon."

For the first time, Rachel's faith wavered, and she wept in the darkness. And for the first time as she prayed, there seemed to be no answer. As she rose the next morning and left the old campsite headed for the north, Fox saw her face, and he smiled and said, "Now you see that Jesus God is weak!"

CHAPTER SIXTEEN

"GOD IS STILL IN CONTROL!"

★ ★ ★ ★

News of Philip's raid swept through the country. They heard almost daily of new massacres after Swansea—Dartmough, Taunton, Middleborough and Sudbury. Fifty men were massacred in Lancaster, and forty homes were put to the torch in Groton. The Indians were set to move with Philip as their head, and New England was totally unprepared—strategically, mentally, and spiritually. A company of ill-trained militia would blunder out to be cut to pieces by an Indian ambush, and no one knew what to do.

When the news of the raid of Swansea came, Matthew and Gilbert were stunned. Praise God came riding in wildly, trying to raise a party to go to the rescue.

"They got my Mercy—and your girl, Master Winslow," he moaned bitterly. "God forgive me for leavin' her!"

"Are you sure they're alive, Pittman?" Matthew asked harshly.

"I helped bury everybody, and we followed their heathenish trail," he nodded. "They left the horse alive, at least, and I'm goin' to git my woman back if I have to go alone!"

"I'll be with you in an hour, Praise God," Matthew said. "We have to go tell Rachel's mother; then we'll be leaving."

As they hurried to the house, Gilbert said, "We'll have to raise a militia, Matthew."

He said nothing, but when they went inside the house he went to Lydia and took her in his arms. "The Indians have raided Swansea—and Rachel and Mercy are captives." He looked into her eyes and said, "I'll bring them back, Lydia. Do you believe that?"

The shock weakened her, but she looked up into his strong face, trembling and whispered finally, "If you say so, Matthew. I'll wait for you."

There was no time for long partings, but as Matthew gathered his musket and dressed in old leather clothing used on the trail, Gilbert argued with him.

"You can't go alone, son. Let me go to the governor. He'll *have* to act now!"

Matthew picked up a bedroll and started for the door, then turned and looked at Gilbert. They were so much alike, yet now there was a hardness in his son that the old man had never seen. Always *he* had been the strength of the family, and now he saw that his time was past. "What can you do, Matthew?"

The blue eyes glowed with the light of battle, and Matthew said, "Militia will never catch up with Philip's band or any other Indians. But there's one bunch who can catch them!"

Gilbert asked blankly, "Why, who can do that?"

"The Praying Indians!" Matthew smiled grimly. "I'll pick up a group of them and we'll find out where the women are. It may take a year, but I don't think so. Some of the Praying Indians have family who haven't come over, but they hear things."

Gilbert nodded, then said, "That may *find* them, but how do you plan to get them out of the camp?"

Matthew dropped his bedroll, walked to the wall and reached up. He pulled down Gilbert's sword, the one he'd used to fight Lord Roth and the mutineers who took over the *Mayflower*. He pulled it out of the sheath, held it up, and looked along the line of light that gleamed on the cold steel.

"I'd like to borrow this, Father," he said quietly.

Gilbert smiled, his eyes burning with a longing to go along. But knowing that he would be far too slow, he said, "Take it, my boy—and God go with you."

Matthew suddenly knelt before his father and huskily said, "Give me your blessing, Father!"

Gilbert Winslow prayed over this son, the last of the House of Winslow—and then Matthew rose and was gone.

The Praying Indians had learned to trust Matthew, but they were slow to respond to his call. "We are but a few, and Philip has the largest army of Indians ever seen since the beginning," James Bearclaw said.

"God will provide a way, James. He has preserved the lives of the two women, and I know that He will help us. Will you go if I promise there will be no battle—not for you?"

After discussion with the others, finally James said, "We will find the women—but you must take them yourself."

"A bargain!" Matthew smiled, and later he told Pittman, "We have a chance, Praise God."

"How we gonna do it, Matthew? The two of us against all them savages?"

"Not by might, nor by power—but by my Spirit!" Winslow quoted. "Let's find them first, then we'll see."

It took only four days to get wind of the camp. One of James Bearclaw's relatives, a young man named Rookna, brought word, and James came immediately to Winslow and Pittman.

"We know where they are, but the band is moving soon. Rookna says they are going to the Nipmuck band, and you'll never find them if they get there!"

"Take us to the place!" Matthew said, and in two hours they were on their way toward the west. They traveled hard all night and at dawn, one of the scouts came back with a word. "They are not two miles away, in a little canyon. Not very many warriors—but Fox is there."

"Did you see the women?" Matthew demanded.

"Yes. They are there."

Winslow gave some instructions and they moved out silently. Praise God asked nervously, "I don't think it's going to work, Matthew. This Fox, he's not stupid, is he?"

"No—but he's proud, and that's what we've got to play on. You just keep your hammer down on that musket. We'll have to win by something other than muskets if we win this one, Praise God!"

Rachel was walking down the path toward the rear of the band when she heard the shout; she looked up to see Fox and the other warriors spanning out with their weapons drawn.

"What is it, Rachel?" Mercy asked.

"I don't know. Let's get closer."

They approached the head of the canyon they'd been walking through, and Fox gave them a savage look and waved them to a halt. He looked up at the sides of the cliff on his right, and then to the left. A thick growth of oak covered the lips of the canyon, and he could see nothing.

Then a voice came from somewhere, a ghostly voice that floated on the morning air.

Fox—you are a Woman! It was the same insult that Rachel had offered to him, but this was no frail girl that called so strongly!

"Come down—and you will see what Fox is!" the stocky Indian shouted.

There was no answer for a moment, then suddenly an Indian called out something, and Fox whirled to see a man standing on the edge of the canyon wall—a white man.

Instantly, Fox gave a command and several of his men leaped to go after the intruder, but halted abruptly when a volley rang out, plowing the dust at their feet!

Fox stared at the dust, then raised his eyes to the man on the wall of the canyon. "What you want, white man?"

"I want the two women, Fox!"

Rachel suddenly gasped, and shielding her eyes she stared at the man and breathed a word: "Father!"

Fox whipped his gaze around, then stared back at the man. "I have the women. We will have you, too, white man."

Again a shot rang out, and the dust kicked up at Fox's foot, not two inches away. He jerked the foot back involuntarily and then scowled.

"That shot could have been in your head, Fox," Matthew shouted down at the Indian.

"I am not afraid to die!"

"I say you are!" Winslow challenged. "You are a Woman, Fox, and all your men are cowards, able only to fight women and children!"

A yell of rage went up, and Fox raised his hand for silence. "We soon see who is coward!"

"I will prove you are a Woman." Matthew said, "Choose your four best warriors, give them a blade, and I will fight them by myself!"

Instantly a cry went up, and Fox knew he had no choice. He was leader as long as the others knew he was not afraid. If he did not take up this challenge, he would be challenged by every warrior in the band.

"Come down, big wind!" he said. "You will not say anything for long."

The silence was broken only by the far-off cry of a bird. Rachel's pulse quickened, beating like a hammer.

Matthew disappeared, then in a moment came walking out of a group of trees a hundred yards down the road. He carried no musket, but there was a sword in his hand that flashed in the sun like silver fire. He wore no hat, his auburn hair catching the sunlight.

Every eye was on the tall man as he walked easily along the trail, as blithely as if there were no band of armed savages lined up against him.

"Fox, I give you good day," he said, and then he smiled and nodded at Rachel. "You are all right?"

Rachel caught her breath, answering quietly, "Yes, we have been well treated."

Matthew nodded, then said, "Fox, you have been good to my people, and it hurts me to destroy your warriors. Give me the women and we will part like men."

It was a good try, and Fox smiled briefly. "That not what you say. Are you liar like other white men?"

Winslow suddenly whipped the blade through the air. It made a whistling sound and the suddenness of it startled the Indians. "This is a magic blade, Fox. It was my father's blade, and he has used it to destroy our enemies. It is not like other blades, and I do not like to see young men die like sheep. But you are the leader. I wait for your men."

He turned, took five steps, then wheeled, with the sword held high over his head.

Fox asked, "Who kills this man for our People?"

Every single warrior cried out, but Fox was cautious. He saw something in the white man he did not like, and he wanted no mistakes, so he named four names—all of them tested warriors, not a beginner in the group.

The four men yelled and tossed all their weapons to the ground except for their knives, then began to advance on Winslow, who did not move except to lower his sword, leveling it at the group.

As they approached one of them spoke, and they began to spread out as Matthew had known they would. It was what he himself would have done, had he been one of them. And it was the problem he had pondered night after night, for this plan had been born of desperation—the only thing he could think of with even a slight chance of success.

He had no plan except to have no plan. The only thing he had in his favor was that these men had never seen a swordsman in action. They had no concept of the speed with which he could lower a blade and send it home, faster almost than a striking serpent.

But not if they were behind him, and not if they threw their knives. But knife-throwing was not an art that Indians practiced.

Now, like wolves, they began to circle, and the scene drew a sob that Rachel had to choke off. Her father looked so alone out there! The savages who moved like cats to encircle him were strong, quick and totally devoid of fear, she knew well. How could he hope to win? *And he came for me—after all my hatred!* her heart cried out, and she uttered a mighty silent prayer to God for him!

Now was the time, Winslow knew; the two braves on his flanks were almost out of his line of vision, while the other two before him stood three feet apart, their weapons ready if he turned to face either one.

Always do the unexpected! The words had been spoken years ago by the master who taught him his lessons with the sword. *The best swordsman in the world—if he gets rattled—can be taken!*

He did the one thing that could be done. Ignoring the two Indians who were moving to flank him, and paying no heed at all to the man on the left, he suddenly lowered his blade and with his right toe lunged his entire body toward the large Indian on his right!

The distance was critical, for if his enemy was too far away the sword would never touch him, and he would stand at full stretch, helpless. If the man were too close, the sword might catch in his flesh, and he would be cut to pieces trying to get the blade free.

Now the power flowed through his leg, and with the speed of a lifetime of practice the tip of his blade leaped through the air with all the force of his body behind it! The Indian was leaning forward balanced on the tips of his toes, tilting forward, and he could not believe that the white man was moving at him. Desperately he tried to reverse his feet, but it was too late!

The stroke brought the sword into his body, penetrating the heart—then it was withdrawn as Winslow whipped his blade back, stained crimson and shouted, "You see, Fox! The blade is magic!"

The man he had run through dropped his knife, and stared down at the small puncture on his breast in disbelief. He looked across at Matthew and tried to say something, suddenly dropped to the ground—dead.

Matthew saw that the savage on his left was paying no heed to him, and he did what he never would have done if the lives of the two women had not been at stake. He shouted and lunged with the same speed. The man had time to get his knife up, but the tip of Matthew's blade rasped over it, entered the fleshy side of the brave who grabbed his wound and gasped. But he was made of strong stuff, for he threw himself at Winslow, who had no choice but to strike the final blow.

But as the second Indian fell, he knew that he had turned his back too long, and even though he made a wild lunge to his left, he felt a line of fire run along his back as a blade ripped through his flesh. A cry of victory went up from the Indians as he went down, and he knew that both men would be on him like animals.

He had time only to roll over on his back before the sweaty body of one Indian fell on him. By catching the man's forearm with his left arm, Matthew managed to divert the knife thrust that would have driven straight to his head.

The sword was useless at close range, so he dropped it and with a mighty lunge of his body, threw the Indian off, and rolled to his feet just in time to see a shape to his left. He had no time at all to think, but simply reached out and grabbed for whatever part of the man he could get. The flesh was slippery but his hands closed on a muscular arm and with all his might he whipped the man around in a giant swinging motion and released him.

As the savage went flying through the air, Matthew reached down with one motion and picked up his sword, fell to his left in time to avoid the wicked slash that would have slit his throat, found an opening, and drove the blade into the body of the Indian who was off balance.

As the Indian went down, Matthew whirled to find his last opponent rushing in, blade out before him. But suddenly he stopped short when he realized that his three companions were on the ground, dead or dying.

Winslow could have killed him where he stood, but he lowered his blade, and in the silence that suddenly fell on the scene, he looked at Fox and said, "There is no need for this man to die, Fox. He has proven that he is no coward."

The man cried out and ran toward Matthew's blade in a suicidal rush, but Fox shouted to him, and he stopped.

Fox stood there staring at the tall white man, then looked at the men on the ground. Matthew knew that if this small Indian gave the word, he would die with an arrow in his heart, but he did not move nor speak.

The Fox said, "Take the women."

Rachel came forward half-supporting Mercy, and Fox gave her one look. He moved closer to her and said in a voice only she and Mercy heard.

"This Jesus man is strong. Few more like Him—maybe Fox become Jesus man, too!"

Then he said, "You go now." For a long time he stood there watching Matthew and the two women as they faded away into the woods.

They did not speak until Praise God and James suddenly appeared, and as Mercy wept in her husband's arms, Rachel turned to her father.

He was smiling at her. Suddenly she threw herself into his arms—and it was like coming home! For a long time they stood there. Finally he kissed her cheek and said, "Your mother has forgiven me and we're together now."

She smiled through her tears and nodded. "Forgive me, Father, for being so—"

He put his hand on her lips and said, "I've found a daughter now—and we must start from this day."

"Yes!" she cried. Great joy filled her heart as she said, "Oh, Father—let's go to Mother now."

Three days later Lydia heard the sound of steps on the porch.

"Mother! I'm back! Father brought me back!"

As Lydia held the girl in her arms, she looked over at her husband and said with a smile, "I knew he would." Then she held out her free arm and as Matthew came to her, she added with misty eyes, "These Winslow men—they do what they say!"

PART THREE

SALEM

★ ★ ★ ★

1691

CHAPTER SEVENTEEN

A NEW MINISTER

★ ★ ★ ★

Miles Winslow raised himself high in the stirrups and, shading his eyes from the brilliance of the midday April sun, stared down the road, then yanked his hat off, exposing a thick shock of yellow hair. "There they are, Howland!" he yelped, and spurred his startled bay into a hard run toward a small clapboard house.

His companion, though, only shook his head and continued the steady pace of his horse. Not an impulsive man, he looked with amused tolerance as he watched young Winslow pull his horse down, spring to the ground with the ease of a natural rider, and throw his arms around the pair who stood outside the neat white fence that enclosed the house.

Not very dignified for Harvard's newest scholar, Robert Howland thought. *A minister ought to be a little more restrained.* Howland was a solidly built man with heavy shoulders and a muscular neck. His square face and strong chin revealed a stubborn streak, which he tried unsuccessfully to curb. His light-gray eyes were wide set deep beneath a broad forehead. His light-brown hair was cut short, and his features were more durable than esthetic. He looked, in fact, more like a strong, active gentleman squire than an intellectual scholar.

He came up to the fence, swung easily from his saddle, then waited patiently while young Winslow finished greeting the couple. There was in Howland a strange mixture of deliberate thought and a sort of ponderous behavior, which covered a quickness of mind and easily stirred emotions kept carefully in check.

"Come, now, Robert," young Miles said, turning the attention of the couple toward the visitor. "This is my father and mother—and this is my friend and teacher, Rev. Robert Howland."

"It's a pleasure to welcome you to Salem, sir," Matthew Winslow said warmly, and the hand he gave in greeting was as hard and strong as Howland's own. "We've heard nothing but your name since Miles arrived at Harvard."

Howland took in Winslow's strong figure with approval. He had heard of Miles' father by reputation, and the man's appearance was impressive. He was six feet tall with the strong, athletic figure of a man in his late forties. He was an older edition of Miles, the resemblance between the two so sharp that it caught Howland off guard. They both had the same sharp features, the light hair with the trace of reddish gold when the sun caught it, as it did now, the broad mouth and bright blue eyes that revealed the Winslow blood.

"I'm happy to meet you, Mr. Winslow—and you, ma'am," Howland said in a deep, prideful voice that would shake the rafters had he cared to lift it. He nodded to the beautiful woman who looked small in the presence of the three large men. She still appeared too young to be the mother of a sixteen-year-old son.

"Come inside, Rev. Howland," Lydia Winslow said. There was a trace of coquetry in her voice and in her black eyes. Her dark beauty and expressive features still bore evidence of the French blood of her father.

They entered the house, and for the next hour sat around the oak table, where Howland discovered the source of his young pupil's wit and intelligence. He had "discovered" Miles three years earlier when the young man had come to Harvard at the age of thirteen. In their first meeting he had been astounded at the breadth of Miles' scholarship and at the same time warmly approving of the modest charm of the young fellow. For three years he had nurtured the boy, who had become known at the school as "Howland's Student," for the older man had been jealous of the lad, not trusting other instructors to do the finishing he felt necessary.

Ordinarily this sort of monopoly would have been forbidden, but Robert Howland himself was on a special footing at Harvard. He was a close friend of Cotton Mather, and such prestige was enough to permit Howland to do pretty much as he pleased. In all fairness, it was not his friendship with the titular head of the Puritan world, but his own brilliance that had made him a legend at the school. Cotton Mather had graduated from Harvard at the age of fourteen, but he had said often, "I got an early start, and Robert Howland got a late one—but if we had begun together, I have no doubt he would have eclipsed my record."

Sitting there at ease as he had rarely been on a first visit, Howland noted that Matthew's intelligence and his wife's ready wit and charm were combined in their son.

"I'm surprised you'd think of leaving your position with Harvard to pastor a small church, Rev. Howland," Matthew said at last.

"It was a difficult decision," Howland admitted. "But I've grown too bookish over the last few years. The Lord has instructed me to go out where the harvest is white. Except for the time I've preached for Rev. Mather, I've been rather tied to my desk."

"Aye, a man needs to be with the people," Winslow nodded. "My father says that there are too many people at universities who have more degrees than they have temperature!"

"Matthew!" Lydia said sharply, "you shouldn't say such things to Reverend Howland."

"Oh, Father can say anything!" Winslow laughed. "He's ninety-one, you know, and he never was noted for his tact."

"I've been anxious to meet him, sir," Howland smiled. "Miles says he has more brains than all of Harvard combined."

Matthew threw back his head and reached over to pound his son on the shoulder, "Son! You've got no more tact than any other of us bull-headed Winslows! Imagine telling your teacher a thing like that!"

"It's good to see a young man who honors his parents, Mr.

Winslow," Howland remarked, smiling at the young man.

They talked a little longer and then Miles looked out the bay window and jumped to his feet. "There's Grandfather and Rachel!" he yelped and dashed out the door. Howland heard him talking excitedly and was amused at how the young man, who had gone to great effort to be dignified at Harvard, had now reverted almost to a wild, puppyish excitement in the presence of his family.

As they entered the cabin, Miles said, "This is my grandfather—and this is Robert Howland, sir!"

Howland looked at Gilbert Winslow, and was in some awe of the man, for this one, after all, was the last living member of the Firstcomers—that intrepid band of Pilgrims who had come on the *Mayflower* so many years ago!

"I'm honored, Mr. Winslow. I believe you knew my grandfather, John Howland?" the minister said at once, and the hand that gripped his was still strong and without a tremble despite the years.

"John Howland!" The old man stared at him. "I did, indeed, and a fine man he was, too! Your servant, sir. My grandson speaks highly of you."

Time had taken a fraction from his height, so that he was slightly beneath his son and grandson, but he still stood straight as a pine sapling. The cornflower blue eyes were undimmed, and the tapering face was browned by the sun. His voice was not strong as it had once been, but there was no tremor as he spoke in a thin, clear tone, and his movement, if not swift as those of his tall descendants, was sure and still graceful.

"Reverend Howland is going to be pastor at Littleton, Father," Matthew said.

"They need a man of God there," Gilbert snorted. "The last one they had had no more backbone than an oyster!" He shot a glance at Howland and said, "My grandson tells me you know the Word, sir. I trust you will preach it undiluted—put the fire back in hell and the fear of God in those half-baked, lukewarm, imitations of Christians in that church!"

Miles laughed in delight, and gave Howland a sly wink. "Don't beat around the bush, Grandfather! Just come right out and say what you think about Brother Howland's new charge!"

"Now you behave yourself, Gilbert Winslow!" Lydia commanded, giving his arm an affectionate squeeze. "I think Reverend Howland can be trusted to take care of his church without your help."

Gilbert had opened his mouth to continue, but at Lydia's words he shut it. Giving her a quick smile, he said, "Still trying to make a gentleman out of me, Lydia? You should know by now how hopeless that is!"

"Reverend, this is my daughter, Rachel," Matthew said, and Howland, who had looked to one side to speak with Gilbert Winslow, turned to face the woman who had entered and was standing quietly beside her father.

"This is Reverend Robert Howland, Rachel—the teacher Miles has been talking about for so long."

"Welcome to Salem, Reverend Howland."

"I'm—very happy to meet you, Miss Winslow."

Howland had stammered slightly, for although Miles had talked almost constantly about his older sister, he had never once mentioned the fact that she was a strikingly beautiful woman. *Why didn't the young pup tell me she was so lovely!* he thought with some irritation. He was a man who didn't like to be surprised, and it bothered him that he had been struck so forcibly with her beauty that he had stammered like a callow youth. At the age of thirty-three, he was fairly hardened to the good looks of young women. Being one of the most eligible bachelors in the country, he had discovered, brought out the worst in most people. Almost everyone had a sister, a niece, or some girl who would make the *perfect* wife for him, and he had long ago thrown up a wall of defense against such ploys.

But this woman shook that hardness, for she was without a doubt the most attractive woman he had ever seen, he admitted grudgingly. He gave her a hard stare, hoping to find some flaw, but was unable to do so.

She was, he knew, thirty years old, but no one with eyes would have taken her for such. *Why, she looks no more than twenty!* Howland thought suddenly. He took in the creamy smooth cheeks, like pale ivory, highlighted by a pair of almond-shaped eyes, hazel except for times when there was a greenish glint which gave her a saucy look. Her hair was black, and it curled rebelliously from under the white cap that perched atop her head. The simple gray homespun dress did not conceal the smoothly rounded form, and there was an intensely womanly air about her, despite the direct look and almost militant posture.

"You'll be staying with us tonight," Miles said slyly. He had not missed the startled look that Howland had given his sister, and it delighted him that the self-assured minister was put off stride for a change.

"I don't want to be troublesome," Howland replied quickly.

"No trouble, sir," Gilbert Winslow offered, "I want to talk to you about a few matters."

"Look to yourself, Reverend" Lydia laughed. "The Winslows show no mercy where theology is concerned."

"And this one is the worst," Matthew stated, going to Rachel and putting his arm around her.

"Got more scripture in her than most of these fools who call themselves ministers have these days," Gilbert nodded. "We'll look for you at supper—all of you."

He turned and left, and Rachel said with a smile, "I'll look forward to seeing you this evening, Reverend Howland." She followed her grandfather through the door, and the minister saw that they were chattering like two school children as they headed down the street.

"I hope you won't be offended at my father, sir," Matthew apologized. "He speaks his mind a little bluntly."

"I've heard so much about him from Miles that I'm rather intimidated," Howland answered. "He's quite an institution, isn't he?"

"We weren't sure how he would take the move here from Plymouth," Matthew remarked. "But my business was here in Salem, and Reverend Findley died soon after we moved; Father practically pastored the church for years—with Rachel's help."

Miles nodded at Howland, adding with a smile, "She's the best minister in the whole colony, according to Grandfather. And I don't much doubt it." He shook his head in admiration and warned Howland with a grin, "Don't get into a theological argument with her, I warn you. Aside from yourself, she knows the Scripture better than anybody I know."

"Can preach a better sermon, too!" Matthew vowed.

" 'Course she calls it *teaching*—but I tell you, Reverend, when she speaks to a congregation, it's a thing to hear!"

Howland frowned. "I rejoice that she knows the word, but the Scripture says, 'Let the women keep silence in the church,'' you remember."

"I'm afraid Rachel has too much Winslow in her," Matthew returned ruefully. He scratched his head, then shrugged his shoulders. "Miles is right, though, and I'd advise you to steer clear of her. She has a way of being more logical than you'd think for a woman so attractive."

"That's what does it, Father," Miles decided. "She's so pretty that men don't think she has any intelligence—or else they get all nervous because she's a beautiful woman. Anyway, I've seen some pretty fair Bible scholars get put flat on their backs—theologically speaking, of course!—and never knew what hit them!"

"You two hush!" Lydia interrupted, then continued, more quietly but with force, "Rachel is a handmaiden of the Lord, Reverend Howland. She'll never marry, so she says, because she can serve God better in the unmarried state, as the Apostle Paul puts it. And you'll not find a woman in these parts—or a man either—who serves God so faithfully."

"That's true," her husband nodded. "The poor bless her, and her prayers for the sick—" He shook his head in wonder and finished, "Well, you'll admire her, as we all do, but she is a problem for some of our ministers."

Howland nodded. "Miles has told me of his sister's good works, and I know you praise God for such a daughter. It will be my pleasure to become better acquainted with her."

Robert Howland got better acquainted with Rachel Winslow that evening, but it did not improve his disposition.

The meal had been excellent, and he had enjoyed listening to Gilbert Winslow tell of the voyage on the *Mayflower*. It was almost as if a witness had stepped forward from the Scripture, for the Firstcomers were, of course, the heroes of the church in America, and to hear the old man say things like: ". . . so Standish said to me. . . !" or "Then I went to Governor Bradford and told him it had to be so!" These demigods—or so they seemed to Howland—had been Winslow's friends; he had known them intimately, and it was a wonder to hear it.

Finally Gilbert Winslow said, "It was a grand crew, and I would to God that some of their spirit would come on this generation!"

"Oh, I think we have a goodly number of dedicated Christians in our own day," Howland said. "It's a common mistake to think that people in earlier times were more spiritual than in our own days."

"Do you really think that, Mr. Howland?" Rachel had said little all evening, but now she faced him directly across the table where they sat drinking tea, her hazel eyes gleaming, with a pronounced tilt to her chin as she shook her head. "You have been leading a sheltered life at Harvard."

Howland flushed, for he was not accustomed to being challenged—especially by a woman. "I think we are not so bad as many say, Miss Winslow."

"I think we are *worse*, sir!" She did not raise her voice, but there was no weakness at all in her tone or her look as she began to speak directly to the tall minister. "Our Fathers gave up everything they had in the world, risked death and the loss of all things for the privilege of worshiping God. And what are men risking today? Nothing!"

"Well, really, Miss Winslow, from a theological point of view, we are not in such bad condition. We have more members in our churches now—"

"More members, yes!" Rachel said instantly. "But what of the *quality*? You are aware of the Half-Way covenant, I trust?"

"Certainly! But—"

"A covenant straight from the pit!" she said directly, and Howland blinked at her bluntness. The Half-Way Covenant had been approved in 1657 by the Ministerial Convention in an attempt to settle a question that was both theological and social. Only members of the church could vote in the Bay Colony, and when the children of the first settlers grew to maturity, they were thought to be saints because they shared the covenant with their parents. But then *their* children came along, and most of them had no conversion experience of their own. The church was in a dilemma; if these unregenerate people were admitted to the church, it meant that no man needed to be converted—but on the other hand, they could not vote if they were not admitted. A solution had been reached in the Half-Way Covenant, which permitted the children of members to belong to the church without a conversion experience.

Howland replied with some fervor, "Certainly, that covenant is not the best answer, and Rev. Mather opposed it, but we must work within the framework of the entire church, Miss Winslow."

"The church, sir," she debated, "is the bride of Jesus Christ, and no man nor any group can by agreeing together soil her garments!"

"You oversimplify!" he answered hotly.

"Jesus said, 'Ye must be born again.' Are you going to say that the Savior 'oversimplified' the conditions for salvation?" she challenged.

"Well—of course I'd not say that—"

"Then the Half-Way Covenant *is* wrong?"

Never had Howland felt so ill at ease, and the fact that he was confused as much by her enormous eyes as by her use of scripture and logic did little to make him feel any better. "I think you would need to do much research and study before you can draw that conclusion, Miss Rachel!" he said lamely.

"The conclusion is simple, sir," Rachel insisted, ignoring her mother, who was trying to signal for her to stop. "Either men are saved by good intentions and moral living—or they are saved by grace through the blood of the Lord Jesus!" She suddenly reached over and plucked up a Bible, placing it before Howland. "Show it to me in the Word of God, sir, and I'll believe it!"

"I tell you, ma'am, it's not so easy as that!" Howland's resonant voice rose, filling the room, and his face was red.

Suddenly the tension that had risen so unexpectedly was broken as Gilbert Winslow slapped the table and laughed. "By my head, Robert! You're your grandfather all over again! He was a dear fellow, John was. I knew him in England, you know, before we came to Plymouth."

Howland stared at him, his quarrel with Rachel forgotten. "I never knew anyone who knew him, sir."

"Well, *I* did, my boy!" The old man smiled at the memory.

"As a matter of fact, you wouldn't be here right now if it weren't for me."

"Sir?"

"Why, your grandfather went up on deck one night, and somehow managed to fall overboard. He caught a rope, though, and hung on for dear life. I came topside and heard him calling, so I got some help and we hauled him on board."

"I've not heard of that!"

"Mr. Bradford tells of it in his history," Gilbert said. "And he was much like yourself—in a physical way, though no scholar. A strong man—a strong man! Once when the general sickness cut us down in that first winter, it was just myself, Miles Standish, John Bradford and your grandfather who were able to stand up. John and I dug many a grave—and he never once complained, he didn't! A good strong man and a faithful companion he was," Gilbert said softly, and then wistfully, "And I miss him to this day."

The old man's words brought a peace to the room, and soon they left, after Howland promised to return the next day to visit with Gilbert. As they were walking back to the house, Miles said slyly, "I told you not to underestimate Rachel."

"I'll remember that," Howland said shortly. "She needs a husband with a strong hand, I think."

Miles thought about that. "Well," he noted, "if there's any man on this earth any stronger than my sister, I'd like to meet him. There's been quite a list of candidates—wanting to marry her, I mean. But none of them measure up."

Howland did not answer, but he thought wryly, *What the woman needs is a good beating.* But he realized at the same time that his own admiration for her beauty would make such a thing difficult, so he put the whole matter of Rachel Winslow out of his mind.

CHAPTER EIGHTEEN

A BROTHERLY KISS

★ ★ ★ ★

"Robert, all this talk of witches—what do you make of it?"

"The devil, sir, is not dead—and he will find an entrance if God's people do not keep the door blocked."

The duties of his church kept Howland close to his village as a rule, but his one recreation in the two months since leaving Harvard had been angling with Gilbert Winslow. The young man had found that being a pastor required a certain amount of practical experience that no knowledge of Latin or Greek would solve, and he came at least once a week to fish with the aging man in the stream that wound its way through Salem.

They sat under a huge chestnut tree and said little until Winslow broke the silence with his question about witchcraft. He was not, however, satisfied with the answer, for he shook his head and said, "I mislike it, Robert. There's something about the subject makes people behave stupidly. Why, would you believe that fool Putnam woman has spread the rumor that she lost all her children in childbirth because Rebecca Nurse put a curse on her? And if there ever was a shrew it's Ann Putnam, and if there ever was a saint, it's Rebecca Nurse!"

"Aye, there will always be ignorance, Mr. Winslow, but Rev. Cotton Mather's book *Relating to Witchcraft* documents the acts of witches well. It's all there, the invisible world, all your incubi and succubi—all your witches and wizards of night and day.

'Thou shalt not suffer a witch to live,' as the Scripture says."

The soft May breeze blew a lock of silver hair across Gilbert's eyes, and he brushed it back. "No good will come of it. What's needed is a dose of good old-time religion. *That* would purge all the silly notions people have of trying to live for God on Sundays and for the devil the other six days."

A laugh broke from Howland's deep chest, and he pulled his cane pole up and began to wind up the line. "Things are always so simple with you, sir! No grays—just black or white, right or wrong."

"Well, I'm an old man now, son," Winslow remarked with a smile as he took his own line in. "When I was your age I was just about like you, running around trying to split hairs on matters. But the closer I get to home, the more I see that living is not very complicated. Jesus said, 'Whosoever cometh not after me and forsaketh all he hath cannot be my disciple,' and that's fairly simple—'all that he hath.' "

Howland reached down and scooped up the stringer of fish they had caught. Then as they walked along the side of the bubbling stream, he mused thoughtfully, "But yours was a different world, wasn't it? Things are much more complicated now than when you came to Plymouth."

"Men are born, they love, they die—and someplace along the way they either meet Jesus Christ and follow Him, or they don't."

"You sound like Rachel," Howland chuckled. "Or I suppose she sounds like *you*. All you Winslows are pretty much alike, aren't you?"

"A stubborn breed, Robert!" Gilbert smiled. They made their way back to his house, and Rachel met them at the door, smiling at the pair.

"More fish to clean?" she asked, shaking her head. "Put them in the back and I'll clean them when I return. I've got to go over to Elizabeth Crowley's with some food."

"I'll clean the fish," Gilbert said, taking the string from Howland. "You go with Rachel, Robert—then come back and we'll have these fellows for supper."

"Why, I'm not sure . . ."

"Oh, come along, Reverend," Rachel urged; then she gave

a little giggle, which surprised him. "I promise not to bite your head off or argue about scripture."

Howland had steered clear of Rachel since their disagreement on his first night, but now took the heavy basket of food she handed him, and they made their way through the village, talking about unimportant things.

Finally he said, "I've been wanting to apologize to you, Miss Winslow, for my sharp words."

She turned to look at him and smiled. "I'm too straightforward, I know that. Forgive me, please."

Then the air was cleared and he told her of his church and the problems until they came to a small unpainted clapboard house on the edge of the village.

Four children were playing in the yard, but they all came running when they saw her, calling her name and pulling at her clothing. It made a pretty sight, Howland decided, and he wondered—not for the first time—why she had never married.

She gave each of the children a piece of honeycomb from the basket, then led him inside. "Elizabeth?" she announced. A small, worn-looking woman came to the door and paused at seeing the tall form of the minister.

"This is Reverend Howland, from Littleton, Elizabeth. Reverend Howland, this is Mrs. Crowley."

"How d'you, sir?" the woman said in a small voice, then turned to say, "Jamie is took bad, Miss Rachel!"

"Let's see," Rachel stated, and the three of them entered the room where a small boy, not more than four or five, was lying on a bed almost hidden by the covers. His face was red, and he was breathing roughly and unevenly.

Rachel sat down beside the boy, started to speak, then turned as if she had just remembered something. "Reverend Howland, will you pray for Jamie?"

"Why, surely." Howland stepped forward and prayed briefly, then stepped back, his duty done. "I trust the Lord will be merciful on your boy, Mrs. Crowley," he murmured quietly. It always made him feel inadequate, praying for the sick, and he had done little enough of it at Harvard. As the pastor of a flock, it was different, however, and it was one of the things that drove him to talk with Gilbert Winslow.

"Please, Miss Rachel," Mrs. Crowley whispered, "won't you say a prayer, too?"

"If you like, Elizabeth." She reached into a pocket and pulled out a small object. Howland leaned over and saw that it was a small vial. Opening it, she put a drop of oil on her finger, closed the vial, then replaced it. Softly she touched the boy's forehead with the oil, and then put her hand on his head. For a long while she said nothing at all, then she said, so softly that he barely caught the words, "Lord, what is your will for Jamie?"

Howland was mystified! He stood there staring, and the silence was so heavy it almost had substance as she continued to wait. The boy did not move and she did not speak again—for what seemed like a very long time. Then he saw her head nod, as if she were agreeing with something someone had said. "Lord, we ask you to heal this child."

The boy's eyes fluttered open. He focused on her and said in a tiny voice, "Hullo, Miss Rachel."

She stooped and gave him a kiss. "Hello, Jamie."

"I've been sick."

"Yes, but you'll be fine now." Rachel rose and there was a peaceful look on her smooth face as she moved past Howland. "I'd not let him stay under that heavy cover, Elizabeth. And don't let him have anything very heavy to eat until tomorrow."

"Bless you, Miss Rachel!" Mrs. Crowley cried out, wiping her eyes with her apron. "God bless you—and you, too, sir," she added as they left the house.

They made their way along the street, everyone they met greeting Rachel by name and nodding to Howland. He waited for her to say something about Jamie, but she did not.

Finally he said, "You think the child is—no longer sick?"

"Jamie?" she asked in surprise, looking up at him. "Oh, yes, he's fine." Then she asked, "Why do you ask?"

"Well—" He gave an embarrassed grin, and despite his manner, which was sometimes heavy, she saw that he had humor. "I suppose that I've had so little success in praying for the sick that it startled me the way you prayed—so *positively*!" He looked down at her, thinking how clear her eyes were, and confessed, "I'd not be able to do that! What if he didn't get well? What would people think?"

"I don't mind what people think, Reverend Howland," she returned firmly. "God didn't call me to be popular, but to do His will. And the instant you start doubting God's word, you're *already* a failure, aren't you?"

He thought about her words, then shook his head. "Well, doubt comes to me, I confess. Don't you ever wonder if your prayers will be answered?"

"God has never refused to answer my prayer."

He stopped short and stared at her in disbelief. An elderly couple passed, stopping to turn around and stare at them standing there in the middle of the street. "God has answered every one of your prayers?" he asked, doubt threading his speech. "I never heard anyone say so."

She looked up at him, the smooth countenance calm and possessed. Her full lips turned up in a smile and she seemed amused by his doubt. "Didn't you teach the eleventh chapter of Mark at Harvard?"

"Why, of course!"

She began to quote it, and her voice was filled with a certainty that held him still.

"Jesus answering saith unto them, Have faith in God. For verily I say unto you, That whosoever shall say unto this mountain, be thou removed and be thou cast into the sea; and shall not doubt in his heart, but shall believe that those things which he saith shall come to pass, he shall have whatsoever he saith. Therefore, I say unto you, What things soever ye desire, when you pray, believe that ye received them, and ye shall have them."

He stared at her, then said, "But—surely that's symbolic?"

"I try to think the Lord Jesus meant exactly what He said."

He shook his head, saying nothing. They began to walk. Finally he broke the silence. "I've never known anyone who says that God answers *all* their prayers."

"Yes, you have!" He stared in surprise at her certainty, and she laughed. "You know my Grandfather."

"He says that, too?"

"Yes, and my mother."

"I can't believe it!"

"Reverend Howland—"

"Please, call me Robert!"

"I like that name!" she smiled at his invitation. "Well, Robert, I don't know if I can explain or not, but I'll try. Years ago," she began, a distant look filling her dark eyes, "I watched Mother as she prayed, and I saw how God always seemed to answer her. But I hadn't experienced that power for myself. It took a crisis—a desperate situation—to bring me to the realization of my own need for Christ and His power to meet my needs."

"A crisis?" Howland's expression intensified as he became drawn into the drama of Rachel's story.

"Yes. I was caught in the middle of an Indian raid on a small village near Plymouth. Someone I cared a great deal about was—" She paused, groping for words.

"Go on," Howland encouraged gently.

Rachel took a deep breath. "Well, in the midst of all the shouting and burning and bloodshed, something happened inside of me. I called out to the Lord, and He answered—really answered—and miraculously saved me and a friend from certain death."

Howland let out a long, low whistle.

"We were held captive by the Indians for some time, but in some ways I was less captive than I had been all my life. I had been adhering to a 'form of godliness,' as the scripture says, without experiencing its power. At last I knew Christ's presence for the first time, and saw Him answer my prayers. Before then my faith—if you could call it that—had been a secondhand experience from my mother."

"Is that why you're so set against the Half-Way Covenant?" Robert grinned, remembering their last spirited encounter.

Rachel laughed lightly. "Let's not get into that again! Let's just say that afterward, I knew Jesus Christ for myself. And since that time He has always answered my prayers."

"But how?" Howland was still mystified.

"Grandfather taught me to pray, and the one thing that makes him different in his praying is that he never asks God to do anything unless he's sure it's God's will."

"I don't quite understand," Howland frowned. "How can he always know God's will? God may choose not to reveal it."

"Then he waits until God *does* choose to speak. So that's the way I pray. When we were with Jamie, I was asking God to reveal His will."

"And God *told* you it was His will to heal the boy?" Howland was skeptical, as he always was of those who had visions and personal words from God, always prefacing their remarks with *God told me to say* . . .

She did not answer immediately. Her face was still as she thought how best to tell him how it was with her. "I don't *hear* God, not as I hear you," she admitted. "But there is a spirit in man, isn't there? And didn't the Lord Jesus tell us that His Holy Spirit would teach us all things?"

"Well, yes, but I don't think that means—concrete things."

"Why not?" she asked simply. "Don't you think Jesus is interested in the things we do? Doesn't He care about Jamie more than you or I ever could?"

"Yes, God cares, but—"

"He said, 'My sheep *hear my voice*,' didn't He?"

All this was making Robert Howland very nervous, and he sought for a way to change the topic, but she did not notice his agitation.

"I asked God if it was His will to heal Jamie—and in my spirit I felt that He said *yes*. So I simply prayed for what God already wanted to do. And he is healed."

Her eyes filled with tears, and she whispered, "Praise the Lord, for His mercies are everlasting!"

All this was a far different thing from studying a dusty book on the subject *Praying for the Sick*, and Howland was certain that the woman was a victim of rank emotionalism. He had been carried away by the charm of the family; now he suddenly re-solved to spend less time in their company.

But he was committed to the fish supper, so he went with her to the home of the local pastor, Reverend Samuel Parris. Parris lived in a small brick house in the center of the village. As they approached the house, a black woman opened the door. "Hello, Tituba," Rachel said. "Is Reverend Parris at home?"

"Yes, he with Miss Betty."

At that moment a thin man with close-set eyes and a harried expression entered the hall. He was followed by two young women, both pale and agitated. Catching sight of the two visitors, he stopped abruptly, gave a sharp look at the two young women, saying, "Abigail, you and Susanna run on now—but come back this afternoon."

"Yes, sir," one of them said, a very pretty brunette with a sly look. "Come along, Susanna." The two of them left, and Rachel introduced the men.

"Reverend Parris, this is Reverend Robert Howland, the new pastor at Littleton. Reverend Samuel Parris."

"I welcome you, sir," Parris said quickly. He had a nervous tic in his left eye. "I trust you will have a fruitful ministry in your new field—but you must watch yourself! These people can be untrustworthy, sir!"

"Why, I think I have been treated quite fairly, Reverend Parris," Howland answered, a little shocked that a minister would be so outspoken in his criticism of his church members to a stranger.

"They have been most unjust! Why, would you believe that they have forced me to cut my own wood, sir, when our agreement was that the church would provide wood for me!"

Howland soon learned that there was a running warfare between Parris and his membership. Most of them, including the Winslows, were sick to death of his constant harping on the wrongs done him.

"I heard that your Betty is sick," Rachel said, changing the subject.

"Sick? Who told you that?" Parris snapped, as if accused of a crime. Then he sniffed and calmed himself. "Why, she has a cold, nothing more."

"Would you like us to pray with her?" Rachel asked gently.

"Not at all necessary!" Parris answered quickly. "Perhaps I could make you some tea?"

"Oh no, I have several calls to make," Rachel informed him. "I wanted you to meet Reverend Howland since you will be brothers in the ministry."

"We must have a visit when you're more settled," Parris stated. As he talked the tic in his eye grew more pronounced, so he placed his hand over it in a habitual gesture.

"Your servant, sir," Howland said, and shook the frail hand

of the minister. After they were out of the house, Robert said diffidently, "Reverend Parris seems upset."

"He is, isn't he? He's a very nervous man, Robert. He's never been happy here. He thinks he's being wasted in a small village like this."

" A minister's life is usually hard, don't you think, Rachel?"

"Why, I don't agree," she returned in surprise. She walked along for a few steps, then added, "What's hard is not knowing the grace of God. If Jesus Christ is with me, how can anything be hard?"

Robert suddenly felt a great admiration for this woman, and he took her by the arm without realizing it, saying, "You have a wonderful spirit, Rachel!"

She flushed, then laughed, "Oh, let's hurry, Robert. I wouldn't put it past Gilbert Winslow to cook those fish and eat them—every one!"

It was a delightful evening for all three of them. After they ate the delicious supper, it was too late, both Gilbert and Rachel decided, for Robert to walk back home. "We have a spare room, a Prophet's Room, we call it," Rachel smiled. "You'll be good company for Grandfather."

They sat around the table until eight o'clock, and Robert kept the old man telling tales of the first days. Finally, Winslow yawned. "I must be getting old! Getting so I can't stay up till midnight." Then he smiled and for the first time there was a little weariness in his voice and a slight tremble in his hand, as he said, "You've given me a fine evening, my boy! I hope you'll come again—very often. You're *very* like your grandfather, John!"

He went to his room and Howland said, "It's so hard for me to remember he's ninety-one years old, Rachel!"

"I know," she said quietly. "He's the strongest man I've ever known, Robert. I shall—miss him."

Howland started, then said, "He's not ill, I trust?"

"No, thank God—but it's time soon for him to go to his Lord. That's what he lives for. And I will rejoice when that time comes, but I'll be . . ."

She got up abruptly and walked out into the warm summer night, and he followed her. She leaned against the side of the house, and he came to stand close beside her.

She said nothing and neither did he. *It is strange,* he thought, *that we don't have to talk.*

"You know, Rachel," he said finally, "you're the only woman I know who can stand a thirty-second silence."

She turned and looked at him, and he saw with a shock that there were tears in her eyes. He had never seen one trace of weakness in her, and he was moved. Suddenly he took her hand and held it tightly, saying, "You were going to say, before we came outside, that you'll be lonely when he's gone?"

"I suppose so."

He looked down at her, and she seemed very small, very vulnerable in the soft moonlight. At last he asked her directly what he had often wondered. "Why have you never married, Rachel? Have you never been in love?"

"Once—I was," she whispered. "At least, I thought I was. But then he died, and I promised God I'd serve Him always."

Howland prided himself on his control. He lived by a code of iron discipline, never yielding to the weakness of the flesh. Years before, he had put all idea of marriage out of his mind, at least until God gave him freedom to seek a wife.

But as he stood there holding Rachel's hand, he was suddenly conscious of her upturned face and was filled with a strange feeling of weakness, causing his hand to tremble.

Feeling the tremor in his hand, she looked up in surprise, her large eyes luminous in the moonlight. "Why, you're trembling, Robert!" she exclaimed. Without intending to do it, she reached up and touched his cheek, and a tear rolled down her cheek, making a silver track on her face. "You mustn't be sorry for me," she said.

But it was deep compassion and the suddenness of the emotion that shook him. He was a man who kept his emotion, as well as anything else, under strict control, but her hand on his cheek released something that had been bound up in him for years.

He took her shoulders, then lowered his head and kissed her soft lips, tasting the salt of her tears.

Rachel had not been unaware of Howland as a man, and his kiss swept through her with a power she found difficult to repress. He put his arms around her and held her gently. Though there was pity and compassion in his caress, there was more. She had stirred something deep within him, and he found his heart reaching out to her.

Like Howland, Rachel had kept this part of life tightly locked, but suddenly the door was flung open, and she was conscious only of his strong arms around her, holding her closer, his lips on hers.

Then she gasped and drew back. Immediately, he dropped his arms, embarrassed. They stared at each other, neither able to speak. Finally Howland said, "I—I must be—"

He could not finish, and Rachel moved to wipe the tears from her face. "Don't be upset, Robert—it's not your fault."

He was shocked beyond reason, and stammered as he said, "I—can't believe that I've acted in such a fashion!"

She gave him a strange smile. "You have a large heart, Robert. And you keep it well caged! But I think I have just seen what a compassionate man you are underneath all that bluster!"

He shook his head. "I'm glad you can think of it like that, Rachel."

"You were just sorry for me—that's all." Then she moved away from him, and as she came to the door, she turned and said, "It was a brotherly kiss, Robert. Good night."

He watched her go inside, and then he walked for a long time beneath the stars, and finally returned to the house. The last thing he thought of before he finally went to sleep was her words: *It was a brotherly kiss*—nothing more!

CHAPTER NINETEEN

THE HUNT IS ON

★ ★ ★ ★

"Robert—come in, come in! Where in the world have you been hiding?"

Grabbing Howland's arm, Miles literally pulled him into the house and began to berate him for his neglect. Howland's face broke into a smile; his affection for the young man dissolved the sober look in his student's face. Robert rode out the storm of words, thinking not so much of what Miles was saying, but of the strange state of mind which had dominated him since his last visit to Salem.

He was not a man given to excessive introspection, but that short interlude with Rachel had impressed him so much that no matter how he tried to put it out of his mind, the scene kept returning. For years he had been on his guard against anything that would be a hindrance to his ministry—and the most obvious handicap, in his judgment, was marriage. Fending off potential brides had become almost second nature to him, but something was different in this case. He could not put his finger on it, nor could he forget. Their last meeting nagged at him, pulling his mind in two ways at once, and for a month his work, his study in the Word, and his sleep had suffered. Finally that very morning, he had set his jaw after another fitful night, and started for Salem. He had no plan of action, but he knew he had to face Rachel, if only to see if his vivid memory of her was a figment of his imagination.

"Are your parents at home?" he finally asked, breaking into Miles' running monologue.

"Why, no, they're not, Robert—and you barely caught me." His face revealed a sudden concern and he said earnestly, "I'm glad you've come—things are in a ferment here. I swear the whole town's gone insane!"

"What's happening?"

"Why, it's this fool witchcraft business!" Miles said in disgust. "Some silly women accused a poor old woman—Bridget Bishop—of being a witch, and the trial is on right now. Come on, it's already started, and you may be of some help."

"I hardly see how," Howland protested, but he allowed himself to be drawn along. There had been much talk of witchcraft in his own village, and he was curious to see how the business was handled in Salem.

They made their way to the largest building in Salem, a two-story structure of red brick, and found a crowd pressing around the outside, excitedly talking and staring through the open windows.

"We'll never get in there!" Howland said, but Miles pulled his arm, and they were admitted by an elderly man who nodded at the youth and opened the door just wide enough for them to slip through.

The door they passed through was in the back of the large room, so few people saw them enter. As they took places along the wall, standing with the others who had missed out on the bench seats, Robert saw the Winslow family sitting together close to the front on one of the benches that was at right angles to the room, facing the raised platform where several elderly men sat at a long table—magistrates, he suspected, and judges for the hearing.

Rachel looked his way, and as their eyes met, he had the strange feeling that she had been as restless as he, for she bit her lower lip in agitation, then nodded and turned back to the scene before her.

An old woman, plainly dressed and so upset that she could not speak without a break in her voice, stood on a smaller platform with a small rail built around it, waist high. She must have been at least sixty-five or seventy years old, and from her speech and actions, Howland judged her to be of humble origins and not especially intelligent.

"And you have heard witness after witness testify that you appeared to them in a horrid shape," one of the judges said sternly. He was a tall, thin man with a long face and staring eyes. "John Cook swears that you appeared to him five years ago, that you struck him on the head, and that on that same day you walked into the room where he was and an apple strangely flew out of his hand into the lap of his mother, six or eight feet from him. What say you to that, Bridget Bishop?"

"Oh, I ain't never hit his mother with no apple—please God, I never once hit 'im."

"He has sworn that you did! Are you calling Master Cook a liar?"

"Oh no, sir!" The old woman trembled so violently with fear that she swayed back and forth. "Please God, sir, Mr. Cook—he was angry with me over the business with the suckling pigs, but I never done 'im no hurt!"

"What is this about pigs?" Every head turned to see Matthew Winslow stand up and face the court.

"Mr. Winslow! We will take care that all the evidence is heard! You are not a judge in this hearing!"

Winslow suddenly raised an arm, pointing it like a rapier at the long-faced man who had gone livid with rage. "Thomas Carlew, you have permitted a dozen witnesses to testify of some ridiculous incident going back ten years, while at the same time you are *deaf* to any suggestion that these people may be as silly as they sound!"

An angry hum went over the room, and Miles whispered to Howland, "Father's all stirred up, isn't he? Look at how mad the witnesses are."

Howland saw that many were boiling with anger at Winslow, and he thought, *Winslow is making trouble for himself!*

There was a heated argument about whether or not the defendant should be allowed to amplify her statement on the pigs, but the direct attacks of Winslow prevailed, and the old woman said, "Please, sir, it was only that Master Cook bought six suckling pigs from me, and four of 'em died—so he come and wanted his money back—and said they was cursed. Only I didn't have none of it—so he said I was a thief and a witch." She began crying, and Matthew turned to a sallow-faced man in the front row.

"Mr. Cook, you are a prejudiced witness—your testimony is worthless."

Cook jumped up and began to scream at Winslow, but the judge said loudly, "Sit down, Mr. Cook! And you, too, Matthew Winslow! Or I will have you put out of this room!"

Winslow stared at him, then said loudly, "You are a disgrace to your office, Jacob Sneed!" He swept his arm over the entire courtroom and cried out, "In God's name, can't you see what a farce this hearing is? Not one trace of *evidence*! Nothing but a bunch of sniveling, silly, witless *gossips* determined to have a Roman holiday with one poor, unfortunate woman! God help you all!"

The room broke into a roar, some being in sympathy with Winslow, but most of the crowd angry at the interruption. Justice Sneed finally quieted the crowd enough to say, "You will leave this room, Matthew Winslow—before I fine you for contempt of court!"

Winslow rose to his feet with fire in his eyes as he called out in ringing tones, "There are not words enough in the world, not brains enough in your heads, to describe the contempt I feel for this—I will not say *court*, for it is none! For this pack of dogs without a single trace of Christian love! I wash my hands of you!"

He stepped to the aisle, and Lydia, Rachel, and Gilbert followed him as he stalked toward the door, his face a mask of outrage. As the party left the room, Miles and Howland joined them. Outside the crowd milled around them, some angry, some saying, "Well done, sir!"

A burly man with a pock-marked face planted himself before Matthew, a sneer on his lips as he said, "Ye had yer say, Winslow, now I'll have mine!" He gave a quick look around and was satisfied to see that he had the crowd's attention. "Now wot about it, Winslow? Ye called me own brother a liar, did ye?"

Matthew lifted his head and looked coldly at his accuser. Something in Matthew's eyes made the heavy-set man blink and take a sudden step backward. "Rufus Cook, your brother is a liar, as is well known in this community. You are a liar and a thief, which I am perfectly willing to prove either in a court of law—or right now with fists, knives, guns, or any weapon you care to name!"

A silence fell over the yard, for Winslow's youthful reputation as a fighter of terrible proportions had not been greatly dimmed.

Rufus Cook backed down quickly. "Aw, yer so good an pure, all you Winslows! But lemme' tell ye, there's talk about the lot of ye, there is! The girl there, why, the hull town knows there's something that ain't natural about the way folks git well when she goes to 'em. And if a body can make somebody *well*, why, they can cast a spell and make 'em sick, can't they now?"

A sinister mutter went over the crowd, and Cook nodded savagely, "And that wife of yers, she prays strange. Some say in some kinda language that ain't good English!—and wot we wants to know is—wot sort of words is it, Winslow—mebbe' the Lord's prayer backwards, could it be, now?"

Matthew's arm moved so quickly that it was difficult to see. His fist shot out, catching Cook in the face with a solid *thunk*! The force of the blow drove the burly man backward, and he fell on his back in the dust. Then Winslow reached down, grabbed his coat and yanked him to his feet. He ignored the blood streaming from Cook's nose, and in a deadly voice said, "You open your mouth about my family one more time, Rufus Cook, and this community will not be bothered with your worthless presence any longer!"

He shoved the man away, and the crowd parted to let the family through. None of them spoke until they were out of sight of the square. "They're mad!" Miles said bitterly.

"They surely won't convict the old woman on such evidence!" Rachel said.

"They might," her father said heavily. "We must have help with this. I shouldn't have struck Rufus Cook!" He shook his head and gave Robert an apologetic smile. "You have any ideas about this, Reverend?"

"I think you must go to Reverend Parris," Howland instructed. "He may not be your idea of a good pastor—but he *is* in a position to do some good."

"Yes, that's true." Gilbert said suddenly. "The man has not much of the Spirit of the Lord, but as pastor, he has authority to disperse those idiots!"

"I wonder why he wasn't at the trial, Matthew," Lydia said.

"His daughter is sick, I believe," Rachel spoke up. "Perhaps he didn't want to leave her."

"Well, I don't like the sound of *that*," Matthew grunted. "In a matter this important, the pastor should be on the scene. We'll wait until the hearing is over; then we'll have a talk with Reverend Parris."

It was a long wait, and Howland felt somewhat awkward being there, but when he mentioned leaving, Matthew objected. "No, you must go with us, Robert! Parris may listen to a fellow minister—for he surely won't pay much heed to *me*."

The morning went by, and Lydia prepared a small lunch. No one was hungry and though the hearing was not far from their thought, they talked mostly of other things. After lunch, Gilbert lay down to take a nap, and Miles left on an errand for his father. When Matthew and Lydia also disappeared, Howland was disconcerted to find himself alone with Rachel.

As he sat at the table sipping tea, she came and seated herself across from him. "You look tired, Robert," she remarked. "I suspect you've been working hard."

He shrugged, started to agree, then a sudden streak of honesty overtook him. "No, I've been troubled about the last time I was here, Rachel." He caught her look of surprise and laughed shortly, adding, "I take it that you haven't been upset?"

Rachel stared at him, a slight color rising in her cheeks—making her even more attractive, he thought. "I've thought of you," she said quietly.

The silence ran on, making the ticking of the clock on the mantel seem very loud. She put her hand on her throat in a feminine gesture, and her eyes found his; for several seconds they looked at each other.

Then she said, "We're alike, aren't we, Robert? I mean, both of us have chosen to give our lives to God. And we've both been very careful to build a high wall around our hearts. I saw it in you the first time we met." She smiled at the memory. "It was like a large sign a man would put on his door: *KEEP OUT—NO LOVE ALLOWED!*"

Howland's face changed, for her words had put his life into sharp focus; he had never thought of it in that way, but now he said, "Why, in that you're right! I do want to give God my life, but I never made a vow about it."

204

"Nor I!" she admitted, then bit her lip and a sadness filled her hazel eyes as she said, "When I lost the man I was going to marry, I thought life was over—in that way. So I turned to God, and since that day, I've tried to think of nothing but serving Him."

He got up and paced nervously around the room, pausing to look out the window. Finally he came to stand before her, looking at her with troubled eyes. "I find myself thinking of you constantly," he said, then added, "I can't forget your kiss."

She rose in agitation, and he caught her before she could turn away. "Robert!" she protested, but he held her fast, and she found her heart beating furiously as they stood there.

"I may be in love with you, Rachel," he said quietly.

"You—mustn't be!" she cried. "This is no time to talk of that, not with all the trouble," she finished bruskly.

"If a man's in love," he said roughly, "the time to talk about it is when he has the woman in his arms—like now." He kissed her again, ignoring her effort to release herself.

She never knew which of them broke away first, for she was lost in the wonder of it. But when he lifted his head and stepped back, she said swiftly, "This can't be! It's too—quick! What would you say to one of the young people in our church who did what we've been doing?"

"We're not children, Rachel," Howland answered. "I know one thing, and that is that I feel about you as I've never felt toward any other woman! If it's not love, I don't know what it is. But answer me this, how do you feel?"

She was caught between two desires, both of them strong, and she could not answer immediately. He waited as he watched the struggle reflected in her face. Finally she sighed and said, "I must pray! It's no small thing, is it, to put your heart in the hands of another human being!"

He smiled as he took her hands. "This is the testing time, Rachel. You say God's never refused you anything? Then the matter is simple. You must ask Him if it is His will for me to come into your life."

"I will," she said quietly. "But this time, I don't think God is going to shout the answer from the housetop. I think the answer will be like the treasure hid in a field. Robert, I think we're going to have to give all we have to find God in this matter!"

Lydia was not ignorant of what was going on between her daughter and Robert. As they were on their way to the pastor's house, Lydia looked questioningly at Robert, but said nothing. There was a light in her dark eyes, though, that made him feel uncomfortable, like a small boy caught with his fingers in the honey jar. To avoid any misunderstanding, he resolved to make his feelings known to Rachel's parents as soon as possible.

Their visit with Parris was brief, almost abrupt, for the pastor was so agitated that he found it difficult to speak. His red-rimmed eyes indicated he hadn't slept in days. When Matthew told him why they had come, Parris cried out, "Oh, I cannot put myself against the court! No, not after what has happened here, in my own home!"

"Why, Pastor, what's the trouble?" Winslow asked in surprise.

The slight man began to moan in distress. Finally he made an attempt to compose himself and began. "I must—must tell you," he said with some pain, "the devil has raised his head—in my own house!"

"What do you mean?" Winslow cried.

"My daughter Betty and my niece Susanna have been attacked by the devil! Betty is in a trance, and her cousin informed me that the two of them have been afflicted by my servant Tituba and two others! Oh, it's worse than you can even think! They have been dancing in the forest, naked! And Abigail Williams—she is involved—and God knows who else! The devil is loose among us, I tell you!"

"Brother! Calm yourself!" Matthew commanded. He stared at the distraught minister and said, "You must be mistaken!"

"Would God I were!" Parris moaned. "But they have confessed, and I have sent for help from Boston. Reverend Hale is on his way, or so I trust."

"John Hale, of Beverly?" Howland asked instantly.

"Why, I believe so," Parris nodded. "Do you know him, Reverend Howland?"

"Yes. He was at Harvard last year."

"He is the most knowledgeable man in the matter of witches in the country—except for Cotton Mather, of course."

"We have not come to that, surely! Sending for *experts* on witches!" Winslow exclaimed. "We are godly men! Surely we can find the truth of this business!"

Parris pressed his lips together stubbornly. "My daughter is in a trance, sir! We must root out the devil—even if he takes the form of a faithful member of the church!"

"That's the danger, Parris!" Matthew cried. "If you had been at the hearing, you might have seen a sample of this smelling out of witches! John Cook points at a poor old woman he's hated for years over a trivial matter and cries out, 'She's a witch!' And others begin to get caught up in the thing, so that before you can bat an eye everyone is anxious to be a part of the hunt!"

"Mr. Winslow, I refuse to discuss the matter!" Parris shouted. "Reverend Hale will find the devil who's taken our people by craft—and then we will deal with him!"

Winslow nodded, "We will see what this man has to say, but we are in danger of losing ourselves in this thing, I tell you!"

They left and the door slammed behind them.

"What sort of man is this fellow Hale?" Matthew asked as they made their way back to the house.

"He's not a bad man, Matthew," Howland said slowly, "but he's obsessed with his subject! Spends all his time reading about witches and studying the invisible world. Now, Reverend Mather is interested in this subject, as you know, but there is no—no *balance* in Hale! He sees a demon behind every bush! But he's a fair man, and one who loves God."

"It's a sad thing—a sad thing, indeed!" Gilbert shook his head and added as they proceeded along the way. "In the old days, on the *Mayflower*, we helped each other, and during the first years, we clung together like children—now Christians seek the life of their fellow believers!" He said nothing until they got to the house, and then he stopped and looked over the village, shook his head and said, "I've lived too long, I think!"

"No, don't say that!" Rachel cried quickly. "We'll see this through, Grandfather!"

"It's a time of darkness, child," he said quietly. "And there'll be many of us who'll get swallowed in this wave of evil!" His prophetic tone sent a chill through Howland, and he left for home depressed as he had rarely been.

CHAPTER TWENTY

BRIDGET

★ ★ ★ ★

Reverend John Hale was a man of forty, small in stature, but filled with zeal for his task. He'd been at Salem only a few hours when, to his complete satisfaction, he found the hoofprint of the devil.

Howland was present when Hale located the problem of Reverend Parris's daughter Betty. Hale had been reluctant to allow Howland's presence, but he could find no good excuse for excluding the young favorite of Cotton Mather.

The small room was crowded. Joining Hale, Parris, and Howland were the West Indian servant, Tituba, Parris's niece, Susanna, and Abigail Williams.

Hale began by saying, "We must be precise in this matter, for the devil is subtle. But we will have him out!"

For over an hour there was a long interrogation of the girls, and the truth, though slow in coming, finally surfaced. Susanna Walcott was so nervous during the first part of the interview that she could hardly speak, while Abigail Williams defended herself angrily. It was Susanna who finally began to weep, crying out, "Yes, we were dancing! And there was a bowl of soup with something awful in it, but Abigail made me drink it!"

Howland happened to be looking directly at Abigail Williams as the younger girl cried out, and he saw an instant change go over her face. She had been sullen and angry, but in the flicker of an eye she assumed an expression of grief and sorrow! *She's acting!* he thought in astonishment, and immediately she began to cry out and gave every evidence of honest grief.

"It was Tituba!" she moaned. "She put blood in the soup and said she'd kill us all if we didn't drink it!"

Hale turned his guns on the black woman, and in no time she was broken down, confessing all that he put in her mind. An air of hysteria came into her voice as she began to scream, "I saw Mistress Mason with the devil! I saw Bridget Bishop with the devil!"

Instantly Abigail began to screech, "I want the light of God! I want the love of God. I saw John Proctor with the devil! I saw Mistress Osburn with the devil."

Betty Parris suddenly began to cry, and she too began to accuse various people. Finally Hale led the men out and said instantly, "We have it now!"

"Sir, what you have is a group of hysterical women!" Howland stated sharply.

Howland's statement offended Hale, and he countered. "I'll brook no opposition, sir! You may be a favorite at Harvard through your friendship with Mr. Mather—but that avails nothing here!"

Howland tried to reason with the man, but he was finally convinced that other means would have to be found. Leaving the house, Robert went directly to see Matthew Winslow.

Winslow and his father listened carefully, then both of them exploded with anger. "That fool!" Matthew cried. "Can't he see that those girls are play-acting?"

"I saw it," Howland admitted. "But Hale is a man on a holy quest, at least in his own mind."

"We'll have to fight it!" Matthew told them bitterly. "And what will happen to the gospel while we are wasting our time with this abomination?"

"Winslow, you must be careful," Howland warned. "This is going to get worse—I've seen it before. I know you want to help, but when things like this are just beginning, they're like a forest fire, and nobody can stop it!"

"But—what would you have me do?"

"Wait, that's all!" Howland spoke earnestly, but he saw the

stubborn lines in Matthew's face, and knew that it was hopeless.

"I played the coward once, Robert," Matthew said with a glance at his father. "I was in Bedford Jail with John Bunyan, you know, and I let my God down—but it'll not happen this time!"

Howland shrugged. "I thought it might be that way, Matthew."

For three weeks, all through the month of May, Salem was a battleground. Denouncing a neighbor for witchcraft became so common that no one could be sure who would be in jail next.

The Winslows and a few others stood against the witch hunt, denouncing the whole thing as a godless affair but their resistance had little effect, for as Howland said, it was like a forest fire, gaining ground each day.

On the seventh of June the blow fell. Howland was with the Winslows, for he had practically given up his own parish work to support them in their efforts. They were all sitting around the table when someone knocked on the door.

"Must be William Gates come about the new shipment," Matthew decided. He got up and opened the door, only to find a company of men, six in all. Instantly he knew their purpose.

Marshall Herrick, a man in his early thirties, held out a paper and said harshly, "I have a warrant for you, Matthew Winslow."

"Matthew!" Lydia rose and came to stand beside her husband.

"Don't fret, Lydia. I'll be back to you by dark—"

"The warrant is for both of you," Herrick interrupted.

Matthew turned pale, and Lydia, fearing his temper, said quickly, "I'll get my coat—don't be upset, dear!"

Matthew set his teeth and bowed his head. *Oh, God!* he cried inwardly, *not again*! The horrors of the Bedford jail flashed into his mind with sickening impact. Finally he exhaled and said, "All right."

Herrick looked relieved and said, "I'll have to ask you to put these chains on, Mr. Winslow—and your wife."

"Chains!" Winslow looked aghast at the irons. Seeing the flash of fire in his eyes, the men in the door readied themselves for violence, but once again, he managed to control himself.

"Miles, take care of your sister," he said, and stood there as they put the irons on his wrists.

"Is there no warrant for me, Marshall?" Rachel asked.

"Well—you've been named," Herrick admitted, "but as yet there ain't no warrant."

"And none for me either?" Gilbert said. Then he lifted his head and said fiercely, "There *will* be one, by heaven! I'll see to that soon enough!"

Rachel went to his side and put her arm around him. The two stood in stunned silence as they watched the group disappear down the lane.

Breaking the heavy stillness, Howland said, "I know this is a blow, but you mustn't despair. This madness can't go on forever!"

"It doesn't have to go on forever, Robert," Gilbert stated. "Just long enough to get people hanged."

"It won't come to that, I tell you!" Howland insisted. "At the worst, some people will have to stay in jail for a few weeks— they wouldn't *dare* execute anyone!"

"In England last year they executed over three hundred people for witchcraft," Rachel added quietly.

"This isn't England!" The thought of it made Howland angry, and he cried out loudly, "There's got to be a way out of this!"

But day after day went by, and matters grew worse. Over a hundred people were in jail by the middle of June. Finally a special tribunal of judges—all prominent men, arrived in Salem to take charge of the trials.

"Now they'll bring some reason into this business!" Howland said. "Samuel Sewall is a just man, I know for certain."

But it was Judge Hawthorn and Deputy Governor Danforth who dominated the legal scene, and their first action was to sentence Bridget Bishop to hang!

Rachel and Miles were visiting their parents in the common cell when the news came. They had brought hot food as usual, but the cell was so crowded that they had difficulty finding space.

Miles was haggard, looking worse than his father, and he ate nothing. "Do you know what's happening now—about confessing, I mean?"

"What's that, son?" Matthew asked.

"Why, they've all gone crazy, Father!" Miles said huskily. "They tried Mistress Raymond, and she confessed to being a witch—"

"What! Why, the woman's silly enough, but no more a witch than I am!" Matthew said in a shocked voice.

"Was she sentenced to die?" Lydia asked quickly.

"Sentenced!" Miles snorted grimly. "She was set free—after she confessed her own guilt and repented of it. She accused Giles Cory of witchcraft, so now Giles is arrested and the Raymond woman is free."

"But—that's monstrous!" Matthew's voice shook, and he stared at Miles in disbelief.

"And three more have 'confessed,' " Miles said bitterly. "All you have to do now is name somebody else as a witch and you're dismissed."

They were still talking about it half an hour later when Howland came in, his face pale as he picked his way through the crowd. He said not one word, but stood there looking at them with an expression in his gray eyes that they could not read.

"What is it, Robert?" Rachel asked, taking his arm.

He looked at Matthew and said as though his voice were trapped, "Your father—he's been named, and they've gone to arrest him."

"God have mercy on them!" Matthew hissed. "I'll have none of it!"

"There's more." Howland face was grim. "Bridget Bishop—she'll be executed tomorrow at dawn."

"No! That's impossible!" Lydia breathed.

"You can hear the hammers if you go to that window," Howland said. "They're building the gallows now."

They waited silently, and in less than an hour, the door clanged open and Gilbert Winslow entered. He saw them at once, and came over to say, "I feel better now. Somehow I felt like a traitor to the family being outside."

Matthew stared at his father, shaking his head in unbelief. "From the *Mayflower* to this place!"

"God's still on His throne, son," Gilbert smiled. He seated himself comfortably and picked up a piece of cake that Rachel had brought. "Now let the devil do his worst—for my Lord Jesus has His foot on the slimy fellow's neck!"

Miles struggled to keep his composure, then looked at Howland, asking, "Robert, can't you do *anything*? You must know somebody who can help us!"

"I'll leave tonight, Miles," Howland said. "I've written Cotton Mather twice, but have received no answer. I can't believe he's gotten the letters, so I'll hunt him down, and he'd better do something about this, or I'll know the reason why!"

"Robert—don't go until tomorrow. Bridget needs you."

The two of them had visited the old woman every day, taking food and trying to cheer her spirits. She had come to lean on them, and Howland nodded. "Yes, of course, Rachel. Perhaps we'd better go now."

They left the common cell, and found armed guards had been placed around the small building where the convicted prisoners were kept. One of the guards knew them, but said, "You can't see the Bishop woman without permission from one of the judges."

Howland and Rachel went to the courtroom, which was mostly empty. The judges, they were told, were eating before the next session, so Howland went to the door at the back of the large room and knocked on it sharply.

It opened and the Deputy Governor Danforth stood there with an irritated expression. "What is it, man? Can't you let us have a moment's peace?"

"I don't think you'll ever have much peace of any sort, Danforth," Howland said, staring at him directly.

Danforth was a tall man, accustomed to having his own way in all things. Anger flared in his pale eyes as he demanded, "What does that mean—and what do you want?"

Howland stepped closer, causing Danforth to retreat, a move that bruised his pride. "I mean that none of you will have any peace, sentencing senile old women to die!" He saw his words strike against the man, but gave him no quarter. "And I've come for a pass to see the innocent woman you've condemned to die."

"Who are you?" Danforth shouted. "Do you dare insult this court!"

"I'm Reverend Robert Howland." Howland began to raise his voice. "Declare me for a witch, if you will, but I *will* see Bridget Bishop."

Samuel Sewall, a small man with a pale face and distressed look in his eyes, had been sitting at the table nibbling at a piece of bread. Rising suddenly he came running over to say, "I know this man, Danforth—let me take care of this!"

Danforth glared at Howland, but said no more as Sewall and Robert stepped outside.

"Robert, control yourself!" Sewall warned.

"But, Reverend Sewall, how can you—"

"You'll do no good by getting yourself arrested, will you now?" Sewall fished through his pocket, but finding no paper, he called out to a guard, "You there! Take this man to Bridget Bishop—pass him and this young lady through at once, you hear me?"

"Thank you, sir," Howland said; then he looked Sewall straight in the eye and said, "I'm going to Cotton Mather. It's too late for that poor woman, but I intend to pull your house down around your head—if I can!"

Sewall closed his eyes in distress and implored, "Go at once, Robert! Would God *someone* would call a halt to this thing!" He said no more, but turned and went back into the other room.

Howland and Rachel followed the guard to the small building and were passed through on his word. They found the old woman sitting down on a small bench. As they approached, she stared at them with a fearful look in her face; then hope came into her faded eyes.

"You won't let 'em hurt me, will you, dear?" She clung to Rachel, weeping. For the rest of the day they stayed with her. In the evening Robert left but Rachel stayed with her all night, quoting scriptures to her. When Howland returned at dawn, both of the women were exhausted.

"We have only ten minutes," Howland murmured quietly. "Is she—"

"She's ready to be with her Lord," Rachel said. She leaned over and whispered, "Bridget, wake up. The Lord is near unto you."

Howland never forgot that time. This old woman, who had

been on the verge of insanity when he left, opened her eyes and looked at him with a quietness she'd never shown him.

She sat up and asked Rachel, "Is it time now?"

"Yes. In a few minutes you will be with Him who loves you more than you can ever know! Will you think of Him as you go to the end?"

Bridget took a deep breath, closed her eyes and said, "I wisht it were over—and I were with 'im now!"

They sat there quietly as Rachel quoted a chapter from the Gospel of John, and then there was a knock at the door. They all rose, and when the door opened and Bridget saw the deputy governor and the hangman with the black hood, Howland was afraid that she would break down, but she did not.

"I'm ready," she said quietly, and without another word, moved to the door. As the crowd made way for her, Rachel went with her, the two holding hands like schoolgirls.

There was a thick silence in the dawn air, and despite the crowd that had gathered at the foot of the rudely built gallows, there was no speech heard.

Howland followed the two women, his throat aching. When they arrived at the foot of the gallows, Rachel kissed Bridget and whispered, "Goodbye, sister! Greet the precious Savior for me!"

Bridget's step was firm as she climbed the steps. As the black hood settled over her head, she said nothing. Her eyes were open and there was a smile on her wrinkled lips as the hood slid down. Then the noose followed.

The hangman stepped back, put his hand on the lever and looked to the deputy governor for a sign.

Just as the sign was given, from beneath the black cloth came a strong voice, crying out, "He is here! I see Him!"

Then the trap fell, and it was over.

CHAPTER TWENTY-ONE

A TIME TO DIE

★ ★ ★ ★

Howland had expected to return to Salem within a week, but it was near the end of August before he entered the village, his nerves frayed and his eyes red-rimmed from the loss of sleep. He went at once to the jail. As he dismounted, the guard exclaimed, "Why, Reverend Howland, I didn't know you was back!"

Howland nodded. When the door opened he went at once to Matthew, who was standing at the window. Lydia and Gilbert were lying on a rude pallet at his feet. Matthew was so engrossed, he did not hear Howland approach.

"Matthew—" Howland said quietly. When the tall man turned from the window, he looked ten years older than he had a month before. His hair was unkempt and he had lost weight. He had lines on his face that hadn't been there before, but his eyes brightened as he saw his friend.

"Robert—you've come back!"

His voice awakened Lydia, and he stooped to help her to her feet. She, too, looked exhausted and ill. She tried to smile, but her voice was not strong. "Have you seen Rachel?"

"No, I came straight here."

Seeing him hesitate, Matthew tried to smile. "I know you have no good news, Robert. From your letters we really didn't hope too much."

Howland said wearily, "Mather was gone, and it took me three weeks to catch up with him. Then when I did find him, he refused to interfere."

"I never thought he would," Matthew shook his head. "They all hang together, don't they?" Then he tried to laugh, adding, "I shouldn't have used that figure—*hang together*—it's a forbidden word."

"How many—?"

"Have they executed?" Matthew finished when Howland could not complete his statement. "Why, it's difficult to keep count. There were five in July and six in August—that makes eleven, doesn't it?"

"Robert," Lydia said quickly, "you must talk to Rachel and Miles—at once! They are denouncing the court in public, by name. It's just a matter of time until they are arrested if they don't stop. I wish they'd go away until—"

"You know they won't do that, Lydia!"

Gilbert was stirring, and he was so stiff from the hard floor that Matthew and Lydia had to help him to his feet. He started to speak, but a spasm of coughing cut off his words. It frightened Howland to see how thin the old man had grown. His face was sallow, unhealthy, and filled with pain.

Howland looked at Matthew with a question in his face, and received a warning shake of the head. It was obvious that Gilbert was very ill. Howland said, "I failed, but I'm not giving up."

Gilbert Winslow stood up carefully as if he were afraid his brittle bones would snap with the strain. Though Gilbert had little strength in his body, he held his head high and his gaze steady. His spirit was strong and unchanged. "Well, Robert, we're still here, you see." A grin touched his tough old lips, and he coughed hard; then he went on, "They haven't killed me yet—and even if they do, they won't kill me but once!"

Matthew smiled, then turned to Howland. "See if you can get better quarters for Father, will you, Robert?"

"I'll try," Howland promised. "Maybe Sewall will help."

"Go to Rachel first," Lydia pleaded. "Try to talk to her, Robert!"

"Yes, I'll do my best—but this stubborn Winslow blood is a hard force to oppose, you know!" He smiled at them, then left at once.

Rachel was at the house when Robert stopped by. Surprised, her eyes opened wide when she saw him. Without a word, he took her in his arms and held her. She clung to him for the first time with complete abandonment, and finally she pulled his head down and kissed him.

He stared at her in amazement, then said, "Well! You know how to welcome a man back!"

She flushed, and then laughed shortly. She had lost weight, as had he, and there was the same strain in her face that he'd seen in her parents. "Did you talk to Reverend Mather?" she asked, looking up into his face.

"Yes—and he refuses to do a thing." Howland answered slowly. "I begged and threatened, but nothing would move him. We'll have to find another way."

Rachel turned and walked to the window. She stood there for a long time and he came to stand beside her. A pair of bluebirds were building a home in a knothole of the oak tree, and they made a vivid patch of blue as they streaked back and forth carrying straws and small twigs.

"Robert—maybe there *is* no other way," she said, continuing to look out the window. "This may be one of those times we have to stand and die. There are times like that, aren't there?"

He put his hand on her shoulder, and the smell of her hair was sweet as he stood there. "I suppose so—but we can't *know* if it is. We have to fight as though it were not. Then, when we've done all the arm of flesh can do, we leave it to God."

She turned and looked up to him, and there was such a trust in her face that his heart was overwhelmed. He could not fail her! "No matter what happens, Robert, at least I found you!" she murmured.

He started to reply, but even as she spoke, her eyes flew open wide, and she gave a short cry, her hand flying to her lips. She whirled and leaned against the wall, her shoulders shaking with grief.

"Rachel! What is it?"

She would not answer nor turn at first, but finally he pulled her around. "I—I said the same thing to Jude Alden—and that same day—he died!"

He put his arms around her and let her cry; then finally, when she stopped, he said, "I have something to say to you, Rachel. Something you may not understand."

"I'll believe you, Robert Howland, even if I can't understand you!"

"Will you now?"

"Truly!"

He smiled down at her, and then grew sober. "We must pray—pray as we've never prayed before. But there are things that can be *done*, Rachel. And I have to try *something*—I must! Now, in the days to come, you may see me do some things that will seem—unusual. Right now, I can't say what they will be, but I believe that God has put me in this place, at this time, for a purpose. And that purpose may be to help your family. I intend to do it, but it won't be easy, and it won't be—respectable, I fear."

She stared at him in bewilderment, then whispered, "I—I don't understand you, Robert."

"You will understand less in the days to come—but I want you to try to remember this—" He took her in his arms and kissed her with almost a finality in his manner. "Can you remember that I love you, and will love you until the day they put a stone over my head?"

"Yes, if you say so, Robert!"

He stroked her hair, then stepped back. "Try to talk to Miles. See if you can keep him out of this. Now, I must go."

He left the house, and she stood there waiting for him to turn and wave as he often did, but he walked straight on. The set of his strong shoulders looked like someone squaring off to do battle. What the battle would be, she did not know. She did know, however, and smiled to herself as she thought of it, that he loved her—and that was enough!

August passed away, and as September rolled over the village, the executions continued—twenty-one in all. Still the jail remained crowded, for no matter how many died, there were always more accused and arrested.

The steamy heat inside the jail, together with the constant dust from the floor and the straw used for bedding, irritated the lungs of all the prisoners. Coughing was so constant that they ceased to notice it. Sickness swept through the cells, and by the first of September, six had died of illness; others were past help, even if they had been freed.

The trials went on slowly, and as prisoners were condemned to die, they were taken from the larger cell and placed in the smaller one. Here there was no overcrowding, for the gallows continued to snuff out the lives as soon as they were transferred to the smaller unit.

Rachel and Miles worked steadily, not only to keep their own family from suffering, but to provide as much as they could for those in prison who had nobody to help. Rachel functioned as both nurse and cook from sunup to long past dark until she was worn almost to a razor's edge.

"Daughter, you must rest," Matthew pleaded with her one night. She had helped wash some of the sick women, and afterward when she came as usual to sit with her parents and grandfather, she fell asleep leaning against him.

She straightened up at once, laughed shortly, and said, "Oh, I'm fine. Just a little tired."

Giles Cory, another prisoner, had attached himself to the Winslows. He was a hearty man of eighty, or had been until the prison had eaten away at his strength. He feared for his wife, who also was charged, and he spent much time discussing the problem of his property with Matthew. "If they convict me, Mr. Winslow, they'll take my property, and my children and grandchildren will starve," he had said. Indeed, Matthew could give him little comfort, for such might well be the case not just with Giles but with all of them.

Gilbert was growing much worse, his cough by this time becoming chronic. Had he subsisted on jail food, he would have been dead. He was sitting with his back propped against the wall when he looked up at Rachel and asked, "Where has your young man been, Rachel? He's been gone—what, a week or more?"

Rachel looked slightly confused, then said, "I—I think he's been very busy with his church, Grandfather."

"The big minister?" Giles asked. "He be in court most of the time, so they say. John Proctor say he do sit there with his book out, writing down what the judges say."

"I didn't know Robert was doing that," Matthew muttered.

"Aye, and it make Judge Hawthorn cry out in open court at him, so John said." He laughed and added, "The judge asked the minister what he wrote, and the minister said he knew that God was keeping a record for judgment day—but *he* was keeping one fer when the world found out about these trials!"

Lydia looked at Rachel and asked quietly, "Did Robert tell you what he was doing?"

"No." Rachel got up and said, "I haven't seen him for a week." Then she left and Matthew stared after her.

"Something is wrong there," he mused quietly.

"Yes. She's been hurt." Lydia looked out the window and watched her daughter walk past the gallows with shoulders slumped and defeated. Her own heart was heavy, for although she had little hope for herself or Matthew, she spent most of her time praying that Rachel and Miles would survive. She was shocked to suddenly realize how much she had depended on Howland to help.

Abigail Williams left the courtroom, and as was always true, the tension had built up in her. She was there every day, and many times over the past months she had been called back to testify. She was a beautiful girl with a sense of drama in her blood. Since childhood she had made up scenes and acted them out when she was alone; now the action was real, and she was intoxicated with it.

She lived with an elderly woman named Mistress Taylor, who paid absolutely no attention to her activities. Until the trials had begun, Abigail had worked out, cleaning houses for people. Now she did nothing but sit in court and afterward talk about the trials to Susanna and one or two other girls.

She turned down the street, unaware of the tall man coming from across the way. Suddenly she ran into him and would have fallen if he had not caught her and held her up.

"Careful!" a deep voice cautioned. Startled, she looked up into the face of Robert Howland. "Sorry to be so clumsy, Miss Abigail."

She was very conscious of his hand on her arm and countered with a smile, "Why, it's my own fault, Reverend Howland. I'm always running into things and stepping into holes."

"Are you going this way? So am I." He fell into step beside her, saying, "I've been wanting to speak to you, Miss Abigail."

She had expected anything but that, for she had kept up with his attachment to the Winslow family as closely as the rest of the small village. She said suspiciously, "To me? I think your friends, the Winslows, would not like that, sir!"

"No." He sighed and remarked, "They are to be pitied, don't you think?"

She thought about that, then answered, "I thought you held

that they weren't witches at all!"

"Oh, that was my position *at first*, as it was with most of the poor wretches," Howland said.

Abigail listened to him talk, and something about the big minister excited her. He was, she had always felt, the most attractive man she'd seen, and now to be walking with him triggered her active imagination. She began to see him calling on her, taking her to the courtroom, while everyone gawked at the two of them.

By the time they got to her house, she knew at least one thing about Howland—he was a man who appreciated a *woman*. She was a beautiful girl and had been aware of male attention since she was fifteen years old. She knew admiration when she saw it—as she did in Howland's glances at her.

"Why don't you come in and have a cup of tea," she smiled up into his face boldly.

"Why, that would be very nice," he said in surprise. "Perhaps you could tell me a little more about your experiences with these frightful witches," he added. "I've really no experience, and to hear the *real* thing would be most helpful—though I can't expect an attractive young woman such as yourself to dwell much on these things."

"I don't mind," Abigail smiled, as he led him into her house.

From that day Howland no longer sat on the front seat taking notes, but seated himself farther to the back. It did not escape the attention of the village that he walked Abigail to and from the court each day, and as often as not had tea with her. It was all respectable, for old Mistress Taylor was always present. But if they had considered that the old woman went to bed at seven, and Howland rarely left until ten or later, there might have been even more talk than there was.

There was little said in the common jail, at least by the Winslows, though the other prisoners picked up the gossip from their relatives and friends.

Howland did visit his friends from time to time, but there was a constraint between them that made his visits very painful, so he came no more after the first of October.

Matthew said only one brief word to Lydia, and spoke to no other: "I have never been so deceived in a human being." Lydia only pressed his arm and said nothing.

Miles was not so tactful. He heard the rumor that his friend had taken up with Abigail, but he refused to believe it at first. Finally he had confronted Howland with it, and when Robert said only, "That is the way it is, Miles. I'm sorry for your family," he had stared at the man in disbelief.

"I can't believe you mean that, Robert!" he said, with color filling his cheeks. He had loved this man, more than anyone outside his family. After admiring him, trusting him, now to see him cast off his ties with the family for Abigail Williams, the central figure of the trials, was more than his spirit could bear.

"What about my sister?" he gritted between his teeth.

"That's none of your business."

Miles drew himself up, his face pale. "You are a scoundrel, Howland!" he cried, drawing back his hand and delivering a ringing blow to the older man's face.

Howland did not move. Looking steadily at his friend, he said only, "Leave it there, Miles. I will not fight you."

Miles wheeled and walked blindly away, his youthful face twisted into a mask of grief and disbelief.

Miles had little time to grieve, for two days later, Rachel was named and arrested. Her accuser was a slatternly woman whom Rachel had often helped, taking food to her four ragged children, nursing her when her drunken husband beat her, and going to her when she had the pox and no one would come to her cabin for any price. The woman herself had been accused of casting spells, but she had endured the jail for only a week before she began to scream. In her fear she had accused six or seven women, including Rachel.

Rachel was brought to the jail, with the few things she could carry. Miles had followed close behind, silently suffering as one by one his loved ones were arrested. Lydia took one look at her, and for the first time in all the dreary weeks broke down. She turned her face to Matthew's chest, her thin body racked with dry sobs. Tenderly he held the frail, sobbing form, willing his strength into her. He remembered those last months in Bedford Jail when he had turned from her, refusing to be comforted. Now, in a small way, he could repay her.

Rachel smiled as she looked at them. "Well, I'll not have to go home every night now, will I?" she said cheerily. "But Miles is all right, and we'll soon be out of this place." Even as she said it, she wondered at the dismal future.

Gilbert sat on a bench, his face gaunt, but a fiery light burning in his faded blue eyes. "I wish your grandmother could see you, girl! She'd have been so proud!"

Three days later, five more prisoners were hanged, and the next day the Winslows went to trial—all except Rachel. She, they said, would be allowed time to repent of her wickedness. They were taken into the crowded courtroom, dirty and sick from the long imprisonment, and it went as they feared. One after another, a line of accusers rose up, but there was no defense against their enemies. There was no *evidence*, so there could be no refutation.

"The accusers are always right," Matthew said wearily after the mockery of a trial was over. The end had come when Danforth had said, "Confess your guilt! Point out those who are your companions in this vile witchcraft! Do this—and you will be set free."

"Suppose I confess that I am guilty and repent," Matthew asked at one point, "but am not willing to incriminate others?"

"Then you have not repented!" Judge Hawthorn said with heavy illogic. "A true Christian will always side against the devil—you will identify those who are witches or you will die!"

Each of them was asked to recant, and each, of course, refused. They were pronounced guilty and sentenced to be hanged.

"There was never any hope, you know," Matthew said quietly as they entered their dark quarters. "Not one soul has been found innocent since this farce started."

They fared a little better physically, since there were beds and more space. But day by day the trap of the gallows fell, and it was only a matter of time before they too would make the last walk to their deaths.

Howland had disappeared, they were told. "I hope I never look on his face again, the traitor!" Miles cried bitterly.

Rachel said nothing at all. Two days later, the jailer came with the announcement: "Your turn tomorrow, Rachel Winslow!"

She was so exhausted that her only reaction was to thank God that it would soon be over!

CHAPTER TWENTY-TWO

THE TRIAL OF RACHEL WINSLOW

★ ★ ★ ★

Morning came in a feeble gleam of light that filtered through the small window. Rachel stood looking out, but she saw nothing, for though her eyes were opened, her mind was in another place.

She turned quickly, startled when the key turned in the latch, and Martin Plummer, the young jailer, came in with their food. "Here's your breakfast, Miss," he said. He was twenty, and had no sympathy for the court; now he said apologetically, "No eggs this morning, Miss."

"Thank you, Martin," Rachel said with a faint smile.

Matthew and Lydia arose, and then, moving very slowly, Gilbert pulled himself up and sat on the side of his bed looking very ill.

As they sat down to eat, Rachel noticed that the young jailer did not move to go. He stood there shifting from one foot to the other, and she asked, "Is something wrong, Martin?"

He bit his lip and shook his head with an abrupt and angry motion. "It's—Mr. Cory!"

"Giles?" Matthew asked, lifting his head. "What is it, young man?"

Martin licked his lips and mumbled, "He's—he's dead, sir. Died last night."

The prisoners looked at each other, and Gilbert spoke up in

a rusty voice, "They didn't hang him at night, did they?"

"No, sir, they didn't. They didn't hang him at all."

They waited for him to continue and finally he cleared his throat and said, "They pressed him!"

"Pressed him? What's that, in heaven's name?" Matthew asked.

"Why, you see sir, Mr. Cory, he wouldn't say aye nor nay to his indictment—because he knowed if he denied the charge, they'd hang him and sell his property. So he said nothing and died under the law—so his sons will have his farm."

"What does that mean?" Rachel asked.

"Why, it's the law, Miss! He couldn't be condemned a wizard without he answer the indictment, don't you see?"

"And they did what, boy?" Gilbert asked, his eyes fixed on the young jailer.

"They pressed him, sir," Martin said.

"Press? Press how?"

"They put great stones on his chest until he'd plead aye or nay."

Gilbert stared at Martin, then said softly, "And he said nothing, did he?"

Martin licked his lips and then lifted his head. "He said, 'More weight!' That's all they got from Mr. Giles Cory!"

"He was a fearsome man, Giles Cory!" Gilbert said slowly, his face lit with an awed expression.

"I'll have to come and get you in an hour, Miss," Martin said. "The rest of you are to come as well, by order of the court."

"We'll be ready, Martin."

After the jailer left they ate a little, all except Gilbert—he could only drink a little liquid from the pitcher.

"I hope Miles will not come to the courtroom," Rachel remarked.

"He'll be there," Matthew nodded. He looked around the room and said, "This room is a lot better than Bedford Jail!" His face grew thoughtful. "I've thought so often of Bunyan these days. Eleven years in that foul den, and he could have walked out at any time."

"He was a fearful man, too," Gilbert smiled. "Gone to be

with the Lord now, but his book about the Pilgrim—it's all over the world, I reckon."

Matthew looked at Lydia and then at Rachel. "I can't see any reason in all this," he said in a defeated voice. "It seems so—useless!"

"All things work together for good to those that love the Lord," Lydia said softly, renewed courage in her voice. She came to stand beside Matthew, placing her hands on his shoulders. "We've had so many good years, and our God is good—no matter what!"

They talked quietly for a time, and when the hour was almost up, Gilbert suddenly said, "Rachel, I'm thinking about Howland."

Rachel stood perfectly still. "Yes, Grandfather?"

Laboriously the old man got to his feet and came over to stand beside her. He took her hand in his and stared at it for a long time, so long that she thought he had forgotten what he intended to say. Then he said quietly, "There was a time in my life when everything I did looked wrong—to everyone."

He said nothing more, but she knew that he was trying to tell her something that he had not words for. Finally she said, "You think he's a good man, Grandfather?"

"What do you think, girl?"

She stared in his eyes, and now it was her turn to be silent. Finally she said slowly, "I thought he loved me—and I know I loved him."

"Rachel," he said steadily, "never take counsel of your fears! If you love a man, then stick with him, and don't doubt if the world is falling!"

Rachel's eyes opened wide, and she blinked and nodded, "All right, Grandfather!"

Then the door opened and Martin said, "The court's in session. Come with me, please."

They followed the guards into the courtroom, and despite the early hour, all seats were filled, and as usual, the windows were filled with the faces of the observers.

The judges sat in their places, and Rachel went forward to the chair indicated by Martin, while the others sat on one of the side benches. Rachel sat down and was slightly surprised to find that she had no fear at all. She was thinking of Gilbert's words about Robert Howland, and it took an effort of her will to bring her mind back when Judge Hawthorn read the charges.

"You have been charged, Rachel Winslow, with using familiar spirits, with using unholy arts, with calling forth the dead, and with casting spells. The witnesses have sworn under oath that you have done these things, and we will now proceed to hear the charges from these witnesses in open court."

For the next hour testimony was taken from five witnesses, and Rachel made no response to any of them. Her immobility aroused the ire of Danforth, who interrupted the testimony to say, "You do not appear to know your peril, girl!"

"I am in none, sir, from this court."

"We have the power to hang you!"

"I do not fear him that is able to kill the body, but him that is able to cast both soul and body into hell," Rachel said calmly.

Samuel Sewall broke in to say, "Miss Winslow, we have heard testimony after testimony of your many good works—"

"For which of these do you condemn me?" she shot back.

"For being a witch!" Hawthorn cried.

At that moment Rachel heard the front door slam, and instantly there was a babble of excited whispers. She turned and saw Robert Howland walking down the aisle in the company of a small elderly man.

She heard a noise from the judge's bench and turned to see all of the judges rising from their seats, their faces white as a sheet.

Howland came to the front of the courtroom, looked around for a seat, then said to two men who were staring at the elderly man, "You two stand by the wall," and when they popped up and scooted away like rabbits, he said, "You may have this seat, sir."

The man, in his seventies at least, nodded and sat down. Howland sat down beside him, and both men looked at the court expectantly.

Judge Hawthorn looked as if he were having some sort of attack. His face was ashen and beads of moisture suddenly appeared on his brow. When he spoke his voice trembled slightly.

"Reverend Mather. . . ?" he said tentatively, then cleared

his throat and asked, "Is—would you like to sit with the judges?"

"No, I would not. Get on with the trial."

"But, really, sir, it would be more fitting if you would join us."

Rachel heard the name *Increase Mather* and looked quickly at the small man. She had never seen the man, but he was the unofficial monarch of the Puritan world, ruling from his pulpit in Old North Church in Boston. His son, Cotton, was the rising star, but it was well known that the son honored the father. There was simply no one in the New World like Increase Mather; he was the American equivalent of the Archbishop of Canterbury— or even the Pope, some had said. In any case, his very presence was enough to freeze the judges in Salem, and it was with some effort that Hawthorn managed to say, "We have two more testimonies, do we not?"

"Yes, sir," the bailiff nodded. "Sarah Marsh will come forward."

This was the woman who had first called out Rachel's name, and was a poor witness for the court. She began crying as soon as she laid eyes on Rachel, and when Hawthorn finally said, "You saw this woman use black arts to heal your child?"

"She came—and she put something on his head—and she prayed—and he got well!"

"Ah, and was it blood she put on his head, Mistress Marsh?" Hawthorn demanded with some assurance.

"No—it was just oil—that's all!"

"You can swear to that?"

"Oh, I seen it, 'cause I asked her, and she let me see—it was just olive oil!"

Hawthorn kept badgering the woman for thirty minutes. She would repeat anything he told her, but there was no substance in her testimony.

"Call the next witness!" he said in disgust. For the benefit of the distinguished guest, he announced loudly, "Fortunately there are more vocal witnesses to show this woman for what she is. Call Susanna Walcott!"

"Susanna Walcott—come forward," the bailiff called, and the girl came forward, looking miserable. She sat down and looked at the floor.

"Susanna Walcott, did you see this woman with the devil?" Hawthorn asked.

"Yes, sir."

"Tell this court about it."

"Well, I was in bed, and she flew in through the window, and there was this awful *thing* with her—the devil, it was! And she tried to get me to sign the book he had, and when I wouldn't do it, she pinched me until I was blue!"

She said all this in a rote fashion, as though she had it memorized, but it satisfied Hawthorn, and he asked for more details.

Susanna opened her mouth, but it was not her voice that began to cry out. "I saw Rachel Winslow with the devil!"

The voice was clear, and every eye in the court swung to where a young woman named Sarah Good was standing up, looking at the ceiling. She began to sway from side to side, and again she cried out, "I saw Rachel Winslow with the devil!"

Several other young girls began to take up the chant, calling out that they had seen certain people with the devil. It had happened often in the court, and Hawthorn stood there looking satisfied.

Finally he said, "The devil is revealed! Rachel Winslow, you stand accused! The evidence is that you are a worker of iniquity and a servant of the Evil One."

He would have said more, but suddenly Sarah Good's voice rose again. This time she came out of her seat and moved in a ghostlike fashion down the aisle. Then she held out her finger and cried in a piercing voice, "I saw Judge Hawthorn in the forest! He was drinking from the devil's cup!"

A deathly silence fell on the room. Not a soul stirred, and then Sarah Good cried even louder, "Judge Hawthorn is the Black Man—he came to me in my room—he made me sign his book! He is the Black Man!"

Hawthorn's face was the color of old putty, and his voice mute. He sat in his chair as the girl continued to cry out terrible accusations against him—things no decent girl would even *know* about!

Then, as before, others began to take up the chant. It was the young girls who had cried out before, and older women, too, and some men. But this time they were crying out, "I saw Governor Danforth with the devil!" "I saw Samuel Sewall with Satan!" One of them began to cry out that she had seen the governor of the colony with the devil!

Then a young girl, no more than fourteen screamed out, "I seen Cotton Mather with the devil! I seen Increase Mather with the devil!"

A gasp went up from the crowd, for Howland's companion had risen. He walked to the front platform and stood there staring at the judges. He said nothing but let the silence build up, and then he said in a silky voice, "You gentlemen are accused of witchcraft, I believe."

"But this is ridiculous!" Hawthorn sputtered. "These witnesses are lying!"

"Have they accused other people?" Mather asked, still not raising his voice.

"Why, I believe they may have—one or two—"

"Have some of those who were accused been executed, Judge Hawthorn?"

A mutter swept through the room. Hawthorn sat as though paralyzed, unable to speak.

"Yes, they have," Judge Sewall answered quietly.

Increase Mather stared at the judges, then said with no emotion whatsoever, "I declare this court dismissed—and I will meet with the judges immediately in private."

He turned and walked to the door in the rear, and the judges followed him with ashen faces.

Not a soul moved to leave, but there was a rising tide of talk, and for thirty minutes the courtroom buzzed like a beehive. Then the door opened and Reverend Mather walked out, his face set like a flint. He was followed by the judges. This time they did not mount the platform but stood there staring out at the crowd.

Increase Mather looked out over the people, his face still, but with a light in his dark eyes that revealed the smoldering anger he kept carefully under control.

"People of Salem, I have received testimony that the so-called 'evidence' used by this court to prosecute defendants is of an illegal nature." A gasp went up from the crowd, but he ignored it, and continued. "I hereby dismiss this court, and declare that all prisoners be set free pending further investigation." He paused again and looked down at the judges. "The judges of this court are relieved of their offices and will report to Boston at once. They will remain there until a full and complete report of these trials has been made by the authorities."

He said no more, but stalked out of the courtroom, closely followed by the sulking judges, who walked with their heads down.

Howland got up and walked over to where Rachel stood speechless. "You're free, Rachel," he said. "Let me take you home."

She turned to face him but couldn't make herself heard because the crowd was coming alive with an accelerated wave of emotion. She raised her voice to cry, "Yes, take me home, Robert!" She looked over at her family who were watching them with unbelievable, joyous shock in their faces. "Take us all home!"

Gilbert was too weak to walk, so they got a carriage, in which he, Matthew, and Lydia rode. Since it was not far to the house, the rest of them walked. Neither Rachel nor Miles could say a word to Howland. They walked in silence. Rachel looked up at a crow clutching the denuded branch of a peach tree, croaking in a gutteral tone as they passed. She breathed deeply, drinking in the fall air, crisp and keen with the bite of winter in it. Oh, the joy of being alive and free. *I'll never take anything for granted again!* she thought.

It was a moment to be treasured when they all entered the house. Matthew and Lydia stood there, holding Gilbert upright, looking around as if they'd never seen the room before.

"I never thought I'd see this room again!" Matthew exclaimed as he assisted his father to a chair. Then with a sudden motion, he turned to Howland. "Robert, you're a wonderful *actor*!" Overwhelmed by the magnitude of Robert's service, Matthew wrapped his arms around Howland's shoulders, tears coursing down his cheeks. He was joined by Miles and then Lydia. Gratitude radiating from her eyes, Lydia took his hand and kissed it.

"Oh, come now, you don't have to do *that*!" Howland protested.

Rachel came and stood before him while the rest watched silently. "Robert, you warned me I wouldn't understand—and you were right. I—doubted you. Forgive me! But you have an advocate here—Grandfather told me never to doubt—and from that moment, I didn't!"

"You make too much of it!" Howland said, embarrassed and humbled by their response.

"I want to know what happened. Tell us everything!" Rachel urged, pulling him to a chair. As the rest of them sat down, looking at him eagerly, he began.

"Why, it's simple—at least it seems so now," Howland stated with a smile. "I'd seen Abigail Williams before—you remember, when we went to Parris's house the first day I came to Salem with Miles. And later I saw her when Reverend Hale examined Parris's daughter. One thing I didn't miss—as soon as it was evident that she was going to be found out, the girl put on an act. It was a good act, but I saw her when she thought nobody was looking!"

"She fooled almost everyone else," Rachel remarked.

"I knew she was lying," Howland nodded. "And I knew Cotton Mather was *not* going to do anything about it. The idea came to me that there was only one man more powerful than Cotton Mather—and that was his father!"

"Did you know him?" Edward asked.

"No, but I knew he'd not interfere in anything his son refused to touch. They're very close. So I put the two things together—Increase Mather could do something to stop the trials, but he had to be convinced. Abigail knew the trials were false, but she wouldn't admit it."

"That's why you started seeing her!" Miles cried. "What a fool I was!"

"We all were," Lydia said quietly. "But we have a lifetime to make it up to you, Robert."

Rachel had a frown on her face, and she gave Howland a peculiar look. "I wonder *how* you got that girl to help you, Robert? She's very clever."

Howland's lips lifted in a wry smile, and he answered grimly, "I used the only thing in the world that would have made her admit she'd been a fraud—money."

"You paid her to admit her guilt?" Matthew said, incredulous.

"It was all I could think of. If I'd tried to threaten her, she'd have laughed at me. So I kept on seeing her, and little by little she let her guard down."

"But wasn't she afraid of what would happen to her if people found out she'd been lying?" Rachel asked. "And wouldn't she be put in jail for lying in court?"

Howland lifted his hand in a gesture of disgust. "That young woman doesn't care what anyone thinks of her—not really. And as for being in trouble with the law, they'll have to catch her first."

"She's left Salem?" Lydia asked quickly.

"Never to return, I'd venture." He gave a shrug and added, "She's one shrewd vixen, I can tell you! When I told her I wanted her to tell her story to Increase Mather, she upped the price high enough so that she can go anywhere she likes and live like a queen."

"You don't have that kind of money, Robert," Matthew broke in quickly. "I'll pay the fee."

"You may have to, Matthew," Howland smiled. "I don't have any money myself, so I had to borrow up to my neck to get the price."

Lydia, sitting near Matthew, shook her head in disbelief. "I can't believe that girl was so wicked."

"She sent men and women to their deaths!" Matthew sighed with aching heart. "Poor old Giles and Bridget and John Proctor—and all the others—dead in vain!"

"But God sent us a deliverer!" Lydia cried out. "Our friend and deliverer—Robert Howland—"

"Could you add to that—*son-in-law*, please?" Howland interrupted. Going to Rachel, he put his arm around her.

A glad cry went up as they all welcomed their new son and brother.

Gilbert looked at Robert, tears in his eyes. "My boy," he said quietly, "you're very like your grandfather! Very like!" He wiped his eyes, then said with a sudden laugh, "I'm very glad I fished John out of the sea! He's given me a good return, he has! A new limb to the family tree of Winslow!"

CHAPTER TWENTY-THREE

TAKE ME HOME!

★ ★ ★ ★

The winter that year was mild, but for Gilbert Winslow it was a time of sickness. He could not shake the cough he had contracted in jail, and by March he was unable to walk without assistance.

"He'll be better in the spring," Lydia said hopefully to Rachel. "The winter air keeps him down."

Rachel did not reply, for she saw it was more than physical weakness—it was weariness of the spirit. He was weak and unable to eat, but the trials had drained him of something.

"He's not fighting as he once did," she said worriedly to her father. "He's low in spirit."

"I've seen it, Rachel," Matthew agreed. He stared at her and then sighed. "He's had more life than most. We'll miss him—you'll miss him more than anyone, I think."

She said no more, but by spring he still had not improved. The doctor visited him but was noncommittal. He knew as well as the fiery old man did—he was wearing out.

Then one night in May as Rachel sat reading, she saw her grandfather sit up and try to walk. He began to lean and before she could get to him, he fell to the floor. His breathing was irregular, his face ashen. She ran quickly to get a neighbor to run for the doctor and the family.

When they arrived, they tenderly lifted him into bed. He

did not move, and the doctor decided Gilbert had suffered some sort of stroke. For three days he lay there without opening his eyes.

Howland arrived as soon as he could and stayed with the family night and day. None of them expected Gilbert to regain consciousness, but he did. Early one morning, while Rachel watched by his bedside, he opened his eyes and said, "Rachel?"

She began to weep, and he smiled and said weakly, "Now, this is not the time for that, is it?"

She left him only long enough to call the family.

Gilbert lay there looking at them. "I take it you're surprised to see me back with you?"

Matthew took his hand. "You gave us quite a scare."

"I'm about to give you another one!"

Matthew stared at him, puzzled. "How is that, Father?"

Gilbert smiled. He looked so much like both Matthew and Miles that Rachel almost cried. "I want to go for a little ride," he said.

"A ride!" Matthew cried in astonishment. "Why, when you get better—"

"I mean *now*, son," he affirmed. "And not a short one, either."

They all looked at one another. Then he continued. "Oh, I'm not out of my mind. But it's a small request—just one ride."

Rachel knelt down and took his hand. "Where do you want to go, Grandfather? I'll take you anywhere!"

"There's my good girl!" he breathed. He closed his eyes and they thought he'd gone to sleep, but he opened them and said, "Take me to Plymouth—to the sea—where Humility is buried."

Matthew started to protest, but Lydia squeezed his arm. He stared down at his father for a time, then said quietly, "I'll get a carriage ready."

Robert and Miles went with him, and in less than an hour they had taken a seat out of a carriage, built a framework, and placed a mattress in it.

By the time Matthew came to the house, the women had dressed Gilbert. "Are you ready, Father?" Matthew asked.

"Take me home, son," he said with his eyes closed.

Matthew went to him, and with easy strength picked his

father up as he would a small child. As he did, Gilbert opened his eyes and smiled. "Once I carried you, my boy—now it's your turn!"

Matthew did not answer, but carried him out, placed him carefully in the carriage, then said, "We'll go slowly."

Miles had obtained another carriage, and they all got in and started out with no more ceremony than if they had been going across town.

They had to stop often, and the inns were not of the best, but Gilbert got no worse. He never complained, and much of the time at night the family would gather around and he would listen as they talked. He said little himself, but from time to time he would mention something that had happened long ago.

They came to Plymouth at midday, and he said, "Take me to the sea, Matthew."

They skirted the town, coming in from the seaward side. When they arrived, Gilbert cried, "Help me up!" As Matthew raised him, he gazed at the rolling waves of the ocean, the scudding white clouds, and then turned his eyes upward toward the village on the hill, soaking in the memories, etching them on his mind.

"Now, let it come," he whispered.

Matthew found a house for rent, and all of them set up temporary housekeeping. It was a quiet, holy time, for as the days went by, they saw Gilbert's face grow more and more peaceful.

On the fourth day after their arrival, just before sunset, Gilbert called with urgency in his weak voice, "Rachel—Matthew?"

"Yes! What is it?" Rachel ran to his bedside.

"It's time to go home," he told her simply, a high expectancy in his eyes. Turning to Matthew he urged, "Take me to the sea, son; the tide is going out."

"All right, Father. Rachel, go tell the others."

Though they had prepared for this day, sadness tugged at their hearts, knowing this might be the final parting. After gently placing his father in the carriage with his head in Rachel's lap, Matthew drove the carriage, while the others followed in another.

"Go to the hill where she is, son," Gilbert directed.

Matthew drove to the high hill overlooking the harbor, and stopped the horses beside an iron fence that enclosed a few worn stone markers.

Carefully he picked up his father and carried him to the plot. The others followed close behind. He stopped at a special marker, holding his father's thin form in his strong arms as the others crowded around them.

Gilbert opened his eyes and looked down at the stone that said, *Humility Cooper Winslow—She hath done what she could.*

He said nothing, but there was a smile on his face. "Put me down here for a moment, son."

Matthew gently placed him on the marble bench and sat beside him. As Gilbert lifted his eyes again to the sea, he said quietly, "There's where we landed that first time. What a crew we were—God-hungry and afraid of nothing—Bradford and Standish and Howland—good old John Alden and his Priscilla!"

Raising his voice, he continued. "This land is like no other—and you are Winslows! You must never do other than serve the Lord Christ with all your hearts—but you will live in this land—a land that offers—freedom—"

He paused and lifted his head as if he'd heard someone call his name, and he smiled and whispered, "Yes!" He opened his eyes and looked around, taking in each of them. "I am proud—of all of you! God—is—good—"

Then he gave a little gasp and his head fell forward. "Father!" Matthew cried, but he knew, as they all did, that Gilbert Winslow had gone to his true home! Rachel stared at the face she'd loved all her life. "Goodbye—for a little while!" she whispered as she kissed his brow.

For sometime they knelt there with heads bowed, tears flowing; then they got up and Matthew carried his father back to the carriage.

The next day, they had a little ceremony and once again, Gilbert Winslow lay beside his beloved Humility.

Rachel walked blindly away from the small plot, wanting to be alone. For hours she walked the shores, thinking of all the times she'd spent there as a girl with her grandfather; how he'd been both grandfather and father to her those years she thought her father dead. The pure joy of living and love for the Lord he had instilled in her. He had given her so much. She would miss him. But as the day wore on, a peace fell on her, and she felt the presence of the Lord. It was as though His loving hand reached down and touched that deep ache within, filling her with joy.

"Rachel?"

She turned to see Robert standing by an outcropping of stone. With a cry of joy she ran to him, falling into his protective arms.

"Are you all right?" he asked gently as he held her close.

She squeezed his hard muscular body with all her strength, then threw her head back. There were tears in her eyes, but she dashed them away. "Yes, I'm all right—as long as you love me!"

He crushed her to him, kissing her tears away.

"Rachel Winslow," he said simply, "if you're all right as long as I love you, why, you have nothing to worry about! I'm never going to let you go!"

She kissed him again, then said with a smile of victory:

"Take me home, Robert! Take me home!"